THE
CONDUITS

ENJOY!

Ariel

THE
CONDUITS

A story of hope and survival
amongst a looming apocalypse.

CONVEYANCE BOOK ONE
DAVID W. DRAPER

TO MY WONDERFUL WIFE CAREN CHANLEY,
who patiently ignores me while I write.
This story would not have been possible without your support.
Thank you Caren, I love you.

A special thanks to ...

My son-in-law, Hank Huculak, for his initial encouragement that got the process started while we smoked cigars in my outside spa in the spring of 2018.

Mardelle Busch for being the first manuscript reader and first reviewer.

Lisa McLaren for insisting a more conclusive ending was needed and sticking with me through the whole process.

Tom Bechtel for providing extensive feedback.

Fred Trent for an encouraging review.

My adult children, Shawn Nicole Huculak and Andrew Draper for reading the story and confessing to Dad they liked it.

My mother Phyllis Ellinger for believing in me enough to read a story outside her genre comfort zone.

My initial draft editor, Bill Thompson, of Stephen King and John Grisham fame, for cleaning up an amateur's mess, and saying, "you have a great story underway."

AUTHOR'S NOTE

We all have our day-to-day routines, goals and concerns. For some, it's how to cover expenses for the month, for others, it's getting son Johnny into Harvard Law School, or deciding which stock to purchase next. You get the point. Our life is about living the best we can within the context of our own realities. Rich or poor, we focus on existing within the realm we control, the natural infrastructure surrounding and supporting us is taken for granted.

What would happen if our reality changed; if our natural infrastructure were to let us down? What would happen if you were told the Earth will be destroyed in ten years and we all perish? Would your life change in the interim, or would you still try to get Johnny into Harvard? Would you be worried about your long-term investments, or would you withdraw your money and have fun? Would you keep your job? Could you keep your job? Would the world turn to anarchy? Would money continue to have value? Would the miscreants take control? For sure, life on Earth would not be the same.

If there was a chance to survive an apocalypse and live somewhere other than Earth, would you help work towards that goal? Would you be willing to move to a complete unknown? Would you be willing to give up your luxuries and comforts to live a life equivalent to the earlier American settlers?

The Conduits introduces the reader to a looming apocalypse happening in ten years. It centers around three children and their parents and guardians, attempting to spread the word and offer hope.

Savannah Davies, a news correspondent and leading character in the story, best sums up the plot when she rants in a moment of frustration, "So here we are. We know three kids calling themselves conduits. They are unrelated and have never met or spoken. Born within the same minute of each other. They live on three different continents yet receive identical information telling us the Earth will fry in ten years. But miraculously, all is not lost. They mark the locations where people will escape the planet and go to who knows where, and they will tell us how to do it. To top it off, these children have no idea who, where, or how they're learning this stuff. Am I missing something here?"

This first book portrays the turmoil bestowed upon the parents and guardians of the conduits as they cope with surreal messages their otherwise normal children are receiving. To many, the children represent a threat and need to be stopped.

This is the first book of a *Conveyance Trilogy*. Thanks for giving *The Conduits* a read … I sincerely hope you enjoy it.

David W. Draper
2020

Cast of Primary Characters
In order of Appearance

Note: The Democratic Republic of the Congo is referred to as the *DRC*.

Chapter 1

Alex Campbell .... Conduit
10 years old
Lives in Ecuador
Son of Spencer and Jack

Sarah Mabaso .... Conduit
10 years old
Lives in the DRC
Orphan

Jacob Mendoza .... Conduit
10 years old
Lives in Indonesia
Son of Indah and Cahya

Chapter 2

Spencer Graham .... Lives in Ecuador
Mother to Alex
Ex-wife to Jack

Rosine Okeke .... Lives in the DRC
Sarah's school teacher and confidant

Cahya Mendoza .... Lives in Indonesia
Father to Alex
Pearl diver

Indah Mendoza .... Lives in Indonesia
Mother to Alex
Homemaker

Chapter 3

Savannah Davies .... From London working within the DRC,
Journalist for London World News
Friend to Rosine

Jack Campbell .... Lives in California
Father to Alex
Ex-husband to Spencer
Ex-SEAL
Billionaire

Locations

In order of Occurrence

Calacali, Pichincha Province, ... Home to Spencer and Alex
Ecuador.   Location of an exodus tower

Mbandaka, DRC .... Home to Sarah and Rosine
                                       Savannah's reporting station
                                       Location of an exodus tower

Lake Arrowhead, CA, US .... Home to Jack

Island of Waigeo (North Shore), ... Home to Alex, Cahya, Indah
Province of West Papua,   and family
Indonesia   Location of an exodus tower

Kinshasa, DRC .... DRC plane transfer hub

Sorong, Indonesia .... Transfer hub to/from Island of
                                       Waigeo Location where Sarah
                                       is hospitalized

London, England .... Home to Maggie and her news
                                       crew at London World News
                                       (LWN)

Halifax, Nova Scotia, Canada .... Where the conduit team is
                                       located during the televising of
                                       the event

Greenwood Canadian Forces .... Exit point leaving Halifax
Base, Nova Scotia, Canada

Sudbury, Ontario, Canada .... Transfer point for team en route
                                       to Vancouver

Winnipeg, Manitoba, Canada .... Transfer point for team en route
                                       to Vancouver

Vancouver, British Columbia, ... Where the team departs Canada
Canada

Naval Station Everett, Washington, ... Where team is interrogated
US.

CHAPTER 1

CONTACT

Alex, sound asleep in his bed, rolls over trying to find solace from the heat his ceiling fan can't remedy. As he completes his roll, his eyes open, his pupils fully dilate. He goes still. Three seconds later he sits up and looks at the red digital display on his alarm clock; it is 3 am. Alex lays back down and falls instantly back to sleep. He won't remember this.

□□□

At the same time in Mbandaka, a town in the Democratic Republic of the Congo, Sarah is sitting in her grade 5 classroom studying her country's history. While reading, her pupils also fully dilate. She goes still. Three seconds later the reading continues; she hasn't realized anything happened. The clock on the classroom wall shows 9 am.

□□□

Jacob lives with his family on the Northern shore of the island of Waigeo in West Papua, a province in Indonesia. After being called by his mother Indah to come in for dinner, Jacob stops playing soccer with his friends on the street and heads for home. While in a full running stride, and as he does daily, Jacob jumps the white picket fence that surrounds the front of his parent's house. On this day, while flying through the air above the fence, he freezes; his motion has instantly stopped as though in suspended animation. His eyes are fully dilated. Three seconds later his running continues; he doesn't realize his sprint home was interrupted. His mother had called him seconds before 5 pm.

CHAPTER 2

THE MESSAGE

Spencer Graham and her ten-year-old son Alex are asleep in their modest two-bedroom flat in downtown Calacali, a small town in the Pichincha Province of Ecuador. Spencer is a United States born expatriate; she moved from California to Ecuador two years prior. If asked, she can't explain why she moved here, other than a love for the non-commercialized ways of the beautiful and natural rural Ecuador, or more likely, she answered a calling she's never understood. Deciding on Calacali resulted from her recurring fond memory of the town she visited as a child with her adventurous and globetrotting parents.

Months before her life-altering move from California, Spencer had revisited Calacali and was heartbroken to see the despair and poverty; not what she remembered. Years of rampant double-digit inflation had taken its toll on the country's fragile economy.

During her visit, curiosity directed her to a local grade school to check out the conditions, hoping a move with her son Alex could some-day become a reality. When Spencer found the school understaffed and in dire need of volunteer teachers, she recognized the time had come; she would move. Getting permission from her ex-husband allowing Alex to relocate to Ecuador from California was no easy task. For most, taking a son away from his father to a foreign country is a non-starter, but anyone who knows Spencer will attest to her ability to always get her way. After much discussion and negotiating to allow Alex's school vacation times to be in the United States with his dad, Spencer's ex-husband Jack, agreed, or more accurately, relented.

The digital buzz of Alex's alarm clock wakes him from his deep sleep; it is 7 am. He reaches over and kills the annoying sound and slides off his bed. Embarking on his morning ritual, Alex walks to the kitchen knowing his mom is doing her magic. He pulls himself up onto his stool at the kitchen's bar counter and, without offering a good morning greeting, blurts out, "My porridge ready?" It is a rhetorical question as he knows the answer.

Without responding to Alex's question, Spencer turns around and places his full bowl of porridge in front of him. "You are so spoiled!" she says with a fake seriousness.

Without acknowledging or saying thank you, Alex asks, "Mom, do you know about the Milky Way?"

Spencer, while continuing to wipe the counter, responds with the knowledge of a grade school science teacher, "Well, it's a bunch of stars very far away. In fact, there are so many stars it looks milky in the sky at night, that's why it's called the Milky Way. Our sun is one of the many stars." Spencer pauses and quizzically says, "Alex, why do you ask that?"

Alex, ignoring his mom's question, continues talking. "It looks milky, Mom, because our solar system is on the outer edge of the Milky Way Galaxy. Most galaxies are just like ours, round and flat, so when you look through it on edge, it's dense with stars. You're right though, there are so many stars, like billions, and they're so dim, it's milky looking. In our galaxy, like most spiral galaxies, there is a supermassive black hole in the center of it called Sagittarius-A. The thing I've learned, Mom, is a long time ago the black hole expanded. When a black hole expands it goes from being a singularity to an unstable entity similar to a neutron star."

Alex reflects for a moment, "Mom, a black hole expansion is something astrophysicists don't even know can happen, but I do. I don't get why I'm learning this stuff, it's weird."

This mystifies Spencer, and before she can respond, Alex continues, "The initial expansion event will be detectable soon by our scientists as a gravitational wave propagating through our galaxy. Regular people will also be able to see this new object as the brightest star in the sky once its light reaches Earth. But get this, Mom - the object was unstable and it only lasted ten years. It has already exploded. It released a huge energy burst so massive it is destroying our whole galaxy from the inside out. At this moment the energy burst from the explosion is coming our way and we only have ten years before the initial x-ray radiation reaches us and destroys the Earth. Mom, that means I'm gonna die when I'm twenty. I never really thought about dying before. I won't get to be old like you and dad, but ten years is still a long way off, right?"

Spencer feels her heart palpitating. Her quizzical expression has changed to sheer and utter astonishment. She stares at Alex, while he continues to devour his porridge. He is unaffected by the bizarre story he has just unloaded onto his mother.

After a few moments, Spencer breaks the silence, "Alex, where are you getting this from? I don't understand what you are talking about. How can you know anything about black holes, neutron stars, and x-rays? I don't even know what that stuff is. Astrophysicists? Where is this coming from?"

Alex routinely eats his breakfast and responds, "Not sure, Mom, I'm just learning it, no clue how."

□□□

The school bell rings and before it stops, the students, as though choreographed, pick up their books, placing them into their matching school bags, stand up, and shuffle towards the exit door. Sarah breaks from the routine and heads to the front of the classroom where her teacher Rosine is still working. Rosine is an attractive middle-aged Congo born native. Her family were landowners and had her educated to be a teacher, a job normally filled by the wealthier and privileged Europeans. Rosine loves Sarah and keeps her under her wing.

Rosine looks up to acknowledge Sarah, and says, "And how is Sarah today? Is that crazy place you're staying at providing you with enough food these days?"

Sarah replies with a sigh, "I don't know, Ms. Rosine. I can't tell anymore if I'm hungry or not."

Before Rosine can think of a response to her sad statement, Sarah continues, "Ms. Rosine, I'm learning real cool stuff."

Rosine responds while continuing to work on grading assignments, "That's good news, Sarah. Are you finding interesting books at the orphanage?"

Sarah ignores Rosine's question, "I've learned we're in the Milky Way Galaxy, and most galaxies have black holes at their center." Talking confidently, Sarah continues, "They call our galaxy's black hole Sagittarius-A; well, at least it used to be. A long time ago Sagittarius-A expanded and stopped being a black hole. Earth people don't realize it yet because it's so far away, and it takes a long time before we can detect it. It expanded over twenty-five thousand years ago, and it went from a black hole to a large entity similar to a neutron star. Scientists will detect a gravity wave soon, and people will see light from where the black hole used to be. The large star, well, it wasn't a true star, was unstable and exploded. When the energy from the explosion gets here in ten years, it will destroy the whole Earth along with our galaxy. Ms. Rosine, have I done a good job of learning this?"

Rosine stops and sets her grading pen on the desk. In her sticky, hot, ninety-degree classroom, Rosine for the first time, gets goosebumps and shivers; she has no response for Sarah.

Sarah accepts the silence, "See you tomorrow, Ms. Rosine," and then skips to the exit where her fellow students and chaperone are waiting, as they do daily, for her to embark on the walk back to the orphanage.

▯▯▯

Cahya enters his house from the back entrance and joins his family at the dinner table. The table is in a single room encompassing a small L-shaped kitchen, a screen door in need of paint, and a small living room with an old tube style TV in the corner. Furniture is old and non-matching, covered with throw blankets, yet the environment is tidy and clean. Cahya has not spent money on his house in years.

He sits at the head of the table facing his wife Indah. Jacob is sitting to his father's right beside his younger brother. Across from Jacob are his three sisters, aged four to eight. Indah, since marrying Cahya has been in a perpetual state of pregnancy; it's not the life she had imagined for herself.

Indah attempts to distance herself from the stereotypical poor wife of five children by ensuring the clothes she wears portray her as a socialite, even if she is the only one who doesn't see through the ruse. Each day she fusses with her hair waiting for an invitation to live the city life; an invitation that never comes. Face makeup is a luxury she doesn't experience; the family budget doesn't allow for it.

Cahya is a handsome man of average height. His long curly black hair frames his face and shows a man who spends his time outdoors. Years of diving for pearls have kept his body lean and strong but has taken a toll on his midlife good looks, and premature wrinkles now defy him.

After a tiring day of oyster diving, Cahya ignores his need for a shower and clean clothes, greeting his family with a smile and kind words.

Towards the end of the meal, Jacob looks at his father and asks if he has time to talk for a few minutes after the dinner cleanup is complete. Jacob is Cahya's first-born and favorite child, so he looks forward to their talks and nods affirmative.

After dinner they go out back and sit in the two old wooden chairs strategically placed to view Cahya's pride and joy - a laboriously groomed tropical backyard. The chairs are under a tin covered porch protecting them from the moderate tropical rain. Cahya, speaking loud enough to overcome the noise of the rain bouncing on the porch's metal roof, asks Jacob what's on his mind.

"Dad, I'm learning stuff, but I don't get where I'm learning it from. Did you ever learn stuff, but you can't figure out where you got it from?"

Cahya, looking perplexed, responds, "Not sure what you mean, son, I don't think so. Watcha learning?"

"I've learned in ten years, events in space will destroy the Earth."

Before Jacob can say another word, his dad interjects, "For God's sake, Jacob, have those crazy religious folks been chatting you up again? I told them not to come back here. They were here, weren't they? I'm gonna kick their asses!"

Jacob boldly continues, "No, nothing like that, Dad. No one has been talking to me about this. I've learned there is a black hole in the center of our galaxy. The black hole expanded into something like a neutron star. The star was unstable and has since exploded, sending x-ray energy this way at the speed of light, which means it will get here in ten years and destroy the Earth."

Cahya, now frowning, is annoyed.

"Dad... I don't understand why I know this stuff."

Cahya has had enough and responds in a stern fatherly voice, "Jacob, I've never even heard of a black hole or what the speed of light means. You've been talking with someone haven't you? Who has been telling you this crap? You have never been interested in this kinda stuff. Somebody is trying to fill your head with crazy shit, and I don't like it. You understand it's crazy shit, right?"

Jacob gives up, realizing he will not get support from his father, and doesn't want to upset him further. "Okay, thanks Dad, I know it sounds crazy. I will think about different stuff."

Jacob does a deliberate deflection to show his father he's dropping the topic, "Hey Dad, is your oyster bed producing well?"

Cahya, thankful for the topic change, responds in a softer tone, "We're just coming into a cycle when a majority of the pearls are getting large enough to harvest. The pearl counts should be steady over the next few months. This will be a good year."

"Great, Dad."

CHAPTER 3

VALIDATION

Spencer spends her day questioning the school staff and older students to determine who's filling her son's head with crazy and nonsensical ideas. As she thinks through Alex's story, she reasons it's not coming from his buddies because the concepts and knowledge are too sophisticated. No one admits they discussed explosions in space with Alex. Spencer goes home troubled.

◻◻◻

Rosine can't handle what she just heard. As Sarah leaves on her chaperoned walk to her orphanage for the night, Rosine picks up her cell phone and calls her close friend Savannah; she knows Savannah can help her sort this out. Savannah Davies is an investigative journalist covering humanitarian stories. Savannah helped open the world's eyes to the atrocities plaguing the Congo over the decades. The world outcry, portrayed by the media exposure Savannah created, helped the locals push back on the repression haunting them.

Savannah stands an enviable five foot eight inches and oozes charisma and self-confidence. Her intelligence and wholesome good looks provide a journalistic advantage enabling her to worm and charm her way into the lives of those surrounding her stories. Honesty and integrity have positioned Savannah as a trusted and popular news source. She has amassed a huge following and enjoys great worldwide viewer ratings when her specials are broadcast over the cable networks by her producers based in London.

Savannah met Rosine years back while covering education, or the lack of it, in the Congo. Rosine was a teacher Savannah had interviewed, and they developed a strong and trusted friendship which has endured.

Rosine explains the discussion she had with Sarah to Savannah, saying remembering the fine details isn't possible for Sarah's age and experience; there is no explanation for Sarah understanding what she just described.

Savannah says she is heading out of town on assignment but agrees to come by and talk to Sarah upon her return in two days. Savannah will then decide if a story exists. Even though she isn't sure this will be worthy of her time, Rosine is her friend, and she respects that.

000

The next morning, Alex follows his normal routine and climbs out of bed and heads to the kitchen for his breakfast. After climbing on his stool, he talks before asking for his porridge. "Hey mom, I've learned more stuff. I've learned I'm special because I'm a conduit. A conduit's job is to tell everyone how to prepare. I'm not alone either; there are two others like me. Their names are Sarah and Jacob and I know what towns they live in. They are near the equator just like us. They will tell people around where they live the same stuff I'm telling you. We all know what we're learning is important to share. We also learned it's important we are distributed equally around the equator, but we haven't learned why yet. It's just so weird I'm learning this stuff, right Mom?"

Spencer is freaked, and steps closer to her son. "Alex, this is really, really important. Listen to me. You need to tell me who is telling you this stuff. You can't go around telling people these types of stories." Without time for Alex to respond, she continues, "Please tell me where you're getting it. This isn't coming from the Internet, is it? This isn't like you. I need to understand where you are getting it from." She is stammering and can't stop herself. In a stern voice, "Alex, where are you getting this stuff from?" Spencer is feeling out of control; Alex's story is surreal.

Alex, now upset with his mom, responds, "You are not listening to me, Mom. I just told you I don't know how I'm learning it. I haven't talked with anyone. Why aren't you believing me?"

Maintaining his agitated tone, "One of the other things I learned is we need to start right away or we may run out of time to save ourselves. We need to hurry, Mom."

Spencer is flustered and emotional, her heart rate has elevated. "Get ready, get saved, and hurry? What are you talking about? Alex, this is scaring me!"

Alex speaks faster, "Mom, something important is happening and you're not believing me, and you are upsetting me. I will learn more and you will need to listen."

He stops for one breath, and continues, "Once I learn it, I can tell you about it and the two of us can tell people. If you don't help me, Mom, I have to find people who will, because I have to do this. I have learned this, Mom, and it's important, and people need to hear it."

Spencer, overwhelmed, doesn't want to alienate her son. She relents, deciding to listen and stay cool. She has never heard Alex talk or act this way - she is baffled. In a softer tone, she gets the conversation back under control. "Alex, tell me more about the others you mentioned. I think you said you and they are conduits? Do you know their last names and where they live?"

Alex, seeing his mother become more accepting, says, "Yes, Mom, they know what I know, and they're learning what I learn; we're all conduits, and we're all in this together. Sarah lives in a town named Mbandaka; it's in Africa. Jacob, the other one, is on an island named Waigeo in Indonesia. I don't know their last names. That's all I've learned so far, Mom."

Spencer says nothing.

Alex breaks the silence. "Mom, I am learning stuff no other kid my age understands, our scientists don't even know some of it, what do you think about that?"

Spencer can't respond; Alex's story has terrified her - she knows this isn't coming from him. She knows if she sweeps this craziness under the carpet, it will drive a deeper wedge between them. The move to Ecuador has taken a toll on Alex and stressed her relationship with him. The last thing she wants is adding to the stress. She realizes as crazy as Alex's story is, she needs to understand its source; she needs to show Alex it's not true. Maybe then he will drop it. She has a knot in the pit of her stomach.

🁢🁢🁢

Alex is asleep for the night when Spencer pulls out her laptop and brings up Google Earth. She enters 'Mbandaka' as Alex had spelled it; she sees it is a town in Africa, the Democratic Republic of the Congo to be specific. Spencer does the same for 'Waigeo'. Again, Alex was right; it's an island in Indonesia. She sees these locations are spread equally around the equator. No way Alex is faking this. She feels her heart racing, something is happening she doesn't understand.

Spencer picks up her cellphone and calls Jack Campbell, her ex-husband. Married for fifteen years, they raised Alex together in California until he was seven. Jack amassed a fortune during the Silicon Valley heydays; a fortune he has grown, gaining him entry to the billionaire's club. The wealth was more a deterrent to Spencer than an attraction; material things mean nothing to her and she hated being number two behind Jack's work. He never wanted Spencer to leave him and was hurt when she did, but he couldn't give her the time she deserved. He understood her need to escape and didn't make it hard. Spencer never figured out if she stopped loving Jack, but needed to get her life back. Starting over after the divorce, she took back her maiden name.

Three years later still loving to hear her voice, he answers happily, "Hi, Spencer!"

"Hello, Jack, how's your evening?" and without stopping, pokes fun at him, "I'm not interrupting you screwing someone right now, am I?"

Jack, after the initial excitement of hearing Spencer's voice, responds with a retaliatory smart-ass quip, "I've got three of the hottest babes right here in bed with me this very second. Two of them are doing each other, and the third is doing me."

"I knew it," Spencer laughs.

"Spencer, why are you calling so late? I'm assuming this isn't a 'Hey Jack, watcha doin' call."

"Jack, I need a no-questions-asked favor. It's important."

Jack can hear the seriousness in her voice. It's a tone he hasn't heard in a long time; it means the conversation isn't ending until Spencer gets what she needs.

"Spencer, you know I can't say no to you. Whatever you need, you know you got it."

"Thanks Jack, you've always been there for me."

Spencer explains the need for Jack to take Alex for a week and to supply her with extra funds to do some traveling. She doesn't elaborate, as she doesn't want to involve Jack until she knows more. He doesn't question Spencer; he knows she will share when the time is right. Spencer brings the call to a quicker than usual end. It's late, and there is work to do.

Starting her favorite online travel site, she makes plans.

After ninety minutes of reserving flights and booking rooms, Spencer packs suitcases for Alex and herself.

Her last computer chore - she crafts an apology letter to the school leaving her feeling guilty and sad. It's not like Spencer to skip out on her volunteer obligation. In addition, the letter excuses Alex. She positions the on-screen cursor over the email send button and clicks. Done.

███

She wakes Alex before his alarm clock buzzes and explains she needs to leave and research what he's told her, and he will stay with his dad for a few days in California. Alex loves to see his father; always a happy time. Spending quality time in air-conditioned comfort is a bonus; Alex hasn't acclimated to the equatorial heat. It relieves him to see his Mom acting on the information he is receiving. He takes the new turn of events in stride.

While Spencer is trying to get Alex ready for his trip, he tells her he has learned more. She cuts him short and asks him to hold off until they are driving to the airport. Not wanting to be late, she's worried any new news at this point will distract her; she continues getting them ready to leave.

███

Spencer slides her stick shift into reverse and releases the clutch with her left foot to roll her old dented Chevy pickup truck down the driveway.

Before his mom can say anything, Alex blurts out his latest knowledge, "Mom, we need three locations on the equator spaced around the planet. They said we live on the equator to act like markers for where things will happen. We haven't learned what the locations are for."

"Alex, when you say 'they', who are you referring to?"

"Don't know, Mom. I'm learning this stuff, but I don't know how I know it or who is providing it. I don't even know when I learn it. It's kinda weird, hey Mom?"

Spencer is thinking 'weird' is a huge understatement. She doesn't respond to Alex and the two continue their drive to the airport. Spencer's is stressed and her head is spinning.

She guides her truck into a space in the airport's long-term parking garage. They scurry to Alex's gate after clearing security. Spencer kneels to Alex's height and talks quietly yet firmly into his ear, "Alex, I promise I will find out what this is all about. Please give me a few days and tell no one, including your father." Without pausing and with more emphasis, she continues, "Especially your father! You and I will tell him all about it together when I return. Okay? Can you promise me? Promise me, not even your father - okay? We can discuss new things by phone, but only with me - okay?"

"Okay, Mom, okay. Geez. But hurry, cause as I said, people need to know about this stuff right away."

Spencer reassures Alex she'll work as fast as possible and reiterates he can call her anytime. She sends him through the gate knowing he will be fine; Jack will take good care. He loves his son.

She heads to the KLM check-in counter.

▯▯▯

After twelve hours of flying and multiple layovers, and accounting for the time zone change, Spencer arrives in Kinshasa at 9 am, the capital and largest city in the Democratic Republic of the Congo and the plane transfer hub. Once off the plane she asks an airline attendant for directions to Congo Airways, who will fly her into Mbandaka, the town Alex had mentioned. After language barrier difficulties, the attendant shows Spencer the way.

Forty-five minutes later, Spencer is on a short hop flight on a Canadian made Bombardier Dash 8 commuter plane to find Sarah, a conduit Alex had mentioned. Spencer's plane lands at 10:30 am in Mbandaka, a town that never recovered from its banner years before the Ebola breakout wreaked havoc on the city in the 70s.

Spencer negotiates with the first taxi driver who approaches her; he agrees to be her personal driver after negotiating a fee.

Alex had told his Mom the other conduits were his age, and Spencer has mapped out each of the eight schools accommodating the grades for typical ten-year-olds. She knows her search is looking for a needle-in-a-haystack but hasn't figured out another way. There is no way the schools will release student attendance information to strangers making queries over the phone from a foreign country. Spencer instructs the driver to stop at school after school, where she talks with the teachers of the grade five students.

When she arrives at what turns out to be Sarah's school, the attendant in the front lobby asks her what her business is. Spencer explains she's trying to find a grade five student named Sarah who knows a story of explosions in space. The attendant, not responding to the story, points and says "Rosine, room one." After a short walk, Spencer knocks on door 'one'. She says, "Rosine?" to the lady opening the door.

In poor English, the woman replies, "No Rosine."

Ignoring the response, Spencer asks, "Is there a student named Sarah in this class?"

Rosine is not there. She had stepped out earlier and found a substitute to watch over her class. Spencer doesn't realize the substitute doesn't know the student names, and worse, the substitute knows little English. Nervous dealing with a stranger, she says, "No Sarah," without admitting she doesn't know. Without further interaction, she rudely closes the classroom door on Spencer.

Spencer walks out to her driver's car; another dead end.

After visiting the eighth and final school, Spencer is tired and dejected. She had reasoned Sarah's teacher should know of the story because a parent or guardian would likely check with the teacher after hearing the child's story, just as she had.

She is thinking maybe it's a good sign she can't find Sarah. Or is it? Struggling with everything Alex has said, she is hoping it's all wrong. Her stomach knot has not gone away.

Spencer asks her driver to take her to the hotel room she had booked in advance. Upon gaining entrance to her room, she lies on the bed on top of the blanket. Without removing her clothes, she falls asleep.

⧅⧅⧅

Seconds after 9 am, Sarah puts up her hand and asks if she can approach the front desk. Rosine says 'yes' without hesitation and Sarah walks to the front of the class. She leans over Rosine's desk and half whispers, "Alex's mother from Ecuador is coming to find me."

"How do you know, Sarah?"

"I just learned it, Ms. Rosine."

"Well, let's hope she finds you okay. It will be nice to meet her. You go sit down now, Sarah, and we'll wait for her arrival." Rosine doesn't handle this well; it is deeply disturbing to her, and she feels scared for Sarah. How can Sarah know if a foreigner is coming to visit?

⧅⧅⧅

It is mid-afternoon and Savannah, the journalist, is late for her meeting with Rosine and Sarah. She is driving her Range Rover faster than she should and comes to an abrupt stop at the school's front doors. The school's state of disrepair saddens her as she enters; it has worsened since the days when she first did her reporting here. She continues, hurrying through the front lobby past the attendant sitting behind the lobby counter. Before the attendant can question her, Savannah blurts out, "I'm late for my appointment with Rosine," and with humor in her voice says, "and a student about some crazy story involving explosions in space."

The attendant, carrying an extra 200 pounds and wearing a traditional colorful full-length dress with her hair pulled up inside a matching head wrap, calls out in accented English, "WAIT!"

Savannah stops dead in her tracks, turns around, and without hiding her exasperation, asks "What?"

The attendant explains the prior afternoon, an American who said she was living in Ecuador had come by the school looking for a ten-year-old child named Sarah. She said she wanted to talk to Sarah about explosions in space. Savannah, raising an eyebrow, asks for the American's name, but the attendant doesn't know. Savannah asks the attendant if she can describe her. She portrays the visitor as a short blond with snug fitting American style clothes and a fit looking figure. She describes a pink baseball cap with a blond ponytail pulled through the back. Thanking the attendant for the information, she continues on to meet with Rosine. Thinking to herself as she approaches the classroom, "Now this -is- getting interesting."

Rosine and Sarah are waiting in the classroom. They are squeezed into two student desks rotated to face each other. As Savannah walks in, Rosine welcomes her and introduces her to Sarah. Rosine moves a third desk over, but Savannah ignores the desk offer and without asking goes behind Rosine's desk at the front and pulls out her chair on casters. She rolls it beside the small desk offered, saying, "Sorry, hon, but I don't believe I could fit there."

Rosine has Sarah describe everything she has learned, including knowledge of two other conduits. She mentions the mother of the one named Alex on a trip to find her.

Savannah explains the front desk attendant had told her there was a lady looking for Sarah the previous day. The person was from Ecuador, a country on the equator.

Sarah blurts out with excitement, "Ecuador is where Alex lives! I told you, Ms. Rosine. I told you his mother was coming to find me!"

Rosine reflects on this, and explains she had stepped away from the school the previous afternoon to take care of personal business. Rosine, under her breath, cusses. "I hope we didn't miss her."

Savannah, feeling the onset of a huge story, is pumping adrenaline. With multiple conduits, from different continents with similar stories, she knows this whole thing is mind blowing; there is someone playing strange head games with these kids. She wants to investigate the story.

Savannah assures Rosine and Sarah she will help them. Saying good-bye, she leaves the school and heads back to her apartment flat. From her cell, she calls her London-based publisher, explaining a need for expense money to chase a big story. Savannah has always produced the goods and has consistently contributed to her producer's profitability. She doesn't take advantage - always receiving a blank check in return. As usual, she gets her approval and settles in doing research on her computer. Savannah wants to find Jacob first.

ᑏᑏᑏ

Spencer and Savannah are at the Mbandaka airport unbeknownst to each other, at the counter getting their seat assignments for the only daily commuter flight to take them back to the Kinshasa Airport hub. They are both in search of Jacob and are planning to transfer in Kinshasa for their next travel leg to Indonesia.

There is no doubt for Savannah, seeing a short American with a pink baseball cap, she is looking at the American Sarah had mentioned. Savannah approaches her and introduces herself by saying with a pronounced English accent, "Good morning, hon, you wouldn't perchance be looking for a conduit, would you?"

Spencer looks up to compensate for Savannah's eight-inch height difference.

"You're shittin' me!"

Spencer and Savannah sit together on their flight to Kinshasa. After settling into their seats, Spencer says, "You said in Mbandaka your name is Savannah?"

"Yes. I'm a news correspondent and have been reporting on the Congo region for the last twenty years."

She does a quick topic change and says, "Oh my God, I really dated myself!" Continuing, "I jumped onto this story yesterday because of how bizarre it is, and now the evidence I see is making it seem credible, which is flat out spooky."

"I can't tell you how much this is scaring me. Mostly for my son. This will ruin everything we have and share. I don't know if he can handle the craziness that will happen if this becomes public; it's unimaginable. Why him? Why us? I hope this ends up being one big nothing, for soooo many reasons." Spencer's eyes are tearing.

Savannah's agenda is different; she feels excitement. Not believing the Earth dies in ten years, she feels a huge story; a story she wants for herself.

Spencer lets out a big sigh and continues: "So, Savannah, how did you get involved in this?"

"I have a schoolteacher friend in Mbandaka. Her name is Rosine, and she teaches grade school. I'm her only trusted friend, and she wanted help shedding light on a crazy story one of her students had told her. So, I came to her school yesterday and interviewed the student named Sarah."

Spencer's heart races as she hears the name 'Sarah'. Her body stiffens - she glues herself to what Savannah is saying.

"Sarah explained she was learning things, but she didn't know how or from where the information was coming. She told me about a black hole in our galaxy that expanded, whatever that means, a gazillion years ago creating a new star, and then the star blew up creating an explosion so immense it will arrive in ten years, at which time we're all toast. Like that will actually happen. She also explained that she's one of three with the same knowledge. My initial thought was where is this girl getting her information? However she gets it, she impressed me, especially her ability to keep details. Now I find you and I'm thinking, 'Oh My God', there actually is more than one, and it's not a coincidence. Sarah is telling the same story as your son, isn't she? Holy shit!"

Spencer can't believe what she just heard. As told, the story from this girl named Sarah paraphrased what Alex has said over the past few days, and these children live on separate continents in areas where outside communication is difficult. It corroborates the story.

"How did I miss finding Sarah's teacher? I went to all the schools."

"Rosine was away yesterday afternoon, you missed her," Savannah responds.

Spencer's thoughts have returned to who is doing this. She wants it to stop. If this will be a huge big deal, she wants it to be someone else's huge big deal. Under her breath, but loud enough for Savannah to hear, Spencer vents: "damn it, damn it, damn it," with an emphasis on the third 'damn it'.

"If we find the third conduit, Jacob, and if these kids keep learning things corroborating each other's stories, we either have to find the people who are doing this or bury it. If this is all crazy enough to be true and we're all going to fry anyway, why not let everyone live the next ten years in peace? If we make this public, every church and government will attempt to discredit and ruin us. We will live the rest of our lives under a magnifying glass, with governments wanting to dissect my child and the others. The haters and the people who feel threatened won't ever leave us alone. We will piss off so many groups, that hell, we could mysteriously just disappear." Spencer reflects and continues, "I am so scared right now. Unless this all stops, this is a no-win. If our planet will die anyway, it's outright mean. I really hope it's a stupid trick and not real. Christ!" Needing to settle down, she passes the baton to Savannah, "So Savannah, do you have a husband or family? Tell me your story."

Savannah reflects for a few seconds, "I'm divorced. My marriage stole fifteen years from my life. Christ, I hated that man! As a single woman, I drifted away from my married friends, which were the only friends I had at the time. Without friends, I went from story to story with my journalism, one of which landed me here in the Congo. The corruption here needed exposing, so I stayed. I'm professionally happy, personally lonely, hating almost all men I meet, and now sitting here with you. That's my story. Okay hon, your turn."

"Well I'm also divorced, the difference is I raised a conduit," Spencer says forcing a smile. "Jack and I were two different people, I had to leave him to maintain my personal sanity. He couldn't give me what I needed due to his work, and he understood that. He was a good enough man that he let me go."

"Guys like Jack are every girl's dream, and every girl's downfall," Savannah muses. She returns to Spencer's current troubles and attempts to comfort her. "I'd like to think there is a reason or grand scheme for the conduits; it has to be a good thing. I don't think we'd be getting an advanced warning if we're all going to fry and can't do anything about it. I'd like to think your son and the two others are Angels and their mission is to save us all, otherwise I agree with you, it's all messed up. We have to keep this under wraps until it's better understood. If there is no solution, no sense broadcasting it. That won't be the case though; I'm too much of an optimist."

Savannah is processing the possible outcomes and is hoping this becomes a bizarre mind control story of global proportion. Her story; the largest story ever written, ever told. She lets out a comfort sigh and imagines the celebrity this could bring.

Savannah's optimism brings no comfort to Spencer.

"It's getting late, where are you staying tonight? Did you get a room booked?" Spencer asks.

"No hon, I'm such a cowboy I do things on the fly. I grab rooms last minute and hope for the best. Amazingly it's worked pretty well for me so far."

"I know we just met, but if you're interested, I have rooms booked for tonight in Kinshasa, and then Sorong. If you stay with me, we can continue figuring this out, forage for edible food, and honestly, I just don't want to be alone right now. I am really creeped out by this stuff."

Savannah thinks about Spencer's offer. Regardless of whether she prefers her own privacy, Savannah knows she's traveling with a mother of a conduit, which could be mankind's biggest story. She wants to keep this person close, and besides, Spencer obviously needs a friend and Savannah is thinking she could use a friend too.

"Yes, Spencer, that would be delightful!"

"I've booked a small private plane to get us from Sorong to Waigeo. You can join me for that, too. Based on research I've done, the best bet is the island's North shore, so we'll fly there first. It's closest to the equator which Alex has told me is important."

"Wow, haven't you become the little surprise! Thank you, hon!"

After Spencer and Savannah arrive in Kinshasa, they grab fast food at the airport and get a cab to Spencer's hotel room. It's a single bed and no sofa. They take this in stride and strip to their underwear as neither of them brought pajamas.

They climb into bed from each side, and instantly fall asleep; the jet lag and mental exhaustion has taken its toll.

ロロロ

The new day brings more hours of cabbing, flying and transfers. No easy way getting to the remote islands of Indonesia.

At 11:10 am, Savannah's cell phone rings and she sees from the caller id it's Rosine. She answers and before Savannah can complete saying, "Hello," Rosine cuts her off. She talks fast and is out of breath, speaking in a heavy accent, forcing Savannah to listen carefully. "Sarah has learned more. I think she just learned it. A few moments ago she put up her hand and asked if she could talk. We went out to the hallway. She says she now knows the purpose of the three locations, and it's wild. Get this - we need three locations so departure zones stay in alignment as the Earth spins. These locations are to remove people from the planet. Sarah speaks with such authority regarding this. Do you believe this? Okay, we can discuss details later, I have to get back to my class. Bye."

Rosine hangs up before Savannah can get a single word in.

Savannah turns to Spencer and repeats what she heard.

Spencer says what they're both thinking, "Where is this coming from? This has me scared shitless! Why Alex? Why me? We're just normal people. I'm so scared."

Savannah approaches Spencer and offers a heartfelt hug. Nothing else is said.

ロロロ

Upon arrival to the Domine Eduard Osok Airport in Sorong, the two women find a shuttle ride taking them to the area of the airport where the smaller private airplanes park, side-by-side in rows, tethered to the ground with straps attached to their wings.

Stepping from the shuttle they observe a well-groomed middle-aged man approaching. He appears Australian with his khaki pants, matching

Columbia shirt, and a worn out Akubra hat, a hat worn by most men who venture into the Australian outback.

Any doubt he is Australian is removed the second he starts speaking. "G'day, I'm hopin' one of you two pretty Sheila's to be Spencer. I'm Brandon. We talked yesterday, yes?"

It relieves Spencer to have found a responsible pilot - she was worried she'd end up needing to hunt him down. She extends her hand as a greeting, "Yes, I'm Spencer. Thanks for being on time, Brandon." She thinks to herself with a smile, "I never considered myself a 'Sheila'."

After shaking Spencer's hand, Brandon looks at Savannah, then back at Spencer, saying, "Assuming your mate here will join us, yes?"

Without waiting for a response, Brandon continues, "It's your lucky day, mates, as me back seats are back in. I get em out when flyin' supplies, and this airport ain't where I keep em."

Brandon's tone changes and becomes more business. "I'm haten be'in rude, but the extra weight causes me plane to burn more petrol. I'z afraid I'z needin a bigger fee to take ya both."

Spencer jumps right in, "I'm sorry, Brandon, I forgot to call and ask if I could bring a friend along. The extra fee is no issue. Sorry."

"No worries."

Savannah is glad this didn't become an issue as she doesn't want to sit out this little adventure. She does an after-the-fact self-introduction by offering her hand.

"Hello, Brandon, as you heard, I'm Savannah. Pleased to meet you and thank you for allowing me to join in the fun."

Not acknowledging the thank you, he responds with, "Follow me, mates."

Spencer looks over at Savannah and whispers, "I thought 'mates' were guys." They both laugh.

Brandon leads them on a short walk over to his 1978 Cessna 172, which he will pilot on the 80-mile flight to the Northern shore of Waigeo. It needs new paint; the equatorial sun has tarnished it over the years.

Savannah climbs onto the worn out back seat with assistance from Brandon, and Spencer jumps in the front. With her longer legs, Savannah would prefer sitting up front, but Spencer didn't offer it up, and it's Spencer's gig at the moment.

Brandon closes the door after the women settle in, then walks around and jumps in like a pro.

After firing up the plane's engine, he does the typical clearance conversations with the tower. The little Cessna taxis the ramp and turns onto the runway. Without stopping, Brandon spins the plane around and goes full throttle; the plane jumps into action. After a short sprint on the runway, the ground falls away. They fly the majority of the flight over the waters of the Northern side of the Bird's Head Peninsula, off the North-Western shores of West Papua. Distances are short, which enables Brandon, just after takeoff, to point out the Island of Waigeo straight ahead near the horizon. The tropical views are breathtaking.

Forty-five minutes later, the little Cessna is bouncing on the unpaved grassy runway near Waigeo's Northern shore edging the Philippine Sea.

While arranging for the private flight arrangements, Spencer asked Brandon about transportation on the island. He was kind enough to set up a local car and driver to meet them upon arrival, and sure enough, a long-haired man with white hair and a white beard wearing a full-length white shalwar and large-brimmed white hat is standing beside an older Toyota Corolla at the side of the airstrip.

Brandon taxis off the end of the runway onto the adjoining grass near the parked car and kills the plane's engine and jumps out.

He yells over to the driver, "Blimey, Peter, you lookin' more like a wizard every time I see you." They laugh.

Brandon helps Spencer and Savannah out of the plane.

After a quick round of introductions, Peter assists Spencer and Savannah into his Corolla and whisks the two down a bumpy dirt road to the local three-room schoolhouse two miles ahead. The school is wooden, with an exterior of horizontal clapboard in need of a coat of white paint. The school is comprised of three rooms, two smaller rooms next to a single large classroom. They connect to an exterior hallway exposed to the weather except for a peaked raised roof running the hallway length.

Spencer and Savannah are hoping to get lucky and find the conduit at school. Spencer had checked if there were language issues, and fortunately, English is one of the mandatory classes taught at the school.

Upon arrival, Peter jumps out of the car first, climbs the three stairs, and walks to the classroom. After looking through the classroom door window and seeing the students are reading, Peter opens the door without knocking. Inside he greets the class with "Hey kids," and walks over to the teacher's desk.

"Mornin' Bree. I brought some folks with me that wanna talk at you. You gotta minute to check them out?"

Bree, without saying a word, has a frown as she gets up from her desk and walks out with Peter to the hallway where Spencer and Savannah are now standing. She says with an edge, "I am Bree. What is this about?"

"Hello, Bree, thanks for seeing us. My name is Spencer and this is Savannah. We have travelled a great distance to find a boy named Jacob who is approximately ten years old. We believe he may be in your class. If he is, he has special information he will want to share. Do you have a student by the name of Jacob?"

Bree doesn't like this. "I don't know who you people are, and I don't give up my students in this way. We have security and privacy protocols we follow."

"Bree, we have travelled halfway around the world for the opportunity to meet the boy named Jacob. We can assure you if he hasn't talked to you about what he knows, he will want to. Can you at least tell us if you have a male student named Jacob who would be about ten years old?"

"If I did, I still wouldn't let you talk to him, so what good does it do if I tell you whether I have a Jacob or not?"

Spencer can sense Bree is protecting her student, and Jacob most likely is in her class. She is frustrated to be so close yet unable to meet. In desperation, Spencer attempts to negotiate, "Bree, if we can't meet Jacob, if in fact he's in your class, would you be willing to approach him personally and ask him if he knows anything about a situation in space he wants to talk about? I know this sounds extremely weird, and you're probably questioning our sanity at this point, but please, your question will be harmless, and the result could surprise you."

Spencer is speaking quickly knowing she will not get much more time before the teacher asks them to leave.

"If he's in your class, and he's the one we think he is, this information is bothering him, and could harm him if he doesn't find someone to discuss it with. It is information about events far beyond the boy's experience or knowledge, more sophisticated than his ability to even look up on his own. Again, if he is who I think he is, he will feel a need to tell you about it, he will feel relief, but only if he feels you can be his confidant."

Spencer pauses for a moment to catch her breath and continues, "Again, I realize this makes no sense to you right now and we're appearing crazy. Frankly, if I were in your shoes, I would think we're crazy too!"

Spencer's tone lowers and becomes more pleading, "But please, it will become clear once you discuss this with him, I guarantee it. We are here on a day trip; we flew in from Sorong. Please talk with him before the day is over. You will understand the importance once you do. I need you to phone me so I know if I'm right or wrong. Would you do that? Here, I'll give you the number," providing a teared off paper piece with her number on it.

"Okay, I'll ask, but it's as far as I go. I'll let you know what he says." Spencer is relieved; she found Jacob.

Spencer reaches out and holds Bree's hand with both of hers and responds with, "Thank you, thank you, thank you! I will be holding my phone awaiting your call later today." Bree, with a 'you are a crazy lady' look, pulls her hand back, nods, and walks back into the classroom.

Spencer and Savannah are elated knowing they have found Jacob as they head outside where Peter has been politely waiting beside his car. They jump in and ride back to the Cessna. After the short bumpy drive, they find Brandon sitting in his reclined plane seat with both doors wide open for ventilation. He is sound asleep with his Akubra pulled over his face.

▯▯▯

As Spencer and Savannah enter their room in Sorong, Spencer's cell phone rings. From the phone's ringtone, she says, "It's my son Alex calling from California!"

"Hello, Alex!" Spencer says with the thrill of a mother hearing from her son.

Alex doesn't respond to the 'hello', and dives straight into his latest learning.

"Mom, we will use the three locations to remove people from the planet. A lot of people will be saved! It's called an exodus."

Spencer, bewildered, asks, "Where will they go?"

"Don't know, Mom, but they will be saved."

Spencer re-asks whether Alex has mentioned this to anyone, especially his father. He says no. They end their call a few minutes later.

Spencer hangs up and looks at Savannah saying, "Oh my God!"

She barely gets those words out, and her phone rings again. She answers the phone and tries to say, "Hello," but gets cut off as Bree starts right in.

Spencer interrupts her, "Bree, slow down. Let me put you on speaker phone so Savannah here can listen in."

Spencer turns on her speaker and lays the phone on the small table in the hotel room. Too hyper to be sitting, they stand over the phone.

Bree starts again, "Oh my god, Jacob, that poor boy. He's been bottling this crazy and amazing information up with no one to talk to about it. His father didn't want to hear it, didn't believe it. He knows about a black hole expansion in our galaxy, he even knows the name of the black hole. I googled it before calling, and it actually exists! He told me an energy wave will destroy the world in ten years, and he just learned there are three locations where people will be saved before it destroys the Earth. He said he's a conduit and there are two others. The conduits live in the locations where people will leave the planet, and they will keep learning to guide us. Is that why you asked about him? Almighty God, where is he getting this?"

Spencer responds, "Yes, my son in Ecuador has the same information and he is also calling himself a conduit. Savannah here has knowledge of a girl in the Congo claiming the same. They all appear to have the exact same message, and they all live on the equator."

Spencer pauses for a second and continues: "My son, Alex, said the conduits were the same age, do you know the age of Jacob? Do you have his birthdate?"

"Yes, wait just a minute, I have all the children's files here in the cabinet." She walks over and shuffles through the cabinet while keeping the cell call alive. "Got it, let's see…, birthdate, birthdate. Ahh, here it is, Jacob's birthday is October 10, 2012."

Spencer pulls out a chair from under the table and plops down.

"Holy shit!" she exclaims to both Savannah and Bree. "It's the exact same birthday as my son Alex."

Spencer, collecting herself continues, "Bree, can you be Jacob's confidant for a while? He will need to talk with you as this stuff is way too hard for him to keep bottled up. Let's agree to keep this under wraps until we figure out what to do with it, okay? These kids seem to learn new information daily, so it would be helpful if you could call us each time Jacob gives you an update. Can you do that?"

Bree agrees to everything and they end the call.

Spencer asks Savannah, "Can you call Rosine and get Sarah's birthdate? She should be at her school about now."

Savannah calls Rosine who answers from within her classroom. Savannah fills Rosine in on the third conduit who provided a corroborating story and asks for Sarah's birthdate. Rosine tells her students to be quiet and leaves them to go to the file room down the hall; she pulls out Sarah's records.

After a few moments searching the document for the date, she says, "Sarah was born on the 10th day of October 2012. They even have her time of birth on the record; she was born at 6:31 pm."

Savannah asks Rosine if she can photograph the document and send it to her. She thanks Rosine and ends the call.

They don't say a word. Spencer breaks the silence, "Savannah, at 6:31 pm in the Congo, what time would that be in LA where Alex was born?"

Savannah opens her tablet computer that doesn't leave her side, and checks the time zones on 'timeanddate.com'. "It would be ten thirty-one am in LA, it's nine hours earlier."

"Fuck! What is happening here?" Spencer shouts. "My son and Sarah were born within the same minute of each other. With the way this crazy fucking story is unfolding, I'll bet Jacob was born at the same time, too. If true, this is beyond coincidence. This is just really really fucking spooky.

What the hell, what the fuck are we dealing with?" Spencer seldom uses the 'f' word.

Regaining her composure, "Savannah, can you forward Sarah's birth-date info to me when you receive it?"

Savannah has been taking this in and doesn't answer Spencer's last request; she's in deep thought. She says, "So here we are. We know three kids calling themselves conduits. They are unrelated and have never met or spoken. Born within the same minute of each other. They live on three different continents yet receive identical information telling us the Earth will fry in ten years. But miraculously, all is not lost. They mark the locations where people will escape the planet and go to who knows where, and they will tell us how to do it. To top it off, these children have no idea who, where, or how they're learning this stuff. Am I missing something here?"

It frustrates Savannah; she's sitting on the biggest story ever told and she can't expose it. No sane person will believe it ... not yet. "We can't expose this! If these kids stop receiving information after we expose the story, they will crucify us! If this is real, we're dealing with forces outside this world, hell, outside this galaxy. This can't really be happening, right? What the hell do we do now? Tell the world Angels have arrived? Tell them Christ has returned in the body of three kids? This just doesn't happen!" Savannah has swerved from her usual cool demeanor.

Spencer has been tuning out Savannah's rant; she has moved into her own private headspace thinking about what is unfolding. "They must have chosen Alex before we moved him to Ecuador because these kids were all born at the same time, way before Alex lived on the equator. They knew he would move to the equator. How did 'they' know I'd move to Ecuador? This is surreal. How were these kids chosen? Have we been manipulated?"

Savannah, who had stopped ranting, and was listening to Spencer's reasoning, simply says, "Wow!"

Spencer and Savannah contact Rosine and Bree, and they agree to connect as often as necessary to discuss the events as they unfold. Spencer tells the group she has an idea for the next plan of action, but doesn't elaborate. They don't ask.

☐☐☐

Spencer flies back to California to meet with Jack and Alex. Savannah returns to the Congo.

CHAPTER 4

JACK

After an entire day of travelling, Spencer digs her phone from her purse, presses the phone's home button and says, "Hey Siri, call Jack." After a few rings, Jack answers and Spencer explains she's landed at LAX and is renting a car. Without asking Jack what he is doing, she tells him to be home with Alex within two hours and have stiff drinks poured and ready. She ends the call as abruptly as she started it.

⌷⌷⌷

Spencer pulls her rented red Nissan Sentra into Jack's U-shaped driveway two hours after talking to him. She gets out and walks to the front door, rings the doorbell and without waiting, enters the house. Jack seldom keeps his doors locked. Secluded, Lake Arrowhead doesn't experience crime.

Alex, hearing the doorbell, comes running to the door. His father had told him Spencer was on her way. Alex gives his mom a big hug and says, "Missed you, Mom."

"Missed you too sweetie," and then asks, "Are we all good here?"

"Yeah, Mom, I've got more stuff to tell you, but I haven't talked to Dad yet."

"Thank you, Alex. Now please wait a few minutes and then you can tell your Dad and I the new stuff at the same time. I need a few minutes alone with your father to fill him in. You will be happy to know I found out a lot about your story and believe everything you've said. I'm sorry I didn't trust your story at the beginning. Now go find something to do for ten minutes; I need to talk to your father."

Alex slumps his head and says, "Okay," then saunters away.

Spencer yells so Alex hears her from a distance, "We'll call you," then she turns and yells even louder, "Jack?"

Jack responds from within his office at the back of the house adjacent to the family room adorned with an A-frame cathedral ceilings and floor-to-ceiling windows. The expansive unobstructed view of the San Bernardino Mountains is breathtaking. "I'm in the office, come on back."

Spencer walks around to see Jack straightening papers on his typically cluttered desk. On one edge of the desk, Spencer spots two drinks and smiles when she notices the ice hasn't begun to melt. She knows Jack will have poured her a 'Seabreeze', a cocktail with a rose color from the Cranberry juice. Following her first sip, she says, "Thank you, Jack, I needed this, and it tastes like the best drink I've ever had!"

"Jesus, Spencer, you look awful."

"Thanks, Jack. I feel awful; it's been a whirlwind."

"I'm assuming you're about to tell me about your adventures that were so important it was worth pulling Alex out of school, correct?"

"Jack, you have no idea, take a big drink and sit."

Spencer and Jack both sink into the two large soft leather lounge chairs in the office. She shifts her body towards Jack and looks straight into his eyes, takes a drink, and says, "Jack, I'm about to tell you a story. Please don't interrupt me until I'm done. You can ask questions after but let me say this uninterrupted. Is that okay?"

"Jesus, Spencer, slow down and take a big breath, you're scaring me. I'm all ears, tell it however you like."

Spencer, accepting Jack's suggestion, takes a big breath, another drink, sighs, and explains in detail the entire story starting from Alex's initials comments to the finding of Sarah and Alex. Jack is expressionless.

"Jack, I'm trying so hard right now to keep myself together. The last message the conduits received is they will get additional instructions on how to pull this all off. Alex also has another message he hasn't told me yet. I thought he could tell us both."

Jack, without saying a word, lifts his glass and downs his drink, which he hasn't touched since Spencer started. She takes Jack's cue and knocks hers back.

Jack gets up and walks out of the office.

Spencer waits expecting Jack to return. After the longest five minutes of her life, she says, "Jesus," gets up, and goes looking for him. She promised Alex the three of them will talk; she needs Jack back.

Spencer looks outside and sees Alex riding his bike on the path he and his Dad had formed around the perimeter of their large property. In an agitated state, she walks from room-to-room in the house calling out for Jack. There is no response. She opens the door to the garage, the last remaining place Jack could be. It is dark so Spencer flips on the light switch. She sees Jack sitting in the driver's seat of his one-year-old BMW M850i.

"Christ," Spencer says to herself, as she walks over and pulls the handle of the passenger door. Her wrist strains as she pulls on the locked non-moving door handle. In sheer frustration she yells, "Fuck." Spencer is tired and her patience has run out. After a tap on the window she hears the door unlock. She opens the door, climbs in beside Jack, and closes the door behind her. The two look straight ahead through the windshield and neither says a word.

Jack is first to break the silence. "How the hell do you expect me to respond to that, Spencer?"

Spencer, now angry, says, "I don't know, Jack. You tell me. I didn't ask for this either. I'm hoping it's a bad dream or someone's idea of a fucking sick joke. Don't you dare look at me thinking this is my fault. Like I said, I didn't ask for this either. Right now I'm the messenger."

"Jesus, Spencer."

"I need you to help me with this, Jack, because I don't know what to do. Our son is here, and he's having to handle it. Do you want him handling it alone? He's expecting to talk with us, and he has more information he needs to tell. Jack, this information will keep coming. We need to do something about it. For Alex's sake, you will need to step up and be strong, Jack, Alex needs his father right now. Let's take it bit by bit and figure out what we're dealing with."

Jack relents and gets back on his game. "Let's talk to Alex."

"Thanks, Jack."

On the walk back to the office, Jack looks at Spencer, "I think we need another drink."

"I was waiting for that offer! I was hoping I wouldn't have to ask!"

Jack rounds up the empty cocktail glasses from the office and takes them to his bar in his large living room and pours refills. Spencer goes to the back door and calls for Alex.

They regroup in the office where Spencer and Jack sit back into the same comfy lounge chairs. Alex turns a smaller stationary chair at Jack's desk and sits to face his parents.

"Mom, is it okay if I tell Dad now?"

"Yes, Alex, I've already told your Dad most of it, tell us the latest stuff you've learned."

"Pretty crazy what's going on, hey Dad? Can you believe I'm a conduit!" Still not knowing what it really means.

"Yes, Alex, it's pretty crazy."

Alex starts his update, "Well, the last thing I learned is it will take at least five years to build three towers, one at each of the conduit locations. The towers are to get people off the planet. They have to be five miles high. Their height will align with the new location where we'll be going. Us conduits will learn how to do it and then show people. We will provide special instructions because this hasn't been attempted before."

Spencer and Jack say nothing. There aren't words to help them understand what they hear; they can't comprehend where it is coming from. In their own way, they are both hoping the situation is a huge farce, and maybe, just maybe, the Milky Way's central black hole is doing just fine.

After a pause, Jack looks at Spencer, and then over at Alex. "Sorry, Alex, as much as we believe you, we will need more than this before we can go public. Just because you kids have the same information and the same birth dates, it will take more to convince people we're doomed before we can build five-mile-high towers, it just is. Maybe, as this progresses and you and the others learn more, we'll have something."

Jack continues, saying in a fatherly way, "Alex, it is very, very important you tell nobody except us about what you are learning. People will use this kind of information against you and us. We need time to sort this out. We will need a plan. Do you understand what I'm asking you?"

"Yes, Dad, I won't tell anyone, but we also have to hurry, because every day we waste, it will mean less people get to escape."

Jack looks at Alex and says, "What are you talking about?"

"The towers, while they are being built, will be the home to everyone who is helping. The entire project will be self-contained. The longer it takes us to get started, the less time there is to recruit and complete construction before the Earth is destroyed. If we run out of time and don't finish the towers, no-one will be saved.

Jack and Spencer are expressionless.

Staying focused, Jack asks, "Alex, you're not describing many people compared to the Earth's population. Who determines who gets to go?"

"We haven't learned yet, Dad, but I think we'll know pretty soon."

Alex looks reflective and says one more thing, "Oh, and I think I learn this stuff in my sleep, because when I wake up in the morning, I know it."

"Alex, doesn't learning all this scare you? You say you are speaking with someone or something outside our world about our demise; and it doesn't seem to be affecting you? How are the other conduits dealing with it?"

"It's strange Dad, we know this is a huge thing, but we're being taught to not be affected by it. I can't explain it any better. It just doesn't scare us; it's like this is all normal."

Jack asks Alex to step out so he can talk with Spencer. Alex again slumps his head and shuffles out. Jack gets up and closes the door, and then paces.

"Jesus, Spencer, is there no way Alex is coming across this information, and then somehow formulating it into a story while dreaming?"

"Come on Jack, and the others? Consider the bigger picture. What are the odds this is one big coincidence? These kids are experiencing the same thing. They all have the same advanced knowledge and they have the same birth dates to the minute. Think about it."

"I know, I know. I don't want to believe it. This is doomsday stuff, Spencer. I want nothing to do with it."

"That ship sailed, Jack. You're in this now. He's your son." She continues, "I'm seeing a quandary here. The longer we wait to get things started, it could fail if Alex's story is correct and we run out of time. If we blurt this stuff out, we'll get crucified, and no one will believe it. The only news coverage will be the tabloids and we'll be laughing stocks. Not liking this, Jack."

"Spencer, do you really believe our son and his cohorts will move people to God knows where? Do you honestly believe this will happen? Come on! No one is going to be building five-mile-high towers."

Jack stops and reflects for a moment. "What if this story is partially true? What if the Milky Way is just fine? What if this is a scheme outside of our realm of understanding to get human slaves for some corrupt government, or worse, for some alien world? Maybe some government is using brainwashing techniques to gain world domination. Or maybe mass genocide. We have to be careful here, Spencer."

"Jesus Jack, I hadn't thought about that. This stuff is so weird, I don't think we can count anything out."

Jack continues to pace, "We need proof the Earth will be destroyed, and if we get it, this is just more fucked up. Where are the people going to go? Alex said the whole galaxy is getting destroyed, not just the Earth. Moving people to another galaxy is Star Wars shit. Fuck! Spencer, if this is for a nefarious purpose, then something is in Alex's head; the kids are being manipulated. If someone has developed a technology to brainwash someone in their sleep, we're all in trouble. But damn, what about the birthdates? No way the bad guys could find three kids born in the exact same minute. No way! Shit, this is such a brain fry. I'll never have a good night's sleep after this."

"I'm so scared, Jack. Nothing is going to be the same again. Why us? Of everyone on this planet, why the fuck us?" Spencer has tears in her eyes.

After an embracing hug, Jack and Spencer discuss and agree they need to keep Alex's life as normal as possible while the situation unravels. Normalcy means getting Alex back to his home environment, including school.

Spencer helps Alex pack up his belongings, and after last-minute late flight arrangements, they say their goodbyes and head back to LAX for the trip home.

$$\Box\Box\Box$$

It's a few minutes after 9 am and Savannah gets a phone call from Rosine. "Hello, Rosine! Watcha got?"

Rosine starts right in, "Sarah has new information, but there's more. It's the weirdest thing I've ever seen. I was looking at Sarah this morning in class. She had gotten off her desk seat to grab a book from her bag on the floor. In the motion of bending over, it looked like she froze. She was in a position where she couldn't have kept her balance; she was leaning way over with one foot on the ground and her body was horizontal and neither hands were touching anything. Her body was suspended there. In a few seconds, she continued moving and grabbed a leg of her desk as if nothing had happened. She didn't lose her balance, picked up her book and continued on. She then raised her hand and asked if she could talk with me. Sarah had more information she wanted to share. I think she received the information while in that creepy suspended position. I've never seen anything like it … it freaked me. When I talked with her, I asked her if she lost her balance while picking up her book. She said no and gave me a look of 'why would you ask me that?' She had no recollection of being frozen in a suspended state."

Savannah, not understanding what she heard, responds with, "Weird!" After a short pause, she asks for the new news Sarah has.

"Sorry, Savannah, I got so excited by what I saw, I forgot to tell you what she said. She gave me the date and time the astronomers and scientists here on Earth will detect an extremely strong gravitational wave and see the new star replacing the galaxy's black hole. We now have a date when we can verify something is happening, people will actually see it," and then with a questioning tone, "if it actually happens, it is December 17th."

"Wow! An actual date. I've got goosebumps!" Savannah says.

She does quick math in her head. December 17th is only twenty-two days away. She is now thinking, do I tell the world what is happening and risk the fallout if December 17th doesn't happen, or do I bury this story until we have the evidence?

Rosine breaks into Savannah's thoughts. "One more thing, Savannah. Sarah says this information needs to be communicated to people right away so when the events get detected, people will believe the story. Sarah told me the story will be more acceptable and believable if it's contingent on us telling our story as a future event. If we tell it after the astronomers announce their findings, they won't believe us, we have to be first. Can you believe we're getting this reasoning from our ten-year-old Sarah?"

"It's mind boggling. Thanks, Rosine, for the update. I'll get back to you." Savannah ends the call.

Savannah says aloud to herself, "Holy Shit."

Rosine keeps her eye on Sarah for the rest of the day but doesn't see additional strange behaviors.

▯▯▯

Alex awakes to his alarm as usual and walks into the kitchen to get his porridge. This morning is different; Spencer isn't in the kitchen. Alex calls out, "Mom!" but he doesn't receive a response. He then walks to her bedroom, and through the open doorway sees Spencer lying face down on the bed with her clothes on.

Alex's adrenaline skyrockets as he runs and leaps on his mother's bed. As he lands, he shakes her and yells, "Mom! Mom!"

Spencer moans, and then much to Alex's relief, rolls over. Looking up at him, she says, "What time is it?"

"It's seven, Mom, I just got up. Are you okay? You scared me!"

"I'm fine, Alex, I was so tired after getting home last night, I guess I just crashed."

"That's okay, Mom, you probably haven't been sleeping."

Full of admiration, Spencer says, "You are wise beyond your years."

Her cell phone interrupts the moment. Still in a groggy state, she sits up and slides off the bed and walks towards the buzz. By the time she finds her purse, the ringing stops. She looks at the caller ID; it was Savannah. Spencer decides she will get Alex off to school before calling her back; she doesn't want the conversation rushed.

Alex strolls into the kitchen a few minutes later dressed for school. While waiting for his porridge, he starts in on his morning update, "Mom, December 17th is the day scientists will detect the events in space I described to you. I learned this. We have to tell everyone about the date, otherwise people won't believe the story. If we tell everyone about it after it happens, nobody will believe us."

Spencer thinks for a minute. Alex has gone from describing specific times and events, to now talking about reasoning and communicating. She thinks back to the previous days' conversation with Jack. If December 17th pans out, it answers the doubts they had been discussing; this would be the evidence they were looking for. "Alex, how do you know it's wise to let people know before the scientists see it?"

"Because, Mom, it needs describing in advance for us to be credible. We need well thought out communication. I learned this."

Spencer turns away from Alex and cries while she finishes making the porridge. She has been bottling up the emotion arising from her crazy journey. For the first time, she can't help showing her emotion. It takes Alex a minute to realize his mom is crying and asks, "Mom! What's wrong?"

"I'm sorry, Alex. When I hear you talk, I realize I'm losing the per-fectly normal ten-year-old son I had. I know you can't help it, but you're changing before my eyes. We're talking about a doomsday and saving mankind, and all I want is to live here peacefully with my boy and enjoy a normal life."

"I'm sorry, Mom, I didn't know this was bothering you so much. Every morning when I wake up I know a bunch more stuff. I can't make it go away. I don't want you crying. Are you mad at me over this Mom?"

Spencer realizes she is putting an additional burden on her son. "Of course not, Alex. I'm not mad. Please don't think that. I know it's not your fault this is happening. Your dad and I will do whatever it takes to help you sort this out. I'm sorry, Alex."

"It's okay, Mom."

Spencer wipes away her remaining tears.

Alex finishes his porridge later than normal, and for the first time without his mother, heads for school. Once Alex is out the door, Spencer calls the school, apologizing for needing to be late. The administrator on the other end of the line isn't sympathetic with Spencer and reminds her the only people getting hurt with her absences and tardiness are the students. Spencer sucks up the reprimand, apologizes again, and then calls Savannah back.

It's a hot mid-afternoon in the Congo and Savannah answers on the first ring. Trying to keep things light, she answers the call without saying hello. "Hey girlie, talk to me!"

Spencer cracks a smile as she pictures Savannah saying that. The fun introduction worked, as the smile has brought Spencer out of her funk.

"I miss you," Spencer says.

"Yes, we became the best little team to beat, didn't we?"

Savannah, after working alone as much as she does, has enjoyed Spencer's company. She has developed a closeness for Spencer and is hoping it's genuine and not simply related to her job of 'getting to the story'. It's a gray area Savannah often can't reconcile.

"Yes, we're the team to beat," Spencer responds.

Changing topics and getting right to business, Spencer continues, "I'm betting you already know about December 17th, don't you? I bet you also know we have to get the word out before the date. Am I right?"

Savannah responds, "It's like we don't need to talk, we each have sources with identical information. So weird."

"I'll call Jack and conference you in. We need to talk about this together. Alex told me timing and wording of the message is important. A week ago I couldn't have imagined my son saying that!"

Savannah agrees a conference call will be great and states she will call Jacob's school teacher Bree, as she hasn't heard from her.

After the call, Spencer returns to the kitchen to complete her after-breakfast cleanup. When complete, she picks up her phone to call Jack. As she picks up the phone, it rings. She looks at the caller ID ... it's Jack.

"Hello, Jack, I was just about to call you."

"Spencer, I've been thinking about this," Jack says without a salutation. "Before we do anything, I need to meet the other two kids and their parents. I have to see all of this for myself. I need the three kids together for this to be real for me." Jack talks fast and doesn't let Spencer jump into the one-way conversation, "If this thing is real, it will consume us. You need to quit your job at the school. I'll swing by tomorrow to get you, and the three of us will fly to..., what was the town's name?"

"It's Mbandaka Jack, and Alex had more information for us this morning. Interested?"

"Don't mess with me Spencer. What did he say?"

"Take it easy, Jack! I think we should both hear these updates from Alex rather than you hear it through me, so this is my last update. Alex says the date the scientists will see the events in space is on December 17th. He also said our message has to go out before the scientist's message, or the world won't believe us. Alex also said we need to craft the message carefully; do you believe that? Our little boy saying that! You said swing by tomorrow. I'm assuming you're flying in? Right? What time?"

Jack learned many years back to stay on point and to filter information so conversations stay on track. His heartbeat raced when he heard the December 17th date, but he holds back talking about it; there will be better times. He says, "Be where the private aircraft are at the airport for 9 am. It's a long flight to central Africa, so we need a decent start time. We can all talk about the message when we get together. If you don't hear from me again, assume we're good for nine tomorrow. I guess my decision to swing by tomorrow is better than I thought, given how little time we now have."

"See you tomorrow, Jack."

Spencer thinks to herself how yet again, Jack is turning this into business; she hears it in his voice and the way he is now acting. It was the trait that pulled her away; Jack was always business, and she was second place. Her job was to raise Alex; Jack was seldom there for him because of his business obligations, or maybe more accurately, his obsession. Spencer is thinking how glad she is she's no longer with Jack, but how grateful she is he's still there for her, helping, and has the means to be effective.

Spencer calls Savannah back to announce the change of plans. She explains that Jack, Alex and she will travel to Mbandaka tomorrow on a private jet, and Jack wants to get the conduits together. It thrills Savannah at the prospect of seeing Spencer again.

"Swanky," she says, "Flying in on a private jet; look at you!"

Spencer smiles, "See you tomorrow and prepare yourself for some travelling and who knows what - I think we're all jumping onto a wild ride. Bye again," and hangs up the phone.

Spencer crafts her resignation letter to the school. In addition, she explains Alex will also be absent for an undetermined time period. She walks the letter over to the school, not looking forward to dealing with it.

CHAPTER 5

THE MEETING

Spencer prepares breakfast for Alex as she listens to him explain the message prepared for the world needs planning. He explains it needs to include forming international committees to manage building the towers, creating processes for deciding who qualifies for the exodus, and the logistics for the transfer of needed materials. He says it will be the largest worldwide organizational commitment ever attempted. He assures his mom she doesn't need to know the details just yet.

"There is one more thing, Mom, I learned building the towers and getting people off the planet is a testament to see if mankind can work together to save itself. This isn't a sure thing; if people don't work together on this, it will fail."

Spencer is thinking to herself, "Wow, so now my family and a chosen few others need to pull mankind together for the profound need to save itself. Just another regular day…"

After breakfast cleanup, Spencer and Alex drive to the airport, and proceed to the area where the private jets are parked on the tarmac. Off in the distance they can see the landing lights of a small plane on final approach. They are hoping it is Jack.

As the plane lands, Alex and Spencer can see it's a large private jet, much larger than the typical Learjet most people visualize.

They watch it taxi to an open area amongst other private jets and hear its engines spool down. The front door opens and the stairs robotically unfold. Emerging from the plane at the top of the gangway is Jack, standing there larger than life, wearing khaki shorts and a brightly colored button shirt most likely purchased at Tommy Bahama. He appears dressed for a tropical vacation.

Jack looks over at the administrative building used by the private jet operators and sees Spencer and Alex waiting on the upper step which slopes down to the tarmac. They wave as eye contact is established. Jack steps back into the plane then reappears with a younger man dressed as a flight attendant with dark pants and a crisp white shirt. They both skip down the gangway and hurry over to greet Spencer and Alex. Jack introduces Andre as his flight attendant as they grab most of the luggage; Spencer and Alex grab the rest. They head towards the plane.

Once aboard, Jack introduces Spencer and Alex to the two pilots. Alex asks if he can sit up front for a while to watch; the pilots are obliged to agree. They strap Alex into the jump seat inside the flight deck.

The engines spool back up, and Andre asks Spencer what her preferred drink is to start off this twelve-hour flight; he didn't need to ask Jack.

▯▯▯

After a quick refueling stop, it is 2:50 am local time in Mbandaka as the big Gulfstream glides towards the runway on final approach. Even though it was only 9 pm Ecuador time, the long flight has taken its toll, and everyone has been sleeping for the last few hours. Andre woke the three travelers ten minutes earlier, so they are now in sitting positions for the landing.

As the jet taxis up to its designated parking spot, the entire airport as viewed from the portal windows of the plane looks deserted. Spencer and Jack had agreed they will stay and sleep on the plane after it lands rather than attempt transportation and accommodations in the dark. Their plan was to sleep for just under six hours so they could be up and active by 9 am local time.

The seats on the big Gulfstream fold and make for comfortable sleeping. Andre ensures everyone has blankets and pillows for a reasonable night's sleep before retiring to his own small private cabin.

000

Andre's is abruptly awakened as his watch alarm goes off at 8:50 am local time. He enters the cabin, opens the window shades and wakes up his three passengers. He provides microwaved warm hand cloths for everyone to freshen their faces and takes drink orders. Spencer and Jack both ask for coffee, and Alex asks for orange juice.

While the coffee is percolating, Andre fetches the orange juice out of the fridge. He pours the juice into a plastic glass and takes it over to where Alex is sitting, handing it to him. Alex stands while reaching out to grab the glass from Andre and just as the glass is placed in his hand, he freezes. Alex, in mid-movement while getting up, is bent over with only one foot on the ground. Andre, believing Alex has the glass, lets go. The glass falls through Alex's stiffened hand to the floor, splashing orange juice everywhere. Spencer and Jack, startled by the sound of the full plastic cup hitting the floor, spin around to face the source of the noise. They see Alex frozen in an eerie position, not moving, and not in a position enabling balance without movement. They notice his huge dilated pupils. Spencer yells, "Alex!" which brings no response. Two seconds later Alex is normal, finishes standing up and notices the orange juice on the floor. He didn't see the glass fall. He sees everyone with bewildered looks, and asks, "What happened?"

No one says a word.

Alex breaks the silence by saying, "Not sure why everyone looks like they saw a ghost, but after we clean up this mess and you two have a moment, I want to tell you about the new stuff I just learned."

Spencer and Jack look at each other, continuing their silence.

Alex, now frustrated, says, "What's up with you two?"

⛶⛶⛶

Bree waits until 5 pm to call Savannah, not wanting to disturb her too early. By habit, Savannah looks at her watch when her phone rings and she sees it is 9 am in Mbandaka as she answers. She sees Bree's caller ID and offers a cheery, "Hello, Bree!"

Bree asks the typical and cordial 'how are you doing' questions and then goes straight into the Jacob update. She tells Savannah everything Jacob has told her, and it corroborates what Sarah and Alex have already said.

Savannah brings Bree up-to-date on Spencer and Jack's arrival today in Mbandaka, and the likelihood they will want to make plans to fly into Indonesia to meet her and Jacob. Savannah says Jack will want to meet with Jacob's parents. Bree responds it needs careful handling as Jacob has not spoken to his father about the conduits beyond his first attempt.

Just as Savannah is setting down her phone, it rings again. This time it is Spencer.

"Hello, girlie, are you safe here in Mbandaka?"

Spencer smiles again upon hearing 'girlie'.

"I don't think I'd call this place safe, but we've arrived. We slept on the plane last night after we landed, and we're just about to get rolling. Do you want to meet us for some food? I'll introduce you to Jack and we can make plans."

Savannah is an early riser, and responds with, "I've already had breakfast, but I can always use more coffee. Should I recommend a place? The hotel restaurants are the safest regarding food quality, so I would suggest Hotel Uvira. Why don't I swing by the airport and pick you up?"

⯅⯅⯅

Twenty minutes later, Savannah pulls her Range Rover to the edge of the airport tarmac. There is no airport security in these small airports, and Savannah, without being questioned, can walk straight to the plane.

While walking, she sees the side door open, and the stairs folding towards the tarmac. Spencer is the first person to appear at the plane's entrance. She hops down the steps, meeting Savannah at the base. They embrace in a heartfelt hug.

Spencer says, "I've missed you."

"Me too!"

⯅⯅⯅

Jack is controlling the conversation in the Hotel Uvira's restaurant. He explains why he wants to get the entire group together. This includes having Spencer, Alex, Sarah, Rosine, Savannah, along with Bree, Jacob, his parents, all meet. Jack wants to do this in Indonesia, as the final destination. He explains he wants Savannah to make arrangements to have Sarah and Rosine, and herself, join them on the next leg of the trip. They agree the meeting location will be Sorong. Jack asks Spencer to book a meeting room in whichever hotel she books the overnight rooms.

Savannah expresses her concern that Rosine, as a teacher, will find it difficult to leave her class with no notice.

Jack replies, "Savannah, explain to Rosine this meeting is much more important right now than the students not having a teacher for a few days. Tell her if she can't get a substitute in the eleventh hour, to just cancel her class until further notice. I know it seems harsh and insensitive, but this situation is more important, and we have to act on it fast. Tell Rosine I will compensate her for lost time and if her school board lets her go, I will subsidize her for as long as it takes. Tell her I guarantee she will never be at a financial loss."

Jack continues, "Tell her to have herself and Sarah to the plane by eleven am tomorrow. That will give her enough time."

Savannah responds, "Jack, that is very generous of you, I will make sure she is aware of it and will explain to Rosine the seriousness and urgency we all feel. The biggest challenge for Rosine in trying to meet your schedule, is getting custody of Sarah from the state; she is not Sarah's guardian."

Jack jumps in, not letting Savannah continue, "Savannah, if Sarah is in agreement, we just take her. If this story unfolds the way I think it will, abducting Sarah will be an insignificant sidebar in this adventure."

"I'll try to convince her Jack, but I can't promise anything. Are you sure we want those optics portrayed given the tremendous pushback we'll get when we publicize this?" Savannah says with an astonished look.

"My experience always works for me is if it needs to get done, regardless of the perception, just do whatever it takes, and beg forgiveness and do the damage control after. We have to keep our eyes on the target, and I think our target right now is getting everyone together without waiting on a bureaucracy, which I'm sure will work at a snail's pace. Hell, if we ask permission to take Sarah, we'll still be sitting at this table in a week."

"Okay, Jack, I'll try, but I can't guarantee Rosine's reaction," Savannah says as she stands up and excuses herself to go to the lady's room. Spencer asks if she can join.

"Let's go."

The women find a single joint sex toilet room with a single soiled toilet and dirty sink. They lock the door behind them and take turns squatting over the toilet to avoid contact. While Spencer is relieving herself, Savannah says, "Spencer, since I'm now the one with the room, why don't you stay with me tonight? I'm guessing you don't want to share a room with Jack, so I'm thinking Jack and Alex can get a room or stay on the plane. I love having you around. How does that sound?"

Spencer smiles, "I was hoping you would ask!"

Back at the table, Jack continues making plans for the remainder of the trip. After discussing the need for everyone to meet, he asks, "Savannah, how do you think we should take this story public?"

"I've been thinking about this a lot," Savannah says. "I will meet with my producers and wow them with a sell job presentation. I'm sure I can get them to the second phase which needs to be this entire team meeting them; they definitely won't agree without meeting the children. The story has to be credible; and given its significance, it will break the agency if it becomes known as a hoax or for any reason goes down the drain. There needs to be complete buy-in and we have to arrange a news conference. We all need to be there. In addition, I will get permission for all the other major news agencies to attend and cover it. I'm a trained correspondent and can present the core part of the story and have it followed up by the correspondents in the gallery asking specific questions. That's when things will get interesting. I'm sure the first questions will be things like, 'where are the messages coming from?', 'is this God communicating with us?', 'are the conduits the children of god?', 'has Christ returned as children?', 'how can a tower five miles high get built?' You get the point. Our responses can't be speculative. We either know the answer, or we say we don't know."

Jack responds, "Well, let's ensure we get your producer interested, otherwise we have a huge challenge ahead. Our announcement, when followed with evidence, will cause a worldwide crisis. The markets will crash as everyone attempts to sell their long-term investments, there will be runs at the banks, and we will panic the churches as they try to remain relevant. Every government will lose control as the people demand answers. I can tell you right now it will be a mess."

No one knows what to say. Spencer, changing topics, asks Jack, "What are your plans tonight? Are you getting a room with Alex, or staying on the plane? I am staying with Savannah because I need to clean up, and I couldn't say no to a gracious offer." She and Savannah smile.

Jack looks at Alex, "What will it be, buddy? Are we getting a room, or hanging on the plane?"

"Let's do the plane, Dad."

Spencer asks Savannah, "Why don't I go with you to talk to Rosine? Maybe two can be more persuasive and knowing another conduit's mother is here will help her decide, and after all, you are just a reporter," she says with a laugh and an eye wink.

Savannah asks Jack if he needs to go anywhere else, offering up her willingness to drive him. He thanks Savannah for the offer and says no. After Jack pays the check by Visa, the four of them head back and drop Jack and Alex off at the plane.

It is mid-afternoon by the time Savannah and Spencer head towards Sarah's school. Savannah calls Rosine from her cell phone while driving; she immediately answers the call. Teachers do not have phones in class to distract them while teaching, but Rosine's is the exception. Being in a high-risk neighborhood, and given how seldom she receives calls, she keeps her phone close.

Rosine agrees to a meeting and says she is looking forward to meeting Spencer.

Upon arrival at the school, Rosine dismisses her class early after arranging for a walking chaperone for the students. She asks Sarah to stay behind to meet Spencer and offers to drive her back afterwards, something she has done often.

They go down the hall to a room with small round tables. There are supplies around the room's perimeter, and Spencer notices she is in a workshop where the students create art and do projects.

Rosine motions to the group to sit. Spencer asks Rosine if it is okay if Sarah waits outside for just a few minutes. Without waiting for Rosine to respond, Sarah obediently leaves the room. Rosine steps over and closes the door.

After quick introductions by Savannah, Spencer jumps right in, "Rosine, I want to hear your take on what you're hearing from Sarah."

"It's surreal," Rosine responds. "She is telling me detailed things more sophisticated than her capabilities of learning or understanding."

"Where do you think this information is coming from?"

"I don't know, nor does Sarah. It's just strange. I've seen her when she receives the information, and it was the most bewildering thing I've ever seen. She froze in mid-movement, and it appeared like gravity had stopped working on her; she was just suspended in mid-air. Once she regained movement, she had more information to tell me. She had no recollection of the moment she froze."

"Oh my God!" Spencer exclaims, "Alex went through the same situation this morning on the plane! He then said he had more information. I wonder if it was at the same time?"

Spencer now gets to the point. "Rosine, my son has been getting the same messages as Sarah, even though she lives almost halfway around the world. Do you believe we have to act on this, over and above anything else?"

Rosine clearly doesn't understand the context of the question. She replies, "Sarah has told me the message needs telling, so people can prepare. She also said the message needs to be broadcast before the astronomers see the evidence of the doomsday event. People won't believe the message otherwise."

"Okay, good," Spencer interrupts. "We want you to take a big leap and join us to meet with the third conduit named Jacob, so all three children can communicate this, just as Sarah has requested. We need to act fast. We know this will be a difficult choice, but it's important for the children to meet, and Sarah won't want to travel on her own. We have to announce this to the world together as a group."

"I could never leave my class!"

"Rosine, I think we're dealing with something much bigger and more important than your students right now. Do you see that?"

"I know, but I can't abandon them; many come from poor and desperate circumstances, I just can't leave them."

"Rosine, we understand you are Sarah's only confidant. If you don't join us, Sarah won't want to come - we are all strangers to her. It's imperative we act fast on this, and we can't do it without Sarah, and she won't do it without you. This will be hard on you, no question - it was hard on me. I'm also a teacher and I had to leave my students too, I totally understand. If you don't come with us, then Sarah will never get her message out, that will distress her. If this story is true, and you blocked her message, you will never forgive yourself and it could ruin Sarah."

The pressure on Rosine is causing her eyes to water, "What do you expect me to do, just disappear and not show up tomorrow?"

"No Rosine, let your school and students know."

Rosine sighs and relents, "Okay, I will come with you, but I have no money to cover my expenses, I'm not sure how I can do this."

"Rosine, my ex-husband Jack has committed to funding us. So, don't worry, we will have food and accommodation throughout this adventure. Jack promised, and he is solid on his word."

"Okay, I'll do it. Please understand I'm not trying to be difficult, but this is hard for me. I'll let the orphanage know Sarah is leaving with me for a few days."

"Are you sure that's a good idea, Rosine?" Spencer asks. "I'm assuming you are not her legal guardian, correct? You will need to get this authorized. We're concerned it could take too long or get denied altogether. Can you agree to meet us here tomorrow morning with Sarah and not mention this to the orphanage?"

Rosine is clearly stressed. "I can't just take her. I could be locked up."

"What are our options Rosine? You know what will happen if you ask permission," Spencer says.

"This is awful. I hate being so underhanded, but you're right, it would be difficult getting Sarah out. My teaching friend will help me with this. I'll ask Sarah to come early. I could go to jail when we return."

"Don't worry, it won't happen. We'll figure it out. Can we have her here at 7:30?" Spencer asks.

"I hate to be deceptive with her, but yes. I'll request she be here at 7:30 so we can further discuss her story. This is just crazy."

⬛⬛⬛

Rosine drives Sarah to the orphanage as arranged. During the ride Rosine asks her to arrive an hour early the following morning. Sarah agrees and tells Rosine she will make special chaperone arrangements for the walk.

Rosine phones her closest friend Jackie to make arrangements with the school and to notify the parents and guardians of the students in her class.

⬛⬛⬛

Back at the plane, Spencer updates Jack explaining Rosine and Sarah will join them on the next leg of the flight to Indonesia in the morning. Unbeknownst by the others, Jack sighs with relief.

Savannah gets to know Jack better while making small talk while Spencer spends time with Alex, talking about the excitement of the adventure.

Andre feeds the group individual frozen chicken stir fry meals warmed in the microwave.

Jet lag catches up with the group, and Spencer heads out with Savannah to her room in town. Jack, Alex and Andre stay on the plane for the night.

▯▯▯

Savannah's home is a one-room apartment in a row of six similar units, on a quiet well kept residential street. The construction is a concrete block with flat roofs. Inside, the spartan furnishings include an efficiency kitchen, a small round table with 2 chairs, and two beds. Spencer notices there is no place to relax other than sitting on a kitchen chair or a bed.

Savannah says, "I'm beat, and I don't know about you, but I could sure use a nightcap."

Spencer smiles while sitting, "We are always thinking the same thing!"

"I hope rum and coke is okay with you, unless you want straight rum," Savannah says laughing. She mixes the drinks, getting the coke and ice from the fridge.

They knock their drinks back quickly and Savannah immediately follows up with, "One more?"

Spencer responds by pushing her empty glass towards Savannah.

As Spencer receives her fresh drink, she says, "With all this craziness, I can't tell the last time I've felt as relaxed as I do right now. It just seems when we're together alone like this, all the other crazy shit just melts away."

Savannah walks behind Spencer and massages her shoulders, saying, "You're my girlie."

After the quick massage, Savannah gets up and undresses to her underwear. She climbs into the bed nearest the kitchen table. Spencer follows suit, also undressing to her underwear. She flips off the light switch on the wall and climbs into the same bed as Savannah.

Sleep comes instantly.

▯▯▯

They wake the children in the orphanage at 6 am. Their strict routine comprises making their beds, tidying their personal space, washing in the common bath with just a wet cloth, dressing into their school uniform, and then going to the common room for their morning meal. The children are allowed free time between their meal and leaving for school. Most of them choose the group activity room for free time where they have access to a two channel TV, game tables and a wall of books to read.

On this day, an assistant approaches and interrupts Sarah during her morning meal, "Sarah, when you finish, please go to the House Mother in her office. She has a message for you."

Sarah responds, "Yes, Ma'am."

Sarah finishes her last mouthful of rice and walks the hall to the House Mother's office. She is worried she's done something wrong, as these types of personal invites are rare. The House Mother is a strict but kind lady, and like everyone, adores Sarah.

Sarah knocks on the House Mother's door and waits for the "Come In," that always follows.

Once inside, the House Mother explains she has received information from Sarah's school, and her teacher has left and they're not sure when she is returning. Until the school has a substitute or replacement, the class is cancelled. She tells Sarah she has to stay at the orphanage during the day until told otherwise.

Sarah is heartbroken and drops her head.

The House Mother says, "I'm sorry, Sarah, I know you were fond of your teacher. That will be all."

▯▯▯

Spencer and Savannah wake up to the alarm clock set to 5:30 am. After a small breakfast and coffee followed by a morning cleanup, they head out. Leaving is difficult for Savannah as she doesn't know if she will ever be returning.

They are on the road in Savannah's Range Rover by 7:10 to make sure they don't keep Rosine and Sarah waiting.

They arrive early at the school but not early enough to beat Rosine who is already there. Rosine walks over from her Nissan Versa carrying a suitcase and gets into the back seat of the Range Rover while Savannah takes her case and puts it in the back. Jackie, a lady of native descent, who accompanied Rosine, drives her Versa away.

While waiting for Sarah, the group makes small talk discussing the adventures that lay ahead.

At 7:30 Rosine says, "It's not like Sarah to be late, maybe she's having trouble finding a chaperone for the walk this early."

They keep making small talk.

At 7:40 Rosine is worried. "There is something wrong. Sarah never does this."

"Maybe she just forgot to get here early," Spencer pipes in. "I suggest we give her until 8:30, which is the start of their school day - Rosine, correct me if I'm wrong."

"No, that's correct," Rosine says. "We can wait, but I doubt Sarah got this wrong. She just isn't like that."

Spencer phones Jack to let him know the schedule has changed while waiting for Sarah.

After an uncomfortable silence, Rosine says, "If Sarah doesn't show up for 8:30, then something *is* wrong. We will need to go to the orphanage. I don't think it should be me, though. They shouldn't see me on the same day my class cancellation notice went out."

Spencer and Savannah turn to Rosine, and simultaneously say, "Cancellation notice?"

"Yes, my friend Jackie contacted all parents and guardians of the students in my class. It was a lot of work; she drove to many homes to get the word out."

Spencer says, "Rosine, perhaps they told Sarah to stay at the orphanage because of the cancellation?"

Rosine has a stunned look, "I am so sorry! All I was thinking of was getting Sarah here early. The notice going to the orphanage flew right over me. Sarah isn't the only student from there."

Rosine continues, "I have just devastated that child, allowing her to think I left without discussion. I am her only confidant. She has no one close to her at the orphanage. Oh my God, this is awful, we need to get her."

Savannah drives the walking distance towards the orphanage. They agree Spencer will be the one who speaks with Sarah as she is less imposing than Savannah.

It is 8:40 am when the Range Rover pulls up in front of the orphanage. Spencer jumps out, walks to the front door and rings the bell.

After a few moments the door opens, and an attendant greets Spencer, asking her what she wants. Spencer explains she needs to speak with Sarah. The attendant lets Spencer in but says in broken English, the House Mother must greet all guests first. He asks her to take a seat. Before the attendant walks away, he says as if an afterthought, "It will be a few minutes, the House Mother is in a meeting."

"How long is a few minutes?" Spencer asks.

"Don't know," replies the attendant as he walks away and closes the door to the lobby behind him.

Spencer phones both Savannah and Jack, to let them know what has happened. Everyone is fidgeting and pacing; they want things to get moving. Alex being a typical ten-year-old, is getting impatient and challenging his father on why they can't get everyone onboard and just go.

⧠⧠⧠

After what feels like an eternity, Spencer looks at her watch. It is now 9 am.

At the same time, Sarah is looking for a book to read. As she reaches up to a shelf, she goes into her episode. Three seconds later she knows she needs to escape the orphanage. She has learned Alex and Rosine will be at the airport. She thinks of a plan.

⧠⧠⧠

In the plane, Alex has also just finished his episode and looks over to his father and says, "Dad, Sarah will escape from the orphanage and find a way to the airport. She knows we're here, Dad!

"How do you know, Alex?"

"I don't know, Dad, I just do. She seems to know what I know, and I know what she knows. This stuff just keeps popping into my head. She knows her teacher will not be at the school anymore and she is thinking maybe it's because she's coming here to the plane."

"Alex, does she know your Mom is in the orphanage right now to get her?"

"Dad, I didn't know she was there, so I doubt Sarah does. You didn't tell me Mom was actually *in* the school, and Sarah will only know it if I know it."

Jack, not believing what he's saying, "Can you tell her your Mom is there, and to let Spencer handle getting her out?"

"It's not like that, Dad - I seem to only learn things once a day. Sarah is the same."

"Holy Christ," Jack thinks to himself, as he realizes Alex must get his insights each morning, like the episode yesterday with the eerie freezing. It's hard for Jack to accept these two kids are somehow communicating, but he has no choice.

Alex interrupts his father's thoughts. "And Dad, I've got more stuff to tell you and Mom."

⬜⬜⬜

Sarah goes to her bed in the dormitory. She looks around to make sure no one is watching, grabs her school bag and empties it under her worn out bed cover. After grabbing the only pedestrian outfit she has and her underwear, she stuffs them into her school bag. Sarah walks inconspicuously towards the side door of the orphanage where the children leave for school. She goes through the door hoping no one notices and hurries to the closest side street where she will be out-of-sight. Her plan is to find the first stranger with a cell phone so she can phone Rosine with the one number Rosine ensured she memorized in case of trouble.

⬜⬜⬜

Spencer's phone rings, and she sees it's from Jack. She answers, and without saying hello, says, "I know we need to get going, Jack. We're doing the best we can. Should get to see Sarah soon now."

"Listen up, Spencer. Sarah knows about us here at the airport. She knows Alex is here and is thinking this is where Rosine is heading. She believes Rosine's travel to the plane is why her class was cancelled. If she hasn't already, she's planning to escape the orphanage to make her way here. She doesn't know you're there to get her. Alex told me all this. Don't ask, I will fill you in later. Get your butt in there and stop Sarah before she takes off. She can't be in this town by herself - Christ!"

Spencer hangs up and says out loud, "Oh shit!"

Spencer walks into the orphanage landing in the group room with other children; she doesn't see Sarah. Not knowing what else to do, Spencer yells as loud as she can, "SARAH!" The loud yell brings two attendants running. Before they kick Spencer out, she tells them Sarah is planning to escape.

The two attendants look at each other, and without wasting time questioning Spencer further, one says, "I'll check the dining room," while the other says, "I'll check her private space," meaning her bed. Spencer didn't understand the local dialect of French the attendants were speaking. She sees they are no longer worried about her presence, so she sprints along behind one. Her random choice leads her to Sarah's private space. The attendant notices the bulge in the bed cover and lifts it up to uncover Sarah's school supplies. He then opens her small end-table sized chest of drawers; they see she has removed her belongings. He looks at Spencer and says, "gone," in heavily accented English. The attendant has seen this a hundred times before with other orphans.

Without saying a word, Spencer sprints back to the Range Rover. At the vehicle, she jumps in while gasping for breath and says, "Sarah has left the orphanage. She somehow knows about the plane and is trying to make her way to the airport. She can't be far. Which way is the airport from here?"

Rosine interrupts with, "We have lots of students from the orphanage trying to leave. They head to a side street out of direct view. She will go there before she heads for the airport. The airport is three miles East. She can cover that distance in twenty minutes if she knows how to find it. If we miss finding her near here, she should be easy to spot as she gets closer to the airport on the only access road. She has my number memorized, and if she finds someone with a phone, I'm sure she will call me. Drive all the streets near here."

□□□

Sarah has spent most of her recent years in the orphanage, and besides her chaperoned walk to school each day, and a few outings with Rosine, she has little knowledge of the surrounding town, let alone where the airport is. She realizes she needs to find someone with a phone and plans to keep walking until she finds someone. Sarah believes a phone will solve everything; she refuses to believe Rosine has abandoned her. She wouldn't do that.

Within two blocks, Sarah sees four boys. They appear older than the oldest boys going to her school. They stare her down as she approaches. When close enough to communicate without having to raise voices, and in her native tongue of Lingala, she asks if any of them has a cell phone. She explains she needs to make an urgent call. Sarah does not understand she is putting herself in danger. She is naïve and hasn't been around evil people.

One boy asks where she's from, and without understanding the danger of her response, tells them she's from the orphanage. She then reiterates she needs a phone to connect with the people she's joining up with at the airport. The boys look at each other and chuckle, "Airport, yeah right!" they sarcastically say in their native tongue.

Another boy, says with a more sincere and serious look, "Seeing how important your call is, you can use the phone in our house, it's right there." He points to the house behind him.

Sarah responds with, "Thank you!"

The boys look at each other with big grins, then saying nothing else, position themselves around Sarah and walk her to the house they had pointed out.

It delights Sarah knowing she will talk with Rosine soon. She is smiling as she walks with the boys to the door of a small rundown flat-roofed house. As she approaches, she notices the number on the outside of the door is 169. The five of them walk through the door together. It disturbs her to hear the door close behind her followed by the distinctive click sound of the door's lock. She is no longer smiling.

☐☐☐

It's now mid-afternoon. The group has traveled every road Sarah may have taken multiple times with no sign of her. When they pass people on the street, Rosine asks in Lingala whether they had seen a lone ten-year-old girl. Nothing surfaces.

Sarah has not made a phone call to Rosine, and this has everyone worried and scared for her. As much as they didn't want the police involved, they requested the orphanage to phone the police. The overworked, under-staffed police want nothing to do with chasing runaway orphans and the call resulted in a small entry on a missing persons form placed on a pile of a hundred similar forms.

Everyone is tired and hungry; they break off the search and re-group at the plane.

Inside and feeling anxious, they discuss the strategy if Sarah never surfaces again, a sad but likely outcome given missing females almost never reappear after being abducted. Dead people don't talk, and in this area, a dead person is much safer for the culprits than someone running around with loose lips. For many of the depraved people in these crowded lands, life is disposable.

Rosine is crying the whole time, she knows how things work. She doesn't know what to do. She is carrying the weight of Sarah's disappearance on her shoulders as she knows it's her fault; if the orphanage hadn't prevented Sarah from going to school, none of this would have happened.

Alex has listened patiently during the difficult discussions on how to continue searching, when to call off the search, and the deadline for continuing on to Indonesia. When he sees the adults have no more to say, he pipes up, "Maybe I will learn about Sarah's situation tomorrow morning, just like I did today when she left the orphanage."

This takes a minute to digest, and the adults say nothing.

Jack remembers how Alex appears to have communicated with Sarah earlier this morning. Now believing what he is seeing from Alex, he knows the only hope of finding Sarah alive is with his help.

"Let's hope it's the case, Alex," Jack says as he excuses himself from the group and pulls out his cell phone while walking towards the plane's cockpit. He places a call back to LA where his friend Jim answers. Jim recognizes Jack's number from the caller ID of his secure communication app, and says, "Talk to me."

"Jim, I need an extraction in Mbandaka in the Congo. Single ten-year-old girl. She's probably in an apartment or small house with amateur punks. A 4-pack should do it. Will provide a specific target location when your team arrives. I will arrange ground transportation. Have them bring an Enforcer and a medic. They need to arrive prior to nine am local time tomorrow. I'll meet them on the tarmac here in Mbandaka. Usual financial arrangements. They can be back home within a day. As usual, make sure your plane is not traceable and the team comes clean."

Jack's mercenary operations always use planes from shell companies owned by fake individuals. To stay hidden, they pay for planes in cash from numbered bank accounts out of Switzerland. Necessary precautions if operations go wrong and planes get left behind. Politicians and bureaucrats disavow any knowledge when operations fail; they always hang mercenaries and operatives out to dry. Jack does nothing without believing he is helping the greater good, but often has to operate on the short side of the law to accomplish clandestine missions.

"Damn Jack, does this kinda shit just follow you around?"

Jack doesn't answer, saying "We good?"

"Team will be there, Jack."

Before Jack had amassed his billions, he had been a Navy SEAL. He moved straight into SEAL training upon graduating with top honors from West Point. As a SEAL, Jack's charisma and natural leadership skills enabled him to quickly climb the officer ranks while gaining the respect of his fellow soldiers. During his tour, the camaraderie Jack experienced with fellow SEALs formed lifelong bonds.

After retiring from the SEALs as a Captain, Jack leveraged his vast network of friends and associates to help him build his business empire. The high-tech hardware appliances his company developed for the military enjoys a worldwide market with sales contracts in the hundreds of millions per client. With his private plane, and his need for continual cross-continent travelling, Jack has often helped his friends who work with the government to execute the clandestine operations needed when American lives are at stake and politics are in the way. He often uses his plane to fly mercenaries into hot zones under the guise of a business trip, typically to extract those who need out.

Jim knows mercenaries throughout the world and has become the go-to broker for teams requiring quick assembly for clandestine operations. On this evening, he places a call to an operative in France; he needs a team geographically positioned to reach Mbandaka in Jack's immediate time frame.

After the meal and a short rest on the plane, the group again takes turns driving Savannah's Range Rover through the streets of Mbandaka. Either Jack or Andre is in the vehicle during the searches to ensure safety; they are armed, unbeknownst to the ladies. Jack always travels, whether legal or not, with weapons aboard his plane, especially when entering less than stable countries. Jack handpicked Andre and the pilots years back because as fellow retired ex-SEALs, they possess elite military training.

Everyone agrees when 6:30 arrives, they will call off the search because of the onset of darkness. If Alex can't help in the morning, they will have to leave without Sarah. They are devastated and heartbroken for Sarah. There is concern for how this will impact the bigger picture.

After postponing the search, everyone is back on the plane by 6:40 pm. The group is quiet and feeling a deep melancholy. They agree to reconvene in the morning at 6:00 am. Jack needs the early start so he can arrange for the rental of two cars prior to his extraction team's arrival. He knows he has to be ready for 9 am to align with Alex's 'experience'. Jack doesn't know what else to call it; the whole thing is surreal for him, and he knows Sarah's fate is riding on the hope Alex can deliver.

The women climb into the Range Rover. No one is speaking, and within a few minutes, Rosine gets dropped at her flat. She agrees to get picked up in the morning at 5:50 am and forces a 'good night' amongst her tears.

Upon arrival at Savannah's flat, it's a repeat performance of cocktails, except this time the subdued mood has paralyzed conversation. Savannah and Spencer knock back their two drinks. Savannah gets up and sets her alarm clock for 5 am, strips to her underwear, and again climbs into bed first.

⬚⬚⬚

It is 5:55 am when Savannah, Spencer and Rosine arrive back at the plane. Jack and Andre are up, they have left Alex to sleep longer. Jack explains he has help arriving to get Sarah back, assuming Alex provides a location. He asks Savannah if she can drive him and Andre into town to rent vehicles. Of course, she agrees.

Jack explains if Alex can't provide an exact location, they will need everyone to assist as their only option will be a vain attempt to canvas every house within a radius of the orphanage.

The car rental agency opens at 7:00 am, and at 6:45, Sarah, Jack and Andre are on their way into town. An hour later, they arrive back driving separate vehicles. Jack and Andre are driving matching black Nissan Pathfinders.

Back in the plane, Jack receives the expected call from Jim who explains the extraction team is arriving from France, and their ETA is 8:30 am. As requested, it's a four-man team plus a medic. They will each have two-way communicators, bullet-proof vests, two 9mm sidearms, and four AK-47s assault rifles.

At 8:30 am, Jack steps out of the plane. Sure enough, off in the distance he sees the landing lights of the extraction team's jet on final approach.

Jack and Andre walk to the location of the approaching plane on the tarmac. After waiting for the plane's stairs to lower, they climb into the cabin to meet the team. Francois, the team leader introduces himself and explains he and the medic are the only English speakers. He then introduces his team. Jack can't help noticing the attractiveness of Alma the medic, and wonders how these women get involved in dangerous mercenary missions; then he smiles at himself, as he knows why.

Francois hands extra communicators to Jack and Andre and they clip them behind their ears. Jack asks if there are more for their companions. Francois hands out an additional two and then starts a quick radio check. He explains the range is just under one mile. Jack notices Alma is also wearing a communicator and is subtly hiding a side arm under her top.

The team looks like they mean business yet are dressed in casual attire suitable for blending into their surroundings in Mbandaka. The bullet-proof vests under their shirts are unnoticeable.

Jack explains it could be awhile until his intelligence source comes through, but the team should be ready and waiting with their equipment in the two Pathfinders.

Jack and Andre walk back to their plane. As Jack looks back, the extraction team is already loading the vehicles.

It's now 8:55 am and Alex is up and has had his morning orange juice. Savannah and Spencer are wearing their communicators, and everyone is sitting around making nervous conversation while keeping an eye on Alex. Alex knows he is everyone's focal point, but he says nothing; he understands.

Sure enough, right at 9 am, with everyone watching, Alex becomes still as they see his eyes fully dilate. They have seen this before but can't get used to it. There is no explanation; it's just surreal.

Three seconds later he is back to normal and says, "Sarah is in trouble."

Before anyone can react, he continues, "She was looking for a phone and four boys took her into a small house for her to make a phone call. She has already recovered from her first beating that almost killed her."

Jack doesn't understand recovering from a beating, but has to stay focused, "Alex, where is she?"

Alex continues, "She was about two blocks from the orphanage when they took her into the house. Sarah remembers the house number was 169."

Jack jumps into immediate action and takes control. He says over his communicator, "Ok everyone, we're going in. We meet in front of the orphanage. Savannah, Spencer and Andre go first in the Land Ranger. Francois, you and your team follow second, I'll drive third with Alma. Rosine, please stay here at the plane with Alex."

Francois repeats the message in French for his team.

Within a minute the three vehicles are speeding down Liberation Road, North away from the airport. They turn left onto Avenue Revolution and take it to Avenue Telecom where the orphanage is to the left. The entire trip is three miles. Everyone is looking out the windows for a house number of 169.

The previous evening Jack studied the area using Google Maps. Google hasn't done street views in this remote and dangerous area, so Jack didn't get house number ranges, but he wrote the street names where he wanted the search to begin. En route Jack gives the group instructions on how he wants them to fan out.

Jack and Alma stay back with the two Pathfinders holding the Enforcer, two folding stretchers and the four AK-47 assault rifles. The others head out on foot, jogging.

Francois, while running up Avenue Bomongo, notices house numbers in the 130's are increasing by two. He is thinking to himself it is looking promising.

A little further up the street, two teenage boys are standing on the curbside. They see Francois approaching and walk towards him. The boys believe Avenue Bomongo is their turf, and no stranger will get past unscathed, or at least without paying a toll. Francois isn't an intimidating or large man at five foot nine inches in height. The two boys approach asking questions in a loud and aggressive manner in their native tongue of Lingala. Francois motions he doesn't understand and asks if the boys speak English. They approach laughing. One boy asks in a heavy Lingala accent, "American?"

Francois shakes his head to show 'no'.

The boys continue to approach and appear menacing and aggressive. As they get within a few feet, Francois puts up his hand in a gesture indicating stay back.

The boys ignore his gesture. When within arm's reach, the larger of the two boys reaches out to grab Francois. Francois instinctively does a defensive arm blocking move while pushing the boy to the ground. The second boy pulls out a knife and lunges. At this point Francois goes into full survival mode. He grabs the boy's arm and twists it behind his back. His arm snaps, and the knife falls to the ground as he drops in pain. The other boy has gotten up and runs at Francois. Francois does a kick to the boy's knee, breaking it; he falls to the ground a second time.

Francois now knows he has a predicament on his hand … anyone who has seen this has most likely called the police, or worse, is rounding up others to help in the fight. He takes a quick look around to size up his situation. During the short moment Francois is sizing things up with his back to the boys, the boy with the broken arm gets up and stumbles to the house they were in front of, enters through the open door, slamming it shut behind him revealing the house number.

As Francois turns to look, he sees 169 on the door. He walks up to the remaining boy with the broken knee who is laying on the ground moaning and kicks him in the head, knocking him out cold. Francois communicates with the team explaining the circumstance and describes his location.

Jack and Alma put their idling Pathfinders into gear and race to the location. Savannah, who is driving her Range Rover, squeals her tires as she spins around and heads over from a few blocks away. The rest of Francois's team start sprinting back to their vehicle.

They all arrive at 169 together. While moving to the target, Francois has been providing instructions to the team on what to do upon arrival.

The team members jump out of their Pathfinders with the Enforcer, a battering ram used to knock down doors.

Jack has told the team if the culprits realize they are in trouble, they will quickly kill their hostage, so the team works fast. Two team members with the Enforcer run for the door. Francois and the other members run to the sides; guns drawn.

Not wanting to impede the professionals who do this as a living, Jack and Andre stay back at the vehicles, guns in hand, watching to ensure no interference.

Francois, without saying a word, holds up a finger, then two, and on the third finger the Enforcer ram hits the door with a loud bang. The old door comes off its hinges and flies into the room. The first two mercenaries charge the room, guns raised in shooting position, while the two handling the Enforcer, drop it, and draw their own sidearms.

Inside, they see the boy with the broken arm sitting on a wooden chair, and a second boy lunging for a gun on an end-table beside a couch. One squeeze of the trigger by Francois and the lunging boy is dead on the floor. The boy with the broken arm is knocked unconscious with a raised kick. There is an adjoining kitchen and two interior doors, both closed. Jack had relayed to the team to expect four or more thugs as told by Alex, so the team doesn't let its guard down.

Francois points his gun at one door while he signals to the team to investigate the other. Just as they approach the door, it flies open and a boy runs out shooting. Before the team can fire on him, the boy gets one lucky round off hitting a mercenary member in the neck, just above his bullet-proof vest; he falls. The boy can't get a second shot off before he is riddled with bullets. One soldier attends to his fallen comrade while Francois calls for Alma over the communicator. With his remaining available comrade, Francois kicks in the second door and finds Sarah tied to a blood-soaked bed. Another boy is standing naked beside her holding up a small bedside table; he is going to smash it into Sarah's head. Francois shoots three quick rounds into the boy's abdomen and he keels over. The table he was holding falls with him and unbeknownst to the boy, hits its target with a loud thud. Sarah, who is unconscious from a preliminary blow, doesn't feel the table smashing her head. She remains still. Francois runs over and checks her for a pulse; it's faint. It saddens and angers Francois to see Sarah's bruised and bloody naked body. He sees there is blood both fresh, and some dry; Sarah has been enduring this for hours.

After a quick glance around the small room, Francois communicates an 'all clear' to the team as he unties Sarah. Francois tells Jack they need the two stretchers from the Pathfinder.

As Jack is grabbing the stretchers, he can hear sirens in the distance. Over his communicator, he says, "We're gonna have company, we gotta get outa here!"

Alma runs into the room where Sarah is lying unconscious and notices a room full of nude pinups on the walls and a dead naked boy on the floor. While Francois continues untying the rope restraints holding Sarah, Alma checks Sarah's pulse and then takes a moist wipe from her kit and clears the blood away from her eyes, nose and mouth. Francois looks at Alma and says, "She is very weak."

Alma, while checking her breathing, says, "Yes, probably a massive concussion and internal bleeding. They were obviously trying to kill her."

Alma can't help noticing the lubricant and blood between Sarah's legs and a plethora of additional bruises on her body. She can't understand how people can take pleasure in inflicting such pain and suffering on a fellow human, especially a young girl. In her medic role Alma has seen it all, but Sarah's age, and the brutality she is witnessing, has brought tears to her eyes.

Francois sees the tears, but there is no time for emotion. He instructs Alma to attend to his fallen soldier.

Jack enters the room and helps lift Sarah onto a stretcher. He pulls off his shirt and lays it over her naked body while saying, "Christ."

Alma holds a compress on the neck of the fallen soldier while the others load him onto the second stretcher. His neck is bleeding profusely, and blood is everywhere.

Outside, Savannah and Spencer have been receiving instructions and have the back seat of one Pathfinder folded down and the rear door lifted open.

Without missing a beat, Francois and Jack come running out with Sarah on one stretcher and the fallen comrade on the other being carried by his teammates. Alma is running alongside holding the neck compress in place.

Jack shouts, "Let's go, let's go!"

Once Francois is free from holding the stretcher, he runs full stride back into the house. The team hears a gunshot from inside; Francois is not leaving with any of the thugs alive. The boy on the street with the broken leg suffers the same fate - after exiting the house, Francois points his side-arm at his head and squeezes the trigger.

Alma, while attempting to keep the compress on, jumps in the back of the Pathfinder alongside the fallen soldier's stretcher. Her ability to keep pressure on his neck wound isn't successful; her hand slips away, and blood sprays everywhere in the back of the SUV. With blood over her face and in her hair, she regains control of the pressure.

Savannah closes the back door and runs back to her Range Rover. Jack instructs the remaining three extraction team members to get into the Pathfinder with the AK-47s and take up the rear. Everyone else jumps into the remaining two vehicles where they can. Jack is driving the middle Pathfinder with Alma and the wounded; Andre is riding in the Range Rover with Savannah and Spencer. As soon as Jack jumps behind the wheel, he phones his pilots waiting in the plane. He tells them to have the plane started and positioned behind Francois's plane on the entrance ramp to the runway. Jack then asks Francois to instruct his pilot to also be ready and position their plane first on the ramp.

Within two minutes of smashing in the door, the entire team is heading back to the planes; the sirens in the distance are getting louder.

Jack communicates with the extraction team and asks them to hold back and block the entry road to the airport. He explains their job is to block all traffic, especially law enforcement who may chase them. He gives explicit instructions to disable vehicles without wounding the occupants if possible.

As the three-vehicle convoy passes where Liberation Avenue turns south towards the airport, and just after the last intersecting road, the trailing Pathfinder skids to an abrupt stop sideways in the middle of the road. Francois and his remaining two soldiers jump out, open the back doors and pull out three AK-47 assault rifles. The team takes strategic positions behind the Pathfinder with their weapons pointing from where they came. They can hear sirens getting louder. They wait.

❑❑❑

At the airport, the two private jets start up their engines. Once they have adequate thrust, Francois's pilot moves his plane onto the ramp leading to the runway. Jack's plane moves in behind. The ramp onto the runway faces West and is positioned halfway along the runway's length.

Jack's copilot opens the door to prepare for the group's arrival.

The airport is so small it only uses a single air traffic controller. Large aircraft arrival and departures are infrequent, so Jack's pilot is hoping the air traffic controller is not on shift. No such luck; while sitting in the tower reading a novel, the noise of the jet engines from two planes catches the controller's attention. He immediately radios the planes and asks for their intentions. Jack's pilot requests clearance for an immediate departure. The controller, with displeasure in his voice, denies the clearance and requests him to file flight plans and customs forms. He tells the pilots to shut their engines down. The pilots ignore his request and the controller responds by making a phone call.

Two minutes later the Range Rover and Pathfinder with the wounded pull up to the foot of the gangway to Jack's plane. Within seconds of the team's arrival, an official looking vehicle with blue flashing lights races over from behind an airport building. It parks in front of the wheels of Francois's plane which is first on the ramp. Two uniformed officers jump out. They have badges on their shirts and side arms at their waists. The officials are taking no chances and have their hands over their guns, ready if need be.

Through the communicator, Jack says, "Everyone stays put, except Andre."

Alma responds with, "You better hurry, Jack, I'm losing these two."

Jack ignores Alma and says, "Andre, we have to take these guys down, and move their vehicle. I'll take whoever is bigger, try to handle the other and don't mess up like you did in Columbia; I'm getting too old to carry you."

Andre replies with a simple, "Shut up."

Jack and Andre jump out of the Pathfinder and walk up to the officials, trying to look casual and non-threatening with smiling faces. As they approach, Jack and Andre size up their opponents. They notice one is older and taller, carrying a few extra pounds; the other is younger and doesn't look experienced. Once close enough to read their shirts, they realize they're dealing with the 'Republican Guard'. Jack is thinking, 'Christ, what are they doing here at the airport?' As in Iraq, most of these third world countries regard 'Republican Guard' as their elite forces.

As a distraction, Jack had grabbed a piece of paper from the vehicle when he jumped out. He waves it in front of himself as they approach the officials, trying to deflect with what he hopes they believe are official documents. Jack says to Andre on the communicator, "I'll do a throat jab to the older on the left. Do what you can with the younger."

"Roger that," says Andre.

Not liking the way Jack and Andre are approaching, the two Republican Guard stop walking and pull out their guns and point. The older guard gestures to lift their arms and says in accented English, "Up."

Jack then says to Andre through the communicator, "Let's try to get close enough for contact," followed by a directive to Alma's communicator, "Alma, we may need a little help here. I need you to distract these two guys. We need to take them out."

While Jack and Andre put their arms in the air, they keep walking towards the officials.

The older guard yells, "Stop! Knees!" Not seeing Jack and Andre reacting fast enough, the guard follows up with an even louder yell, "Now!"

Jack and Andre drop to their knees as they see the guy means business. Jack says to Andre, "when we get our distraction, go for the smaller guy. I'll go for the big one. It's up to you, Alma."

Bang! The noise of a gunshot reverberates off the metal sided airport buildings, and the large guard who had been barking the orders falls to the ground. The echoing noise makes it difficult to know the source. Jack leaps from his knees towards the shorter guard, but the guard has his gun at the ready as he sees Jack's advance. He turns, aims, and shoots. The team instantly hears a third gunshot. Both Jack and the shorter guard fall to the ground. Andre, up off his knees, leaps to Jack's aid. Alma is running over from the Pathfinder. Andre reaches Jack first, who is lying on his back with one hand over his shoulder.

Jack sees blood oozing out between his fingers and yells, "Fuck! We have to get out of here - fast." He follows up with one last, "Fuck!"

Andre can tell Jack's state of mind because Jack seldom uses the 'f' word. He responds with, "That's my Jack."

As he stands, Jack asks, "Where did the gunshots come from?"

"That would be me!" Alma says after reaching Jack and hearing his question. "How bad is it, Jack?" she says as she puts two fresh bullet rounds into her gun.

This isn't the first time Jack has been hit, and he replies with, "It stings like hell, but it's just a flesh wound."

Jack continues, "Andre, get Francois and his team back here. We have one minute before the sky falls in. And get their fucking car moved," referring to the guard's car stopped in front of Francois's plane.

Alma says, "Jack, you're not dying, so you're on your own, keep pressure on it. We need to get the other two wounded onto the plane, stat!"

Jack takes back command, and says to Andre, "Go!"

Over his communicator, Jack says, "Ladies, it's up to us to get the wounded on the plane."

Jack runs towards the Pathfinder still holding his shoulder and Alma takes the cue and runs behind him.

Andre runs to the guard's car while trying to get Francois on his communicator. There is no response after three attempts. Andre then hails Jack, saying he is going back up the road to get Francois and his team.

"Okay. Keep me posted. If I lose contact with you, you'll have two minutes before this bird takes off. You know the drill, Andre."

Andre doesn't respond, he knows the drill; unlike the military who leave no one behind, mercenaries do not bring back fallen comrades on private planes. There is no way to explain to immigration officials after landing why dead people with gunshot wounds are aboard.

Relieved to see the keys still in the ignition after jumping in the official's car, Andre hammers the gas and propels the car onto the grass adjoining the ramp. He then does a full out sprint for one hundred feet to the Pathfinder to help remove the two wounded who they placed behind the vehicle on the ground. Andre then jumps in the Pathfinder, hits the gas and squeals the tires heading back towards the extraction team.

□□□

The wait for the sirens by Francois and his team was less than a minute. Three police vehicles come screaming up the road with sirens blazing and lights flashing. Francois and his two soldiers are ready with their AK-47s aimed up the road at the oncoming cars. Francois is kneeling behind the engine's hood, and the other two are standing on the Pathfinder's running boards. They lay their guns across the cargo carrier rails on top of the roof.

As the speeding police cars approach within range, the team opens fire, aiming at the first vehicle's radiator and tires; the goal is to disable the vehicles and not cause casualties if possible. It works; a 7.62mm round from Francois's AK-47 shreds the first car's front tire. The team stops shooting as the driver loses control and the car careens into the ditch where it smashes against a fence post, steam hissing from the shot-up radiator. Two police in the shot-up car jump out and crouch behind it, shielding themselves. Francois notices the car trunk open. He sees a rifle pulled out. Francois swears in French under his breath, "Merde."

The driver of the second police car hears the gunfire as the first car veers into the ditch. He hits his brakes hard and after leaving a long skid mark, comes to a full stop in the road's center. Francois's team prevents the officers in the stopped car from getting out. Each time the police try to open their doors, an aimed volley of bullets from AK-47s foil their try.

Francois knows he needs to disable all the police cars; it's the only way the planes can leave. The problem is they have no direct line of sight to the third car. In the interim, his team shoots up the front of the second car, which now resembles a vehicle in a war zone; it isn't going anywhere. Francois knowing time is of the essence, decides to draw out the third vehicle by ordering his men back into the Pathfinder. They take turns shooting covering rounds back at the police while jumping into their vehicle. In the driver's seat, Francois fish tails as he floors the Pathfinder and turns up the road towards the airport. He will allow the third police car to chase them to the airport's entrance.

As they are pulling away, the officer in the ditch with the rifle takes careful aim at the back of Francois's vehicle and shoots. It's a skilled shot; the bullet penetrates the Pathfinder's back window and strikes the rear seat soldier in the back of his head, killing him instantly. Francois's remaining colleague yells "Aller, Aller", meaning "go, go."

Four police officers jump into the third car that hasn't sustained damage and pull around the destroyed car to take up chase. Francois sees this from his rearview mirror and says, "Yup, they have balls." He is hoping he has time to stop and take out the remaining police car with the AK-47s. He knows he needs to keep the gunfight away from the planes. Francois then hears Andre calling him over the communicator. Francois explains he's racing back to the plane, being chased by a police car. He also tells Andre he has a man down.

Andre processes this information and tells Francois to keep heading to the plane and explains he will drive by in the opposite direction. He can then turn around and pull up the rear to help out if needed. He has the fourth AK-47 in his Pathfinder.

Within a minute, Francois is back to the airport's entrance gate. It's as close to the planes as he wants to get and hammers on the brakes. The anti-lock brakes vibrate the pedal under his foot as he brings the heavy Pathfinder to a full stop. The remaining soldier leaps out with his AK-47. Francois grabs his and follows suit. The police car is heading straight for them at 100 miles per hour. Francois is thinking not a bright move; these guys are amateur.

They both open fire on the police car as it approaches. The two AK-47s blast away at the car's front. Glass and material scatters every-where from the impact of the bullet rounds, but the car isn't slowing. The driver, hit from the first salvo of bullets, has his head slumped over the steering wheel and his foot pressed further against the accelerator pedal.

The remaining police are frantically attempting to gain control of the car as it careens towards the Pathfinder. It's too late. At high-speed, the police car smashes into the back of the Pathfinder with the sound of a large explosion. Metal shrapnel flies everywhere.

A rear axle from the Pathfinder breaks free during the collision and flies out and impales Francois's remaining team member. The soldier looks at the spear piercing his chest and tries to pull it out. Seconds later he is on the ground dead. Francois just misses the impact of the two vehicles; it was a close call.

Francois runs over to his fallen comrade just as Andre arrives. After a quick check confirming his man is dead, Francois grabs his gun and jumps in with Andre; they speed off to the plane. Neither man says a word. They screech to a halt beside the plane and jump out. Just as Andre hears more sirens in the distance, Jack says over the communicator, "Status please."

"We're at the plane and we have more company coming. We gotta go now! Is everyone onboard?" Andre asks, as he runs up the steps to the plane carrying two AK-47s.

"Yes. Get on. Let's go," Jack yells back.

Andre closes the plane's door while the pilots taxi the jets onto the runway. Jack moves up to the cockpit so he can see out and help in decision making. The plane has to taxi to the North end of the runway where it will turn around and accelerate South. Jack is communicating with Francois and has told him they will both turn around as they approach the runway's end, which will place Jack's plane first for takeoff, the reason Francois's plane was first at the ramp.

Jack looks out the jet's starboard side window and sees six police vehicles racing South along Liberation Avenue towards the airport entrance.

Jack looks at the pilot and says, "Can we hurry this thing up just a bit?"

Without responding, the pilot gets on the radio to Francois's pilot, and the plane in front accelerates. Jack's pilot follows suit. The pilots stay in tight communication during the high-speed taxi maneuver to avoid colliding.

It takes less than a minute to get to the end of the runway, where Jack's plane spins around first and without a delay, the pilot pushes the throttles to full power.

Straight in front, Jack sees six police vehicles speeding up the ramp towards the runway. The police cars are travelling so fast they fishtail as they turn right from the ramp onto the runway. They are now charging full speed straight at them.

Jack asks the pilot, "Can we make it?"

"Don't know," is the terse response. The pilot does not relent.

It has now become a game of chicken with the approaching police cars. The police in the cars see the plane is not stopping. Four of the cars drive off the runway - stopping the plane isn't worth their lives. Breaking hard, the two center cars come to a stop as the police occupants leap out and roll away. The huge Gulfstream lifts up and soars over them but doesn't have enough height; its center landing gear wheel hits the top of a windshield, blowing the glass out. The plane shudders and dips, but the pilot maintains control and continues. Jack asks the pilot, "Do you practice for that sort of thing?"

The hot exhaust from Jack's plane forces Francois's pilot to wait a few seconds before he also goes full throttle. It's a fatal wait. Jack's plane is blocking Francois's view as they accelerate down the runway. They don't see the stopped police cars until after the big Gulfstream in front is airborne. As soon as Francois's pilot sees the stopped cars in front he at once pulls back on the wheel attempting a premature liftoff. It is too late; he doesn't have adequate lift and the landing gear snags the broken window of the police car Jack's plane had hit. Francois's plane spins and tips sideways. The first part of the plane to hit the pavement is the port wingtip as it tumbles and breaks apart loaded with Jet-A fuel. The vaporizing fuel, ignited by the hot engines, erupts into a huge explosion.

Jack feels his plane shake from the shock wave of the explosion behind him. The looks on his pilot's faces tell the story. They know what happened. In a vain attempt, Jack's pilot tries communicating again with the other jet. There is no response.

A key strength of Jack is his ability to focus and push things out of his head while in combat. It allows him to compartmentalize and continue making strategic decisions. This is the case now; he ignores the explosion of Francois's jet.

He asks the pilot, "How low can we fly this baby until we're out of Congo airspace? I'm not sure if this country has any jets to scramble, I've heard they don't, but if they do, they will be after us. I'm sure they're pissed; we left a mess back there. Can we stay under the radar?"

The pilot says, "Jack, you're assuming they have radar. But yes, we'll fly at four hundred feet. We'll be low enough in this terrain; line of sights will be short. We'll head northwards towards South Sudan and Ethiopia. As we leave the Congo's airspace, we'll climb to fifty thousand feet. Unless Sudan and Ethiopia pull out a surprise, they shouldn't have any military aircraft capable of bothering us up in the thin air."

The pilot continues, "Have you verified our fueling arrangements in Yemen?"

"No, been a little busy today," Jack quips. "I'll do it right now. Just keep us from being shot down."

The pilot goes on the intercom and tells the passengers to remain seated and seat belted until the plane is out of Congo airspace, which will take two hours. He explains the low altitude flying requires evasive flying maneuvers around the ground terrain, and the thicker low altitude air mass is much bumpier because of thermal variances caused by surface temperature and pressure fluctuations.

No one pays attention to the pilot's request for seat belts. Andre is providing dampened warm cloths to help Alma clean Sarah and the wounded mercenary. Spencer is going through Alex's bag trying to find clothes to borrow for Sarah, who is Alex's size. Everyone is stumbling and holding on while moving within the cabin as the Gulfstream bumps and swerves along at low altitude.

As Savannah looks out the window, she shouts out, "Holy shit!" seeing the terrain pass by just a few hundred feet below and to the side while traveling at over four hundred miles per hour. They are all feeling the quick turns push them side-to-side in their seats as the plane winds its way through the valleys. The plane remains out of sight from prying eyes of line-of-sight radar. Newer jets have terrain displays showing the pilot an artificial forward-looking synthetic view, needed to swerve through the hills. At four hundred feet, Jack's pilots depend on this advanced technology.

As Alma attends to the wounded mercenary, she looks at Andre and says she doesn't think he will last much longer. Andre responds with a pensive lip-tight-together shrug; there is nothing he or the team can do.

Jack comes out of the cockpit to check on the passengers. He walks up to Andre and asks, "Were any of the AK-47s recovered?"

Andre quips, "Jack, hey, it's me, Andre!"

He continues, "Francois took one, lost one in the collision I haven't told you about yet, and I put the other two in my cabin. I can't believe you even had to ask me," as he winks at Jack.

Jack asks Alma how the fallen mercenary is doing. She tells Jack what she told Andre.

"If he doesn't make it, we leave him in Yemen. We'll be leaving the guns there too, which is why I asked about them." Jack knows he's in trouble if the wounded mercenary survives. He will need a story to explain the bullet wound when they land in Sorong. For the team's sake, he is hoping this doesn't become an issue.

"Andre, I'm borrowing your cabin to make a call, I'll try not to sit on a gun."

Jack walks to Andre's cabin and closes the door. He pulls out his iPhone and calls Jim. The Gulfstream has the latest technology installed, one being a two-way satellite antenna distributing the satellite signal within the plane as both WI-FI and a cell signal. This enables the passengers to communicate with the outside world transparently using their iPhones, just as on the ground.

Jim again sees Jack's caller id, and says, "Talk to me."

Jack jumps right to it. There are never chummy personal conversations between the two. There is huge mutual respect and trust, but it's always business.

"Lost the whole team except the medic, Jim."

"Christ, Jack, how do you lose a whole team? Were they ambushed?"

"Nope, lost them pretty much one at a time. Francois and his pilot were the last to go when their plane exploded." With morbid humor, Jack continues, "You need to send me better soldiers next time Jim, it's not acceptable when they all die like that."

Jack continues, "Well actually, Jim, they're not all dead. Alma the medic has survived, and she saved my ass by shooting two Republican Guard. She's also nursing one of Francois's team who got shot, but she says he won't make it."

"Damn it, Jack," Jim responds. "It's because of clients like you that I will run out of operatives, so don't whine the next time you need a team and there are none to be had."

They both know they're kidding. It's a high-stakes game with no guarantees. Mercenaries get paid a hundred thousand dollars for missions seldom spanning more than a few days; they accept the risks to earn big money.

Jack asks Jim if the Jet-A fuel arrangements in Yemen are ready. Jim is a preeminent pro-active professional and has checked the fuel arrangements. He takes this opportunity to snipe back at Jack, "Dude, don't ask questions like that! It's me ... Jim."

Jack gets Jim to text him the latitude and longitude coordinates of the airstrip, just to be sure. He has them, but he can't be too careful. Jack knows running a big jet out of fuel because he can't find the airstrip in the desert will ruin everyone's day. The big Gulfstream has a large range, but it can't make their destination to Indonesia without running the fuel significantly lower than the safety margin.

Sarah remains in a coma, but her vitals have strengthened. Alma, who came well equipped, has Sarah on a saline drip to keep her hydrated. She tells the group she doesn't know if Sarah will ever come out of her coma. If her brain is bleeding significantly, she will die if care doesn't come soon.

As the jet leaves the Congo airspace, it climbs to fifty-one thousand feet and the flight smooths out and becomes routine. At this altitude the plane is above commercial traffic, above most storm systems, and most importantly, above the service ceiling of the capabilities of the old military planes the poorer African countries have in their arsenals.

ꟷꟷꟷ

It's been five hours of flying since leaving Mbandaka and the big Gulfstream throttles back and starts its descent as it approaches its fueling airstrip in the deserts of Yemen; it's 5 pm local time.

Three hours earlier Alma had notified Jack the fallen soldier had died. Andre put a sheet over him. Jack is saddened when a soldier falls, but for the better good, he is glad he has to make arrangements to get the dead soldier off the plane prior to landing in Sorong; so much easier this way.

Jim has used the Yemen airstrip for many years when the clandestine operations he's handling can't use regulated airports because of illicit cargo.

The operator of the airstrip has managed over the years to keep his business out of the local spotlight by paying bribes to the government officials, making it a favorite refueling stopover point when customs and immigrations need avoiding. The airstrip is a mile and a half long ribbon of pavement in the desert. There is no tower, landing lights or electronic guidance. Landing here requires pilots who can fly their planes without help from glide slopes and other electronic navigational instruments; a skill private jet pilots learn, but never use.

After dropping to a thousand feet, Jack's pilots do a flyby of the airstrip to make sure it's safe. They then do a large low altitude loop for the final approach. The Gulfstream's wheels screech with a puff of smoke as they hit the airstrip surface. There is no fanfare at the airstrip. It is in an isolated desert with nothing but an 80-mile dirt road leading up to it. Nobody knows who built the strip or for what reason, but Jack assumes it was for illegal use. It is isolated enough to not be affected by the civil strife and war engulfing the country.

As planned, a fuel truck holding the needed three thousand gallons of Jet-A fuel is waiting at the end of the airstrip.

After the jet stops, Jack skips down to meet the fueler. The fueler only speaks Arabic so Jack uses his electronic language translator to communicate. Jack types into the translator, "Have a dead body onboard. Please bury. Will pay with two AK-47 machine guns."

He shows the translated message to the fueler, hoping he can read. As the fueler is looking at the message on Jack's device, Andre is stepping down the stairs with the two AK-47s. The fueler looks up from reading the message, sees the guns, and shakes his head 'no'. He rubs his thumb and index finger together, the universal meaning for money. Jack puts his finger in a 'wait one minute' gesture and runs back into the plane. He comes back out and shows the fueler one thousand dollars in American cash and then makes a gesture as if asking 'is this okay?' The fueler nods an affirmative, takes the cash, and continues on with his fueling chore.

Jack goes back up the gangway and reenters the plane. He reappears a few minutes later and steps down the stairs with the fallen soldier over his shoulder. He drops the body on the back of the refueling truck; it has now become the driver's problem. In the meantime, Andre places the two AK-47s on the passenger side seat of the truck.

In the distance Jack sees the dust clouds of vehicles approaching the airstrip. He yells at Andre, "Let's go!" and follows him as they sprint up the gangway and into the jet.

With just a minute to spare, the jet is back in the air on its way to Sorong with a full load of fuel. Jack sighs in relief.

▯▯▯

Twelve hours later Andre is waking everyone for landing in Sorong Indonesia. They have traveled through six time zone changes and the local time is noon.

As the plane shakes and bounces upon touching the runway, everyone is less stressed although the burden of Sarah's serious condition is weighing on them. The calamity back in Mbandaka has taken its toll on everyone, both emotionally and physically, and they are now hoping the worst is behind them.

Jack, sporting a blood-stained gauze pad on his shoulder, isn't wearing a shirt; he wants his wound to heal and dry more before ruining any of the few shirts he has onboard. While the plane is taxiing, he stands in front of the group and reviews the instructions he has given everyone throughout this leg of the trip. Jack's fit and buff body doesn't go unnoticed by the ladies.

It is important for everyone's story told to customs and immigration to align. Jim set up the story they will tell, as requested by Jack. Experienced with visa issues, Jim set up a fake humanitarian conference hosted at a local hotel where the group is staying. Jack explains this to everyone, hoping no one screws up the message. The fake story is needed because of the disparate nature of the plane's occupants; immigrations will be suspect.

Jack knows they need to get Sarah to a hospital immediately and has decided they will tell the truth about her condition. They will say she was assaulted during their stay-over in Mbandaka and they didn't trust the local health services. With luck, they can use her condition to explain she lost her passport and hurry them through customs and immigration interviews.

One privilege of private jet travel is the convenience of having immigration officers come to the jets needing clearance. Andre opens the plane's door once the official arrives on his modified golf cart. As he ascends the plane's entrance stairs, Andre looks past him and notices the ambulance he had arranged while inflight, racing towards the plane's location.

Jack's wound has been re-bandaged and is not visible behind his clean shirt. The stories everyone tells the immigration officer come across without a hitch. The officer understands the urgency when Jack explains the near-death condition Sarah is in, and the need to get her to the hospital fast. A quick look by the officer at Sarah and the sound of the approaching ambulance ensures the procedure goes quickly.

As the immigration officer leaves, the ambulance attendants hurry in with Andre's guidance, carrying a portable stretcher. Rosine and Savannah accompany Sarah in the ambulance for the ride to the hospital.

Staying on the plane, Spencer and Jack make arrangements for the private plane flight to meet Jacob. Jack suggests to Alex he fill Alma in on the events leading to here. Alma is looking out the window as Alex says, "Do you want to hear what I've learned?"

▯▯▯

The ambulance attendants race Sarah straight into the ER. Running behind them, Rosine and Savannah try to keep pace. One attendant calls out to the triage nurse, "Possible subarachnoid hemorrhage. Attention stat!" The ER staff know only thirty percent of hemorrhage patients come out unscathed, thirty percent don't survive, and the remaining are left with permanent disabilities.

The nurse picks up the phone and preps the MRI room for an emergency visit. Taking over from the ambulance attendants, the ER staff whisk Sarah away through a pair of swinging double doors displaying a sign declaring "Patients Only", in multiple languages.

Savannah is told she will be notified when Sarah is ready to have guests in her room.

Rosine has been in a constant state of sobbing ever since the ordeal with Sarah started and continues on unrelenting. Savannah doesn't talk or console her; she is providing her the space she needs to grieve on her own.

After the longest ninety minutes of their lives, a nurse comes out to tell the women Sarah is being prepared for surgery. She tells them Sarah has hemorrhaged, and the pressure needs relieving in order for her to survive. It will be after 5pm when the surgery takes place ... the hospital has to call the physician and wait for him to arrive.

Upon hearing from the nurse, they're told they can visit Sarah in her room while waiting for surgery. Savannah and Rosine are less stressed. The nurse instructs them to follow her, and when they walk into the acute care room accommodating Sarah, they see a bruised comatose little girl who appears to be connected to every device and life support system the hospital has to offer.

At first sight, Savannah says aloud, "Oh God," and is thinking Sarah looks like Frankenstein waiting for his high-voltage zap bringing him to life.

The nurse suggests they take a seat in the guest chairs. She says it could be a while before the surgery staff comes to take Sarah away. It is now near 3:30 in the afternoon.

Exhausted, Savannah falls asleep in her chair. Rosine is running on pure adrenaline and continues to stay awake while holding Sarah's hand. She has dropped back from crying to her steady state of sobbing.

It has been ninety minutes since Rosine and Savannah sat in the chairs. Savannah has remained asleep the whole time and is now snoring. Rosine is still holding and stroking Sarah's hand.

Rosine is suddenly startled as she looks at Sarah. Sarah's eyes have opened with dilated pupils, and her bruises vanish. She comes out of her coma and sits up. Rosine is so freaked she yells out "Sarah!" as loud as she can; it sounds like a scream. Seeing Sarah sit up and her bruises disappear is as shocking as seeing someone come back from the dead. Rosine is shaking.

Savannah wakes out of her deep sleep, sees Sarah sitting up and Rosine, who looks like she is seeing a ghost. There is no longer any noticeable bruising on Sarah's face; she appears normal.

Sarah looks up at Rosine and says, "Hi, Ms. Rosine. I knew you would come for me."

It is 5 pm.

▯▯▯

Alma is listening to the detailed story Alex is unfolding. She knows Jack wouldn't be going to this much trouble if he had doubts, so she is accepting the story on its face value. While Alex is talking, Alma notices him stop moving and his eyes dilate. Three seconds later, he finishes his sentence as though nothing has happened. Alex apologizes and excuses himself from his conversation, turns, looks at his father to check if he is off the phone. He is.

"Hey, Mom and Dad," Alex calls out. "Sarah is in the hospital with Rosine and Savannah, and she will be okay. They cured her!"

Jack, realizing Alex has just communicated with Sarah again, asks, "How could the hospital have cured her already?"

"It's not the hospital that cured her, Dad; it's who's teaching us. They nursed her back to health. She was in terrible condition. Those boys almost killed her. She will be fine now, though. Good news, hey?"

As usual, Spencer and Jack can't get their heads wrapped around what they hear. Jack now knows the conduits are communicating, but it's just for a few seconds. How is it possible Sarah got cured in the handful of hours since they took her to the hospital?

Spencer chimes in, "Alex, Sarah left in the ambulance about six hours ago. How is it possible *they* had time to nurse her back to health?"

"It's really weird Mom. We don't remember where we go, or who teaches us, but we're there for a long time. It's like we're living in two places at the same time. They had time to cure her. We were there for longer this time."

Spencer just doesn't understand what she heard. Her simple response is, "What is longer?"

"Not sure, Mom, but I'm pretty sure it's different every time, I think it's like a few weeks. It takes a long time to teach us the stuff we're learning."

Jack asks, "So Alex, if you're leaving for a few weeks at a time to learn stuff, when exactly is this happening? You have been with me or your mom almost continually."

"I don't know, Dad. It's like I said, we're living in two places at the same time."

Spencer feels she has lost her son. Something has taken over Alex and she doesn't feel he's her son anymore. She is saddened.

Jack gives up on this craziness and phones Savannah.

ⵔⵔⵔ

Savannah looks at her phone and sees it's Jack. She answers and says without a greeting, "Christ, Jack, Sarah has just made a miraculous recovery. She's fine. I'm betting the staff here will want to keep her for observation, they don't understand what is happening. These folks are very perplexed; not too often they get to witness a miracle. Jack, this is scary shit. The horrible bruising she had, it's all gone. A few noticeable darker spots here and there, but mostly all gone. She is talking, appears normal, and says she feels fine. What the hell! What is happening?"

Savannah's last question is rhetorical, and Jack doesn't answer it. He attempts to calm her by responding in a soothing voice, "I know all about it, Savannah. We talked to Alex. These kids are communicating, Savannah, and that's not the half of it. We will fill you in later."

Savannah says, "Christ," again followed by, "It's just so hard to understand and believe."

Jack continues, "Savannah, we need to get Sarah out of there before someone opens their mouth and this finds its way to the media. They will not discharge her without another scan; they will need to see for themselves she is okay and cured. My concern is they will want to study her to find out why their initial diagnosis was so wrong. That can't happen."

Jack's voice becomes slower and commanding, "Savannah, get her out of there."

"I know, Jack. If we walk out'a here without a discharge, I'll phone you first. We will most likely need help. We'll try hard for a quick discharge first."

Jack thinks to himself, 'God, I hope we don't have to do another forced extraction.'

"Okay, Savannah, keep me in the loop. Bye."

After the ruckus in Sarah's room following the loud shriek Rosine made, the story finds its way to the lead neurosurgeon who has just arrived at the hospital and is now reviewing Sarah's MRI results. He walks into Sarah's room holding the results of Sarah's first scan and stands by her bed. "Hi, Sarah, how are you feeling? I hear you have made quite the recovery."

"I feel okay, doctor. I don't feel any pain or anything like that."

"This scan I'm holding shows you were a very sick girl when you arrived here."

Sarah doesn't respond, she doesn't know what to say.

The doctor then asks Sarah a series of questions to test her cognitive abilities. She answers them without hesitation. Looking at the head nurse, the doctor instructs him to order another MRI. He is not happy; he is upset when the hospital makes mistakes. As he walks out the door, he says, "I'll talk with you all after I review a new set of scans. Let's hope we get the correct results this time."

As he leaves, Savannah calls out, "Doctor, how long will that take?"

The doctor, not happy driving to the hospital for nothing, brushes Savannah off with a terse, "I don't know, ma'am," and walks away.

Savannah, put out by the doctor's callus response, shouts back with a cynical, "Thank you!"

She then asks the head nurse the same question. Savannah needs to put a strategy in place to decide whether she waits, or just leaves before being discharged.

The head nurse explains the MRI will take somewhere between ten and forty-five minutes depending on whether others are waiting. If the doctor gets tied up in another case, no telling how long it will be until the MRI is analyzed.

It's all Savannah needed to hear. She walks out of the room and phones Jack.

Jack answers with, "Tell me a story."

"It will take too long, Jack, I'm getting her out of here. Can you arrange an Uber and have it waiting out front?"

Jack asks, "What's your plan?"

"I will wait until everyone has left Sarah's room and then I will set off the fire alarm. The second the alarm goes off, Rosine and I will rip off all the monitors connected to Sarah and the three of us will walk straight to the front door. We will have a plausible excuse for leaving the building while the alarms are on. We're on the third floor and I know where the staircase is."

"Wow, Savannah, you know how to do things in style!" Jack responds. "Okay, I will provide the Uber driver with the destination hotel address and we'll meet you there. I don't want us to go back to the plane."

He continues, "I will give the driver instructions to wait out front and I will call you as soon as I see he is there. How long will it take once I phone you?"

Savannah pauses for a moment to think it through, "It shouldn't be but two minutes, Jack."

"Okay, I'll await your call, then I'll order an Uber."

"Okay, Jack, I'll call you right back." Savannah's adrenaline is pumping; it's not every day she sets off fire alarms and pulls people out of hospitals.

She goes back to the room's doorway and motions for Rosine to join her in the hall. Savannah fills her in on the plans. Rosine reluctantly agrees. The two of them go back into the room and Rosine goes up to Sarah and whispers instructions into Sarah's ear. Sarah nods she understands.

The head nurse and his attendant stay in the room. They are still discussing the strange turn of events. Savannah is pacing and just wants them to leave.

Another attendant walks into Sarah's room and says, "Good news, young lady! We're ready to take you back for another MRI. Ready for a ride? Just need to get you unhooked."

While the head nurse and his assistant watch, Sarah's saline drip and the myriad of monitors are unhooked.

The new attendant says, "Let's go! They're waiting. It seems everyone is anxious to see what's happening with you."

He then moves the gurney Sarah has been lying on towards the door.

Savannah has to think on her feet and act fast. She phones Jack back, "Jack, things have changed, they're taking Sarah right now for another MRI. Call the Uber. I'm pulling the alarm now."

"Okay, I'm on it," Jack says.

Savannah leans over to Rosine and says, "We're doing it now."

As the gurney clears the door, Savannah follows and looks for a fire alarm switch. She sees one thirty feet up the hall. It is the opposite direction of where Sarah is being taken. She approaches Rosine again and says, "After the alarm goes off, I will distract the guy pushing the gurney. The second I distract him, you two head as fast as you can to the nearest exit."

Rosine looks startled and doesn't say a word. She looks for an exit.

Savannah walks briskly towards the fire alarm switch trying not to draw attention to herself. She looks up and down the hall to see if anyone is watching her. She sees no one and pulls the alarm lever, breaking the glass cover. The alarm wails. Over the noise, Savannah hears a male voice shout out, "Stop!" She doesn't hesitate and runs to catch up with the gurney. As Savannah approaches, she puts her hand on the gurney attendant's shoulder pulling him back to get his attention. Pointing to a door, she yells over the wail of the alarm, "There's an old lady on the floor in there screaming for help!"

The gurney attendant yells back, "Wait here," and runs into the room.

As the attendant turns his back, Sarah jumps off the gurney, and she and Rosine scurry towards the exit. Savannah is right behind them. They fight their way through the people who are rapidly filling the hall.

The attendant comes out of the room, sees his empty gurney, and just barley glimpses Savannah as she steps into the stairwell exit. He runs to the exit but stops at its entrance and gives up the chase when he sees the stairwell is full of people exiting the hospital.

While shuffling down the stairs, Savannah calls Jack to get an Uber update. He tells her it's a white Isuzu Panther SUV and it should be there in two minutes.

The stairwell empties outside onto a grassy area flanking the building. They make their way through the crowd as they hear fire truck sirens converging on the hospital from every direction.

Taking their best guess on the direction to get them to the front of the hospital they proceed. There is no direct path and they have to walk around fences and across groomed lawns. It is taking longer than two minutes to reach the main entrance and Savannah is hoping the Uber driver remains patient.

Savannah can now see the fire trucks and is thankful they made the right choice after leaving the exit. The fire alarms become silent as they approach the front. The group sees two fire trucks at the entrance and more arriving. The sirens heard from the arriving trucks stop before reaching the hospital entrance; Savannah assumes they now know it is a false alarm.

There is no white SUV near the front entrance and Savannah notices a lineup of vehicles trying to get into the hospital from the main road out front. As a result of the alarm, she sees the hospital security have blocked the hospital's entrance road, not allowing traffic to enter.

She sees a white SUV ten vehicles back in the lineup. They walk towards it stepping past a security guard as they exit the front gate. They turn towards the white vehicle, hoping it is their Uber.

As they walk past the security guard, Savannah notices him stare at her and then pick up his two-way radio microphone from its clip on his upper shirt pocket. It unsettles her.

As the three walks towards the Uber, Savannah senses the guard is following them. She turns and takes a quick glance over her shoulder. Sure enough, the security guard is keeping his distance, but is following. Savannah calls Jack again.

In a humorous way, Jack says "What now, Savannah?"

"Jack, we're almost to our Uber, at least I hope it's our Uber, and we're being followed by a security guard."

"You and your clan are definitely trouble magnets," Jack quips.

"This isn't funny, Jack. What if he stops us?"

"Not happening because Andre and I came in our own Uber, and you are walking beside us right now. We thought you might need some extra help."

At that moment, the door of a red Honda Accord opens and Jack steps out.

Without looking at them, Jack says, "Don't look at me or acknowledge we're here. Just continue walking to your Uber and leave."

Savannah quietly says to Sarah and Rosine, "Wow, Johnny on the spot or what?"

They keep walking and are relieved to see the white SUV is their Uber ride. They jump in and drive off to the hotel with no additional fanfare.

While the three were completing their walk to their Uber, the security guard had sped up his pace to catch them. Before he caught up, Jack steps in front of him forcing him to stop.

The guard says, "Get out of my way."

Jack knows he has to take him away from the scene to provide time for the others to get away cleanly, so he says to the guard, "I have a gun pointing at your belly. Get in that red car and I won't kill you. Don't test me."

The look in Jack's eyes scares the guard, who says, "Okay, just don't shoot me."

Without resistance, the guard gets in the Accord. Jack tells him to move over and slides in beside him. The guard can see Jack's gun pointing at him.

While Jack is pushing the security guard in, Andre is making room and is jumping out of the back seat on the other side. Andre then opens the Uber driver's front door and points his gun, concealing it so only the driver sees it.

"Get out!" Andre yells at the driver. "Don't touch your phone or you're dead."

The driver steps out of his car, and Andre jumps into the driver's seat. He abruptly backs up until he almost hits the car behind, then speeds out into the roadway and accelerates away. The stranded Uber driver helplessly watches his car drive off.

Two blocks ahead Andre stops the car and Jack kicks out the security guard.

"We have to ditch this car ASAP," Jack says as Andre speeds off.

Andre pulls into a small strip mall. He drives down its side road to the back where garbage dumpsters are carefully aligned. He parks the car between two of them. They get out and throw wigs, hats, fake mustaches and sunglasses they were wearing into a dumpster. They can't be identified when doing illegal clandestine acts, and Jack always has various paraphernalia on his jet for situations like this. He's always one step ahead.

While walking back towards the front of the strip mall, Jack is on his phone ordering another Uber. He uses a different credit card.

□□□

Jack knocks on the door of the hotel room he and Spencer had arranged. Spencer looks through the peephole and opens the door. Jack sees the news has everyone glued to the television.

"Well, that was quite the day," he says.

Savannah looks up from the couch and says, "It's not over yet, Jack. Look at the TV. I'm royally screwed."

The news channel they are viewing is covering the day's events at the hospital. A correspondent is explaining a video showing a person setting off a false alarm. Sarah and Rosine are also visible in the video. The correspondent is interviewing the hospital attendant who had seen Savannah pull the alarm, followed by the gurney attendant who is explaining how Savannah had distracted him as they ran off with Sarah. Everything reported has a supporting video.

The head nurse is telling the interviewer how Sarah had a miraculous recovery. She goes into detail describing the child's wounds and bruises, along with the brain hemorrhage that had her comatose, and how it all went away.

The news broadcast is interrupted with a "Breaking News" banner across the screen. A news correspondent outside the hospital is interviewing the security guard who explains he identified the false alarm suspect as she walked by him from a still image taken from the security video sent to the guards. His orders were to follow the suspect but not apprehend, but when he explained over his radio they were heading for a vehicle, he was instructed to stop them. He tells how he was accosted at gunpoint and forced into a car. The Uber driver got pulled out, and two armed men drove off with him, kicking him out a few blocks later.

The news correspondent holds up his phone and shows a still image containing Rosine and Sarah. He asks the guard if those were the other two accompanying the false alarm suspect. He nods and says, "Yes, that is them."

The news switches to the main anchor who says, "So there you have it. Stay tuned, this is a breaking story."

Jack says, "Shit," and picks up his phone to call his pilot. He tells him to get the plane out of the country ASAP. Jack knows as soon as the immigration officer who had cleared them upon arrival sees Savannah on TV, he will make phone calls, and the authorities will head straight for the plane and hold it.

As Jack gets off the phone, another breaking news banner displays on the TV. This time the anchor is explaining they have heard from reliable sources the person who set off the fire alarm at the hospital is Savannah Davies, a news correspondent working for London World News out of London.

Jack, who is still standing, says, "Okay, listen up everyone. We have to move fast tomorrow. Because of Sarah's miraculous recovery and Savannah's growing notoriety, this story will get world coverage overnight. They will look for us."

Jack continues, "Savannah, you need to manage the damage with your employers because their phones are all going to be lighting up right now."

After a pause for breath, "I've ordered my plane to leave because they will look for it once the immigration officer recognizes Savannah. While we're away tomorrow getting Jacob, Jim will coordinate another jet prepped and waiting for us at the Sorong airport here. We will leave on it and rendezvous with my jet elsewhere. In the meantime, nobody leaves this hotel room except for Alma and Andre - understood?"

Everyone nods.

For clarity, Jack reiterates the plan to the group. "Spencer, Alex and I will leave tomorrow to meet Jacob, and we'll hopefully be returning with him and his father. We'll be back within hours. I will coordinate with Andre during the trip, and we'll regroup at the airport upon returning. You will already be aboard the new jet waiting for us. Christ, let's hope this goes a little smoother than the last couple of days."

Jack asks Spencer to call Jacob's teacher and get his home address. He then calls Jim and instructs Jim to have an operative at Jacob's house in the morning to help Jacob's family in his father's absence. Along with other skills, operatives know how to handle themselves if the need arises.

ⵔⵔⵔ

The following morning, Jack, Spencer and Alex climb into an Uber and drive to the Domine Eduard Osok Airport for their trip to Waigeo. This time Jack made the flight arrangements and chartered a Cessna Grand Caravan. The Grand Caravan is one of a few mid-sized planes capable of landing on short unpaved airstrips while accommodating a dozen people.

The repeat flight to the island provides Spencer time to reflect on how much her life has changed and how uncertain the future is. Spencer wants this to go away.

The Cessna lands on the bumpy airstrip and comes to rest where the wizard man had picked up Spencer a few days earlier. This time, Jacob's teacher Bree is waiting for them in her Toyota Camry. The pilot assists with getting Spencer and Alex out of the plane. They walk over to meet Bree, leaving the pilot behind to attend to his plane.

Spencer introduces Bree to Jack and Alex, and they climb into Bree's car for the short ride to the school.

While driving, Bree explains to Jack she has requested Jacob's father, named 'Cahya', to come for a parent and teacher meeting. She didn't mention to Cahya what the meeting is about, other than she needs to discuss Jacob with him. She warns Jack that although Cahya is a nice and kind person, he is strict and intolerant of things he doesn't understand or doesn't want to believe. Bree asks Jack to approach him with kid gloves. She says he will be feeling manipulated.

Jack understands and acknowledges he'll be careful, but he remembers his own reaction to the story when he heard it for the first time from Spencer; he knows it will be a challenge.

Bree parks her car in her usual space and leads the three into an area serving as a small lunch room for the teachers. Cahya and Jacob are sitting at the table as they enter. Upon seeing Alex, Jacob jumps up from his chair, runs up and gives him a big heartfelt hug. Everyone knows these kids have never met and are surprised by the interaction.

Cahya is already upset; he was not expecting others. He gets even angrier observing his son greet a strange boy he personally has never met or seen.

Bree says, "Cahya, some people are here to meet with you. It is about Jacob, and I apologize I have caught you off guard. This is Jack, his wife Spencer and their son Alex, whom you can see already knows Jacob."

Cahya stands from his chair and extends his hand to Jack and then to Spencer. Although disturbed by the unexpected meeting, it does not affect his manners. He sits back down and looks at Bree, "You know I don't like this, Bree. You should have told me."

Jack jumps right in, "Cahya, I asked Bree for this meeting; it's not her doing. After we explain a few things, I think you will understand."

Collecting his thoughts, Jack continues, "I will warn you, what we're about to discuss with you, regardless of what you think, will change your life forever. I know this sounds rather ominous, but the same thing you will hear has already happened to Spencer and myself a handful of days ago."

Jack continues, "About a week back, our son Alex learned some strange things. Stuff he wouldn't have had any knowledge about. My understanding is Jacob approached you about something similar. Is that correct?"

"Yes. He was saying crap, and thankfully he stopped. How do you know about that?" Cahya says defensively.

Jack, trying to stay calm and choose his words, says, "The things Jacob is learning are happening at a daily rate. It's the same information my son is learning, and there is one more ten-year-old, named Sarah, who is also learning the same stuff. This is no coincidence, Cahya; the information is far too detailed, and these children are learning it together."

Cahya jumps in, "You can't possibly know what Jacob is learning!"

Bree explains, "Cahya, Jacob needed to tell someone about what is happening. It is way too much for him to keep bottled up, so he has been telling me. Spencer was here looking for Jacob. That's when I confronted him, and he admitted these things. I have been corresponding with Jack and Spencer since. They have travelled from Ecuador to discuss this with you. Will you hear them out?"

Cahya responds with a disgruntled trite, "Well, I'm here now. Bree, you know you went behind my back with my son."

Spencer ignores Cahya's comment and takes her turn. "A week or so back, Alex told me an event involving something they call a black hole in the Milky Way had happened and it will destroy the Earth in ten years."

Cahya concedes, "That is what Jacob told me, too."

Spencer continues, "Each day Alex has been telling us more stuff. We know the three children live in homes on the equator equally spaced around the planet. Now hold your breath on this one, Cahya; we know they are learning things to save millions of people from extinction when the planet gets destroyed."

Cahya gets up from his chair, paces and then says, "You travelled around the planet to tell me, a pearl diver, my son will help save mankind from extinction?"

Before he can say more, Bree interjects, "Cahya, you don't need to hear it from them, hear it from Jacob. Please just listen to him. He didn't make this up. It's coming from somewhere, and it's not from anyone he has talked with."

She takes a breath and continues, "Jacob knows everything Alex here knows. These children are being taught together and communicate with each other daily. We don't understand how, but they do. Just talk to your son, Cahya."

Cahya is a proud man, and he doesn't want to admit or appear to be a bad parent. He knows something is happening here he won't be able to brush off; he becomes more subdued and looks at his son, "Is this true, Jacob, are you learning these things daily?"

"Yes, Dad. I can't explain how or where, but there are three of us, we're called conduits, we meet every day and are learning tons of stuff. It's gotten to where it's too detailed to discuss. We're learning a lot of engineering like the formulas for compression loads and beam spans. The thing we don't understand is how we can leave for weeks to learn all this, yet never seem to go anywhere."

Jacob looks over at Alex, "That is weird isn't it, Alex?"

Spencer looks at Alex; she is hearing this for the first time. "Alex, are you learning about engineering?"

"Yeah Mom, we have to show people how to build five mile high towers. That hasn't been done before. Not even close. I already mentioned it to you."

"And you are actually learning how to do it?"

"Yup. Jacob is learning it, too. Sarah is a bit behind. She took a few weeks to heal from her wounds. We sure felt bad for her Mom. She was almost dead."

Spencer, with surprise, says, "You mean you were *with* Sarah as she got better?"

"So was Jacob," Alex says.

Cahya, who is now sitting back in his chair, interjects, "What the hell are you talking about?"

"Sorry, Cahya," Jack says, "this has gone a little off track. Sarah is the third conduit. We picked her up in Africa on our way here to meet you. Unfortunately, four boys attacked her and over two days pounded her to within an inch of her life. She was in a coma. We flew her to Sorong where we admitted her to the hospital. They gave her an MRI and based on the results they scheduled an emergency surgery to fix a brain hemorrhage that would kill her. While waiting for the surgery, Sarah somehow became cured, they are calling it a miraculous recovery. I'm just hearing for the first time now my son Alex was with her during the time needed for her recovery, yet he hasn't left our side. This is all over the news right now. Shit is happening, Cahya, shit we don't understand."

Jacob jumps in, "I was with her too, Dad."

Cahya says, "So what do you folks expect from me? Why are you here? To tell me my son is visiting aliens, but never leaves?"

"No, Cahya," Jack says as calmly as possible, "we're here hoping to take you with us. We need to understand and coordinate how to get this message out, and we need Jacob, and Jacob will need you. Like us, you are in this now, Cahya; you have no choice. When this gets out, you will feel the world landing on your doorstep. If you work with us, maybe we can figure it out together, making it less difficult for you."

"I can't just up and leave my family," Cahya says with defiance in his voice. "I feed them. We have no savings."

"I understand that. I have been lucky and I'm able to support you and your family for as long as this plays out. I have already made arrangements for a house maid to assist your wife in your absence. Everything will fall apart when the world hears it only has ten years left; no one will buy pearls, and there will be lots of jobs lost. We all have to do this together, Cahya, and I don't mind assisting because I can't take my money with me when this story ends."

"This is too much for me," Cahya says dejectedly. "Give me a few days to talk with my wife and son and think about all this. I'll get back to you."

"Here's the thing, Cahya," Jack says, trying to sound convincing, "we need a leap of faith from you. Scientists will see the gravity event and the new star soon, and they have told the conduits to get the word out before the science community makes it public. If we don't get the word out first, no one will believe us. I understand you don't believe this stuff yet, but you need to trust us for a few days until you see it for yourself. We have little time. Please explain to your wife an emergency has come up and you and Jacob have to leave now. Today. As we sit here talking, the housemaid will have already arrived at your home. Your wife will be in good hands."

Cahya ignores the request for leaving and rants, "You have a housemaid at my house? When did *that* happen? There is a stranger in my house with my wife? No one asked if that was okay!"

"I'm sorry, Cahya, it's the only way I could swing it so you could leave with us. Don't worry, the housemaid is highly recommended and will be of great help for your wife and can protect your family while you are with us."

Astounded, Cahya says, "You actually want me to leave with you right now, don't you? Are you out of your mind? I can't do that ... I wouldn't do that to my wife."

"Look at the bigger picture here, Cahya. Spencer and I had to leave. Spencer had to quit her teaching job with no notice, I walked out of the business I've been building for years. Back in Sorong is Sarah's teacher, she also walked out on her job and students. We all walked away with no notice, Cahya; we had to. You need to do the same. You have my word the moment you and Jacob want to be back here, I will fly you back. No one out there will ever question my word. I built everything based on reputation. Come with us, Cahya, I will fly you back tomorrow if that's what it will take. Your wife's assistant will keep your family safe and will provide considerable help."

Cahya, now confused and talking fast, "Christ. I've never done any-thing this crazy. I need to pack. You say there is a housemaid at my house now? What do I say to my children? Ah, hell, I can't do this!"

"Slow down, Cahya," Jack says. "Just grab clothes for a day. We'll pro-vide you with toiletry stuff. We'll all buy more clothes and necessities on the way. I'll provide you a cell phone so you can call your family whenever you want, and I'll put one-hundred-thousand dollars in your bank account for you and your wife. Money will never be an issue for your family again. Don't worry about your job."

"Say what?" Cahya says in a higher pitch.

"The money will be in your account tomorrow. Now let's get going!"

Cahya, conceding, looks over at Jacob, "You good with this?"

"Yeah, Dad, this will be amazing," Jacob says with excitement.

Jack asks, "Cahya, I'm assuming neither you nor Jacob have pass-ports, correct?"

"I've never had a passport in my life."

"It's okay," Jack says, "I will take passport pictures of you two and it will be handled. After the photos, take Jacob back to your house, pack for a day, and say your goodbyes. Bree will swing buy in forty-five minutes to pick you up. We'll see you at the airstrip in an hour."

000

As promised, a Hawker 900XP jet flies into the Sorong airport that morning and refuels. Andre is coordinating through Jim and receiving the information for ensuring the group can meet up with the jet.

Alma left the hotel room earlier to buy a few things to help Savannah be incognito when she steps out of the hotel room. She brought back large sunglasses, a wide-brimmed hat, large earrings and hair pins enabling Savannah to pull her hair up. Savannah's picture is still consuming much of the air time on the news channels. The authorities are asking for the public's help in locating her for questioning; they can't be recognized getting onto the new jet.

Just after 11 am, they are in an Uber van en route to the airport. They are driven to where the private jets are accessible on the tarmac. The pilot has the passenger manifest he received from Jim, who had gotten it from Andre. Using the manifest, the charter pilot has made arrangements for the group to pass through customs and get onto the plane. Just after 11:30 am the group is aboard the chartered Hawker.

Six minutes later the large Cessna carrying the other half of the entourage lands. The pilot taxis the plane over beside the larger jet where once aboard, Jack introduces Cahya and Jacob. All ten seats on the plane are occupied.

Thirty minutes later the group of ten are soaring at forty thousand feet toward Kuala Lumpur in Malaysia, where they will rendezvous with Jack's big Gulfstream that had flown out the previous day.

The plane has five rows of individual seats with an isle in the middle. It is the first time the conduits have been together outside of their *episodes*. They are trying to figure out how they have spent time together and know each other so well without ever leaving their normal lives.

Jack is filling Cahya in on the events of the past few days. After hearing the stories, Cahya says to Jack, "James Bond wouldn't be able to keep up with you."

Jack laughs; it surprises him Cahya even knows of James Bond. He is sure Cahya now understands the reality of the predicament he's caught up in.

Savannah has been on her phone steadily, settling the firestorm at the office in London and making preparations for the group's arrival at the studio. She is nervous having to handle her involvement in the fire alarm fiasco.

She makes one last call, then leans forward and says to Jack who is in the next row, "We're a go for the first interview." Savannah closes her eyes and falls asleep exhausted.

Jack then says over the roar of the jet engines, "Listen up everyone. Savannah has arranged for us to talk with her producer in London. We're heading there non-stop after we switch back to my plane in Kuala Lumpur."

Cahya looks over at Jack and says, "I've never travelled further than one hundred miles from where I live."

Jack turns to Cahya and says, "Those days are over, my friend", then thinks to himself, "Wow!"

⫿⫿⫿

The transfer to Jack's plane in Kuala Lumpur takes place without a hitch, and the entourage settles into the Gulfstream for the remaining twelve-hour leg to London.

Jack spends time on the phone with Jim, instructing him to make accommodation arrangements for the group upon arrival. He asks him to arrange for a large twelve passenger van with a driver, to be waiting for them. On a roll, he also gets Jim to arrange for cell phones and to prepare for the money transfer to Cahya's bank account.

Jack moves through the cabin and sits by Alma. They had never discussed the extraction mission in Africa and losing her team; he doesn't know how she's feeling about it. After a few minutes of talking and consoling her, Jack asks Alma to join Andre as an addition to his personal security detail. Jack explains with the future events likely to unfold, additional security will be prudent, and having a qualified medic on hand would be a useful bonus. He has seen Alma in action, making quick decisions saving him from ending up in a Congo jail. In Jack's world, when someone has your back and saves your butt, it forms a bond. Alma thanks Alex for the opportunity and says yes without hesitation.

Andre heats frozen one-dish meals for everyone; no one has eaten in hours and are famished. A few hours after the meal, Andre helps everyone convert their seats into beds and provides pillows and blankets. The group settles in to their makeshift beds and conversation subsides. They all sleep restlessly, going in and out of consciousness as their minds spin thinking through the transpiring events and what lies ahead.

At 5 pm Sorong time while sleeping, the three conduits open their dilated eyes. Three seconds later their eyes close and they remain fast asleep.

Six hours later, Andre emerges from his cabin. Most of the travelers are now awake, and Andre takes drink orders and assists with the cabin setup back to regular seating.

The adults are drinking coffee and eating oatmeal when the last of the conduits wake. Alex looks at Jacob and says, "Do you want to tell them?"

Jacob responds with "Sure," and then gets up and goes to his father and sits on the seat's arm. He announces, "We have learned about stuff that was confusing us."

Jacob has everyone's attention, "There are things about space-time even our astrophysicists don't understand. Our teachers know how to travel between boundaries to places that work on a different time than what we experience. When we learn new stuff, they take us across these boundaries for sometimes weeks at a time. When we return, it's like we didn't even leave. That is how Sarah got cured yesterday. It wasn't an instant miraculous recovery, we went for what seemed like at least three weeks, and they nursed her back to health. It happens to us every day. We all just learned this while sleeping."

Cahya looks at his son and says, "What do you mean, 'they take you'?"

"We don't know, Dad. We don't remember going or returning, or what it's like when we're there. It's like they decide what we will remember."

There is a silence while everyone tries to comprehend.

Spencer breaks the silence, "Do you see people when you're there?"

"We don't remember that. We only know we're together. We don't remember what we do, we just come back with a memory of what we've learned."

She then says, "Do you miss us while you're gone? Three weeks is a long time gone." Spencer can't believe she's even saying this; Alex leaving for another world for weeks at a time is science fiction, she is struggling with it.

"I know we're happy when we're gone, Mom, but I don't remember thinking about here, when we're there. It's just like we don't think of there, when we're here. It's just weird."

Spencer, thinking this through, asks, "If gone for weeks at a time, do you age while you're there?"

Jacob replies, "Yeah.. We are aging the whole time we're gone, it's why they choose kids, we're young and have a longer time to live."

Spencer tears up. She is sure she had noticed changes in Alex's appearance, especially how fast his hair is growing. This news devastates her. She doesn't want this for her child.

Jack asks the next question, "Will the aging stop? Will they stop taking you at some point?"

Jacob responds, "We don't know. I think the length of time we're gone is different each time, because sometimes it seems like we learn a lot, while other times not so much."

Rosine looks over at Sarah, "You believe this too, Sarah?"

"Yes, Ms. Rosine. We learn it together and have the same thoughts about it."

CHAPTER 6

LONDON

A few hours later the big Gulfstream lands at London's Heathrow Airport and taxis to the private jet terminal.

Before the engines stop, a man approaches the plane. Andre lowers the entrance stairs for him, and he hands over passports for Sarah, Cahya and Jacob, and quickly disappears.

Jack's pilot places a call and requests customs and immigration clearance. Within ten minutes, two officials arrive at the plane for visa clearances - a benefit of flying privately.

While the clearance officials are doing their job in the plane's cabin, a white Ford Transit van arrives. It is a large extended model with a raised roof, providing seating for twelve.

Within thirty minutes the conduit entourage team is speeding along the M4 from Heathrow to the Caesar Hotel in downtown London. Jack is sitting up front with the driver. Andre and Alma stay behind on the plane, at the ready.

The driver drops the group off outside the hotel's front entrance. While everyone pulls the luggage out of the van, Jack runs in to take care of the hotel reservation. Upon entering, Jack looks around and decides he likes the place; he enjoys hotels with a boutique atmosphere.

With lots of help from Jim, Jack arranged four rooms with double beds. He and Alex will take the larger one, Spencer and Savannah in another, Rosine will be with Sarah, and Cahya will be with his son Jacob.

The group congregates in the lobby with their inadequate luggage while Jack completes their check-in arrangements. He walks over and hands out the electronic room entry cards to each room couple and tells the group they can eat within the hotel or order whatever they want delivered to their rooms, charging everything. He asks them to rest and wait until tomorrow to do much-needed wardrobe shopping.

Before the group disperses to their rooms, Jack makes one additional comment, "I want everyone to meet in my room at 8am tomorrow. I will have a room service breakfast brought up, and we can discuss our plans for the day and our go forward strategy. I don't want Savannah's producers dictating our message, so we need to maintain control and be smart about this before we meet with them. We'll start those discussions after shopping tomorrow. See you all in my room tomorrow at eight."

ꟷꟷ

Jack talks with Alex and then tucks him into bed. The boy falls asleep instantly unaffected by the events now surrounding them.

Once Jack sees Alex sleeping, he places a call to Jim. Jim's immediate availability is why people use his services; he answers promptly day or night.

As usual, Jack doesn't partake in any pleasantries, and gets straight to business, "Jim, things will get crazy here, and I now need you pretty much full time. Can you make this happen?"

Jim, surprised, responds, "Christ, Jack, what are you doing? You're overthrowing the British government, aren't you?"

Jack, ignoring the snide remark, says, "Jim, I'll need lots of help with logistics, moving people around, and with providing security. Security will be a challenge."

"Well, Jack, imagine that! Just happens to be what I'm good at. Yeah, I've got a project winding down - should be able to dedicate my time."

Jack, hurrying, says, "Okay, good. Now listen up, things will happen like nothing you've seen before. There will be a stock market crash, a run on the banks, and it very well could cause a global infrastructure melt-down. I wouldn't rule out outright anarchy before this is all said and done. It may take a few years, but this will piss off lots of folks."

"Jesus, Jack, it's not a country overthrow, you are starting a global war, aren't you?"

"Take me seriously, Jim. You need to liquidate all your investments as fast as possible. When the money hits your bank accounts, take it out as hard cash. If they have daily withdrawal limits, just keep withdrawing every day; get it all out and don't take the bank's bullshit why you can't withdraw large amounts. They will fight you on the withdrawals, but it's your right to have the cash. Hide it and tell no one. If you ignore me, Jim, there will be a run on the banks, and you will lose it all. You know me, Jim, I'm being dead serious; if you can only get fifty cents on the dollar, do it. Getting half is better than losing it all."

"What the fuck is happening, Jack? That's a pretty tough recommen-dation. Can you be so kind as to fill me in before I lose half of everything?"

"Look, I don't know when it will happen, it's at least a week away, but I guarantee there will be a global news broadcast about a cataclysmic event happening in space that will destroy the earth in ten years. I know this is mind blowing news, but I know it's happening because Alex and I are in the thick of it - not a place I wanted to be."

Jack continues, "If the earth doesn't get destroyed, it sure as hell will be a mess after the newscast. Play it safe, Jim, get your money out. I'm doing the same. And you know me. I wouldn't be giving up anything if I wasn't one hundred percent sure."

"Holy Christ, Jack, ten years? Please tell me you're shitting me? Fuck! How did you get into this mess?"

"Long story. I'll fill you in soon. I'm dead tired and need sleep. Save your money, Jim, and be ready to help."

"Okay, Jack, I'm on standby. Ten years? That's fucked up!"

"I'll call you tomorrow."

Jack then sends a text message to Robert, his financial handler. "Urgent … call ASAP." He wants to act on the same advice he gave Jim and will delegate Robert to do his bidding. Robert has been with Jack since the beginning and an implicit trust exists between them. Robert knows Jack always keeps an eye on his business transactions and would never risk messing with him.

Most businesspeople who have amassed huge wealth move in a circle of wealthy and influential people; Jack is no different. He writes the names of people he will warn of the impending market downturns. This is a tough call for Jack; if the wealthy get their money out first, it screws the little guys who will lose everything. Jack knows this, but if the big guys don't get their money out first, they won't be able to help. He knows it will take big money to fund and execute the conduit's plans. He also knows the governments won't be much help; there is no direct political benefit for politicians in countries where towers are not being constructed. At the highest levels in the US government, there will be skepticism and gridlock bickering. The worst-case scenario is governments weaponizing anti-conduit campaigns and using social media for fake news to discredit the message. Jack sees it every day; the US president has become a master of the art.

Jack goes to bed wondering why, as Jim had asked, he ended up in the middle of an event culminating with the planet's destruction. He is reasoning that along with the conduits themselves, *they* must have also chosen him and Spencer; but who are *'they'*? How would they know Alex would be in Ecuador? Lying in bed, Jack's head is spinning. If conduits and parents are chosen, has it ever happened before? Are we working with God? Are we being guided? He falls into a restless sleep.

▯▯▯

The following morning the group gathers in Jack's room, on time for 8am as requested.

Within minutes room service arrives with a breakfast on carts - scrambled eggs, Canadian bacon, biscuits, fruit, coffee and juices. The group is quiet while eating; evidence everyone is hungry.

Jack is first to finish and starts the conversation, "Alex, you kids say you're learning engineering, and the purpose is to build three towers you have mentioned. You also said on December 17th scientists will observe a significant gravitational anomaly. That's all correct, right?"

Alex replies, "Yes, but there will also be bright visible light where Sagittarius-A used to be."

"Okay, before a news conference, we round up three separate and reputable structural engineers and sit them one-on-one with each of you for a debriefing. In this way we will have three independent evaluations of the information you kids have. I'm hoping the information the engineers capture is the same, thus proving you kids are learning the same complex stuff."

Jack continues, "In the meantime, Savannah, if you could work with your folks and understand from their perspective how this will unfold. I mean, what will they need to gain enough confidence to expose this story."

Jack pauses, reflecting for a moment, then continues, "Alex, there is something bothering me; they will ask it at the news conference. You said x-rays will reach the earth in ten years, which will then destroy the planet.

I know astronomers can't see anything, whether it is visible light, x-rays, gamma-rays, or any radiation for that matter, until it actually reaches us so they can observe it. None of this stuff is detectable until it gets here. Obviously, if we don't see it until it gets here, it's too late. How do we get a ten-year advanced warning?"

"I kinda explained this to Mom at the beginning so I don't think you have heard it yet, Dad. A black hole is collapsed matter and is therefore very dense. They are surrounded by an event horizon extending ten million kilometers from their center. The event horizon is like an invisible line, anything crossing it gets sucked into the black hole, and can't ever leave, or so the astrophysicists thought. Nothing gets out of a black hole, including gravitational waves, light, or other radiation. It's why they're called black holes, they're not directly detectable - they can't be seen. We don't know what caused it, but a huge event happened and the collapsed matter in the black hole, called a singularity, expanded out to something similar to a neutron star. It didn't explode, it expanded out. The expansion removed the event horizon and the resulting event created something like a star, producing massive gravity waves and visible light. Our scientists and astronomers will see the light and detect the gravity waves on December 17th. This event happened over twenty-five thousand years ago, and it's taking this long for it to reach us and be detectable. The thing is, Dad, the star-like entity created from the black hole was huge, like a billion times larger than our sun, and extremely unstable. It exploded ten years after it was created. Even though we haven't even seen it yet, it has already come and gone. It's this secondary event that was cataclysmic and we won't see it until it hits us ten years from now. It's the x-rays from the secondary event that will destroy us. The galaxy is currently getting destroyed from the inside out, but we can't see it. Like I said, Dad, we have ten years."

Sarah jumps in adding to the story. "Our scientists developed the technology to detect gravity waves back on December 14th, 2015. They detected the collision of two small neutron stars. These two stars were two hundred and thirty million light years away; much farther away than

Sagittarius-A. The explosion Alex just mentioned is an entity millions of times larger than they detected back in 2015 and it's only twenty-five thousand light years away - much closer. The gravity waves they will detect are hundreds of millions of times stronger than what our scientists have seen so far. They will cause the earth to shrink and expand ever so slightly, and the shudder will be detectable by the average person if they put their hands on the ground at the precise right second. If this event is known in advance and happens as we say it will, the 2nd part of the story is believable; it will show we know of future events."

Looking towards the conduits, Spencer asks, "All three of you understand this?"

The two boys nod and Sarah says, "Yes, ma'am."

Jack says, "Wow, careful what you ask for. I guess I don't need to worry about *that* anymore."

Just then, the room phone rings. Jack picks it up, says "Hello," listens, and then says, "Please have it delivered to my room," and hangs up.

Jack says, "It appears we have a delivery," followed within seconds by a knock at the door.

After interacting with the person at the door, Jack walks back to the group holding a large shopping bag. He reaches in and brings out a small white box with Spencer's name on it, and just as Santa Claus would do, he gives her the box. Jack hands a box to everyone, each containing a pre-activated iPhone. Jack wanted everyone to have the same reliable means for communicating. He shows the group a special app he had installed on each phone, and instructs them to use it when calling each other rather than using the regular phone capability. He explains the app encrypts the calls so if people eavesdrop, they won't understand the conversations. The group learns the app is how Jack communicates with Jim while facilitating their travels. Jack reaches back in and pulls out waterproof phone covers for everyone; years of clandestine operations and learning from the school of hard knocks has taught him a thing or two about cell phones.

Everyone says thanks and starts putting the covers on their phones.

Jack gets back to business. "So along with the engineers, we need to line up three astrophysicists and three astronomers who will also get debriefed. Is that okay with you kids?"

The conduits, confident with what they have learned, nod their heads in agreement as they continue fussing with their phone cases.

Jack continues, "Savannah, I want all this done before the news conference, and based on the outcome of the debriefings, I would like to have these folks available for questioning as part of the newscast. What are your thoughts?"

Savannah responds, "I hadn't thought of that, Jack. It's brilliant. It will add significant credibility to what we'll be saying. Lord only knows, anything will help."

Cahya, has been quiet through the breakfast, adds a humorous snipe, "Someone will ask us if we're Jehovah's Witnesses."

"You got that right," says Spencer.

Everyone laughs except the conduits; they don't get it.

Jack talks logistics with the adults and they decide on the tasks needed leading up to the news conference. They ask Savannah to schedule interview times, hopefully for later in the day.

As the meeting wraps up, Cahya phones his wife Indah with his new phone. He needed instructions from Savannah, as he had never owned a smartphone before, and most of the behaviour and capability of the phone is alien to him.

When Indah answers, she doesn't wait to hear Cahya's greeting and blurts out, "The bank called me this morning, Cahya. Someone has deposited a hundred thousand dollars into our account!"

"Wow, I didn't expect it that fast. Jack is a man of his word."

"You mean you expected it? What have you gotten us into, Cahya? You are in over your head and it's scaring me. There is a person in our house helping me, and I think she's carrying a gun. What's happening, Cahya?"

Cahya, who now understands and believes the gravity of the situation he is in, knows he has to keep Indah calm. There is no rational way to explain what is happening, so he resorts to simplicity, "You know me, Indah. You know me. You know I would do nothing wrong. Trust me. It's too complex to explain right now. Please hang in there."

Cahya changes the conversation back to the money. "Indah, I don't think I'll be working as a pearl diver anymore. This money is our retirement. Please don't spend any of it until I get back. We can plan things out together, okay?

"Okay, Cahya, but I don't like this."

After a few minutes of Cahya describing their adventure, the call ends.

❚❚❚

Savannah is on her phone, coordinating with her producer at the office, a non-stop activity since moving into her hotel room. She knows if she says too much, it will sound unbelievable. If she says too little, she won't get enough of their time and attention to move this story along fast. Having to explain the fire drill in Sorong hasn't helped.

Savannah ends her phone call, looks at Spencer who is wasting time in front of the TV, and says, "Got it!"

She then dials Jack who immediately answers. "Jack, we're on for 4 pm at our studio. It's about forty-five minutes from here. This will get interesting."

"You have no idea!" Jack exclaims. "I'll have the driver waiting out front at 3 pm. We'll meet in the lobby. I'll call Cahya."

□□□

Its 3 pm and the group has obediently congregated in the hotel lobby. Jack walks in and tells everyone the van is ready out front.

Traffic is heavy as they make their way to the studio - the ride is otherwise routine. Views of London have everyone glued to the windows.

As the van pulls up in front of a modern four-story building, they see a large neon sign over its front doors - 'London World News'. Under the sign they notice the trademarked moniker of 'LWN'. Off to the right, the building has an adjoining lot filled with a half dozen large satellite dishes of varying sizes and orientation. The dishes stream and receive live broadcast signals to and from news affiliates around the world.

Inside, the front lobby attendant provides the group with personalized name tags needed to gain access, then leads them through a locked door to an elevator. On the third floor the elevator opens directly into a large and modern boardroom. The attendant sits the group at the table along one side and then takes a beverage order. After requests for soda and water, he leaves the room.

A few minutes later, Savannah's management team enters through a side door. The tallest person of the group, enhanced by her stiletto heels, introduces herself. "Hello everyone, thanks so much for coming by, my name is Maggie McGee and I'm the executive producer and owner here at London World News. This is Ang, my associate producer, and behind him is Janet, our news director. Savannah here has told me some surreal world news is happening. We have a great deal of trust in Savannah, so we're interested and looking forward to hearing your story."

Savannah steps right in after Maggie finishes. "This story is about these three children here. They have been told they are conduits, a term that will become obvious as this story unfolds. Before we begin, why don't we all introduce ourselves and explain our role or purpose for being here. Why don't you go first, Spencer?"

One by one, the conduit team introduces themselves and explain their role to the LWN team. When finished, Savannah asks the conduits to state their birthdates.

Alex says, "I was born on October 10th, 2012."

Sarah says, "That's my birthdate too."

Followed by Jacob, "Me too, we all have the same birthdates."

Savannah says, "Thanks, kids," and then looking at her team says, "you will hear a lot of remarkable and surreal things discussed during this session here today. The first amazing thing is these kids come from different parts of the world, they are not related and never knew each other before this story unfolded, and not only do they have the same birth date, they were all born in the exact same minute on that day, and I'm not talking about the same time within their respective time zones, I'm talking about the exact same minute, period."

Maggie looks at Savannah and says, "Seriously?"

"We have verified with the original hospital records and birth certificates. These kids were chosen, and Maggie, this is just the beginning."

Maggie's team's interest has become tweaked. They are tuned in and are not saying a word.

Over the next hour, Savannah unveils the story of the conduits. Savannah had asked them to save their questions for the end and they sit stone faced, listening to a story difficult to accept.

As Savannah finishes her account, Maggie says, "So you actually believe we can tell this story? Do you have any idea what you're asking of us? This is doomsday stuff, Savannah. You're talking about the apocalypse, for Christ's sake."

Jack jumps in, "Maggie, as you heard explained, if people don't hear about this before the scientists detect the disturbance, the story won't appear credible. Your studio can take the normal position of taking no responsibility for the message; you are just reporting what you've heard."

Maggie responds, "Jack, you know it doesn't work like that. If it's perceived we're covering a grossly misleading story resulting in mass hysteria, the courts will shut us down. If this December 17th thing doesn't materialize, the damage we would sustain will be unrecoverable. I'm guessing no one here can say they are one hundred percent positive, beyond a shadow of a doubt, this gravity event will happen. Am I correct?"

Spencer jumps in without acknowledging Maggie's question. "Maggie, do you think this could be a hoax? With everything you have heard here today, along with the things these kids are learning, and how they're learning them, and the fact they actually get together daily even though they have been living eight thousand miles apart from each other, it's hard to doubt the credibility of this story. These kids have independently, yet simultaneously learned about what happens when black holes expand, and how to build five-mile-high towers. Who would do this if not true? If you don't help, you will set us back significantly. I'm not threatening, but do you want to be responsible for holding this up if it's true? Millions of lives are at stake."

Maggie responds, "I reiterate, do you understand what the reaction will be to this story? The governments will destroy it, the churches will destroy it, the haters will destroy it, and everyone else will either deny it or just go crazy. I don't think I've described it accurately; it will be worse."

"Maggie, regardless of how surreal this story is," Jack interjects, "Most people don't have significant savings and require their cash flow to exist. For this reason alone, the middle and lower classes will remain working and I predict things will remain stable even though the markets and banks will take a dive creating a recession the likes of nothing we have experienced before. Yes, some will not accept it, and no doubt the upper class will flip out and call foul. Shit is happening, Maggie, that we can't explain and it's not going away whether you cover it or not. We can demonstrate these kids know things our advanced scientists don't understand. We can show they are learning additional information daily, and it's a compelling story.

Isn't it your job to report the news, or are you more concerned in playing it safe and protecting your reputation and interests rather than covering a controversial story the world needs to hear? If it's not you, then we will find someone else; we need to tell this story. Protecting yourself will be short term, as we're all doomed anyway."

Maggie, ignoring Jack's tone, says, "Can you assure me the story is valid? How will you do that?"

Jack, getting more aggressive and challenging, says, "If you tell your audience you are just reporting a story and you are not responsible for whether the evidence appears as forecast, and further explain the risk of not covering the story is greater than the risk of telling it if it becomes true, you are just doing your job, which quite frankly is what we need right now. Hell, even without the evidence, what you have heard today, and what we can show, makes a noteworthy story."

Maggie frowns.

Jack continues, "I totally get the effect this message will have. I also understand the effect this event will have on our planet, and without some early cooperation, the endgame is far worse. We will have experts debrief these kids and I think you'll see what is happening here is undeniable, or at the least credible. Your best correspondent, Savannah here, has seen and heard the evidence. She believes it. Yes, this is surreal, and yes, it will create chaos, and yes, most people will treat the story with denial and accuse you of irresponsible reporting. Maggie, if we hold off until after the evidence, the challenge of convincing people will be insurmountable. I'm telling you this story is true. How do you want your agency positioned over the next ten years? Leading this story, or following?"

Slowing down and in a calmer voice, Jack asks a final question, "What do you suggest?"

Still frowning, Maggie says, "This is an impossible situation. Damn it."

She thinks for a few moments, then says, "Could we record the conference, with credible witnesses in attendance, and then broadcast the conference after they detect the gravity event?"

Savannah jumps up and paces. The group watches her with anticipation. She doesn't disappoint. She stops pacing and adds, "That could work, especially if we let the scientific community know what is about to happen so they can confirm they got advance notice. They won't be able to explain how an advance notice could have been possible, which will bode well for our story. Spencer and Jack, what do you think?"

"It works for me. I think it's a good idea."

Spencer adds a comment normally in Jack's realm as the business mind, saying, "Maggie, can we get something simple in writing saying you will unconditionally broadcast the taped conference if the event takes place on the day it happens? I hate to ask this, but I don't want to see us having to renegotiate this or have to talk with another agency after the fact."

Jack chimes in, "I concur and would take it a step further. I would like a copy. If it doesn't air, there won't be time to fight this thing."

Maggie says, "I understand, it's business, and I don't think it will be an issue."

"Okay, thanks, Maggie. We need to schedule the experts to talk with the kids, we need to notify the scientists, and then we need to tape a conference. Maggie, do you think we should involve other news agencies in the pre-taping?"

"It won't be necessary, Jack. If the pre-event pans out as you say it will, we will provide the recording to the other networks who I guarantee will give it lots of air time. Maybe when we air it the first time, we can have correspondents in the audience to ask questions live. This story will dominate the news networks worldwide for days; hell, it may have airtime for the next ten years. They will dissect it as will everyone else. I see additional conferences being necessary as this plays out."

Maggie looks over at her associate producer. "Ang, please arrange to have correspondents and a camera crew at each of the locations where these events will be detected. I want this captured and I want to be notified the instant you have results. I want this aired within hours of the events; if we're doing this, let's make sure we're first and it's ours."

She pauses for a moment, then says, "I'm sure you all have considered this, but this story will create an upheaval the likes of nothing we have seen before. You all know that, right?"

"Yeah, we know," Jack says in a saddened tone. "Nobody wants to hear about the apocalypse. I can't imagine how people will react to this. I would suggest to all the adults in this room if you have investments, you liquidate them and try to take as much hard cash out of your accounts as you can before the story gets out. Stockpile as many supplies as you can. For your own personal security, it's really important you tell no one you are doing this. This news will shut down the stock markets and create a run on the banks. Who knows what will happen after? As I mentioned, I think things will remain somewhat normal for at least a few years because of everyone's dependence on income, but the world will change. You will see it in everyone's eyes."

"Shit," Maggie says. The rest of her team look like they've just seen a ghost.

Savannah offers, "I'll start writing the story."

Maggie says, "Make it a good one, Savannah. It may be the last big story ever told."

□□□

Maggie is keeping her team busy calling and scheduling experts to debrief the conduits. They are notifying the key scientists involved in running the Laser Interferometer Gravitational-Wave Observatory (LIGO), an experiment built at two facilities in the United States for detecting gravity waves. Maggie's team tells them the first gravity waves from the Sagittarius-A event will happen at 13:07 Greenwich Mean Time (GMT) on December 17th, and will coincide with a visible light source replacing Sagittarius-A. It bewilders the scientists, as they are doubtful of the pre-notice. There is no known science for predicting this event in advance, and they don't believe in magic. They have agreed to an on-site news crew; the scientists crave public attention to ensure continued funding. The Hubble Telescope operations team is also notified and are equally skeptical. They also agree to an on-site news crew. No one believes it will happen.

Maggie requests the two scientific teams write a public relations memo stating they were pre-notified and alerted of the forthcoming events. Her on-site news crews will capture this added information.

Savannah is spending her time behind a closed door at the studio writing a transcript for the pending news conference. It is by far her largest story, the impact of which has given her a pit in her stomach.

▢▢▢

While waiting for the scheduled debriefing meetings to start, the conduit team, less Jack and Savannah, spend their time driving through the streets of London enjoying the scenery as typical tourists. They haven't seen London before and are making good use of the van and driver Jim provided. Old world views through the van's windows are providing a much-needed diversion, and the driver is doing an excellent job as a tour guide.

As Spencer stares out her window, she ponders where her life will lead once this story broadcasts. Viewers will see hers and Alex's faces on every television and smart device on the planet. She is wondering if she will have to hide her identity when going out and will the paparazzi stalk her and Alex. She fears many will see Alex and the other conduits as the return of Christ, while the rest will denounce them as the devil incarnate.

The new reality has Spencer thinking more about their safety. She is gazing out the van's windows without seeing the view; her need to keep her strength and composure has her distracted. Her son still needs her, it's not the time to get depressed.

In between the driver's informative narrative, and as a coincidence to Spencer's thoughts, Sarah blurts out they have learned the conduits will need protection once the news broadcasts. Spencer says, "This will be a nightmare."

Spencer picks up her phone and calls Jack to tell him the conduits have specifically learned of and called out their safety concerns.

The van driver, unaware, continues his narrative of the city.

⊓⊓⊓

Back in the hotel room, Cahya phones his wife Indah to touch base. There is no answer. This concerns Cahya because his wife seldom leaves the house. After thirty minutes of calling attempts, Cahya phones Jack to confirm his new cell phone doesn't have issues with international calling. Jack assures Cahya the phone can call anywhere. After hanging up with Cahya, Jack calls Jim, and asks him to call Indah's new assistant and find out what is happening.

A few minutes later Cahya gets a return call from Jack. "We have a situation, Cahya," Jack says. "Indah got a ride into town earlier and hasn't returned. Her assistant thought it strange because Indah took a lot of stuff with her. We're making a few calls to see if we can figure this out. Don't worry, Cahya, I have amazing resources at my disposal for solving things, and I'm sure this is just a misunderstanding. I'll call you as soon as we know more."

Jack didn't tell Cahya what his gut is telling him. He makes a call to his financial handler, Robert, and asks him to check and see if the financial deposit made for Cahya earlier in the day is still there.

Jack's intuition was correct. Robert calls back and says Indah has transferred the entire balance to a different account Cahya can't access. Jack keeps Robert on the line and calls Jim to create a three-way conference call. Jack explains he wants them to work together to have Cahya's money traced and returned. If it means threatening Cahya's wife, then so be it; Jack has no tolerance for the pathetic behavior Indah just exhibited. He wonders how she can toss her family aside and take everything.

But he's also sad realizing Indah has dug herself a grave. Jack knows they will locate and return the money, leaving her with nothing. He wonders if she has a family to help her. He knows she didn't think this through and understand how it would end.

He is not looking forward to calling Cahya back with this news. He picks up the phone and presses the speed dial button of his encrypted talking app.

Cahya answers with, "Tell me some good news, Jack. These last few minutes have been hell."

"Cahya, I need to talk to you about this. I'm sending Alex to your room to be with Jacob. Can you come to my room?"

"Oh God. It's bad isn't it, Jack?"

"Just come down. The door is open."

Cahya walks to Jack's room and passes Alex on his way to see Jacob. Alex gives Cahya a smile, but they don't speak. Cahya walks straight into Jack's room as requested and closes the door behind him.

"Take a seat, Cahya."

As Cahya sits in a chair at Jack's table, he says in despair, "I just knew bad things would happen as soon as I got involved in this damn mess, I just knew it. What has happened, Jack?"

"Well, cutting to the chase, Cahya, it appears Indah has transferred all the money I gave you into a private account and has left. She moved out, taking only clothes with her. We found out she has flown to Sorong, and the trail ends there. We will get the money back, I have people to handle it. They will return it to you. Please believe me when I say I'm really really sorry this has happened."

Cahya's slumps as the news sucks the life from his face. He tilts his head and goes quiet. He is broken.

Jack says nothing more, giving Cahya time to think. He goes to his fridge and grabs two beers. He puts Cahya's beer on the table in front of him.

Cahya looks at the beer and then up at Jack and says, "I need to leave, Jack. I have to get home. My children are all alone now."

"I knew you would say that, but we need Jacob to stay with us until after the news conference. We will take good care of him. I will move him into our room. Will you allow us to keep him?"

"Jacob has never been away before. I don't like it, but it appears there isn't much choice and I know it's what he would want. I can see he will be in good hands. This thing we're dealing with is changing everything. I wish it would just go away. I'm used to having control in my life."

Cahya stands up and continues, "I need to get my things. Can you help me with the flights back, I have no means to pay and no clue how to book airline trips."

"Cahya, my plane will fly you home. I promised you that. Go get your stuff and I'll call the pilots. The van will drive you to the airport. Maybe the conduits will keep you company and join you for the ride to the plane. Oh, and here is a few thousand in case more shit happens before we get your money back to you." Jack hands Cahya twenty one-hundred-dollar bills.

"Come back here once you're packed. I'll have the others come in so you can say goodbye. Geez, this sucks. I'm sorry man."

Without having drank any of his beer, Cahya walks past Jack with his shoulders drooping. He takes the money and says, "Thanks," and heads for his room.

□□□

Andre remains on the Gulfstream on its way back to Sorong with Cahya. Alma moved off the plane into Cahya's room at the hotel, and Jacob moved in with Alex and Jack.

Over a period of days, the conduit team meet with engineers, astronomers and astrophysicists, many from the University of Cambridge, for knowledge debriefings. The depth of knowledge the conduits have amazes the interviewers and they need multiple days to digest and transcribe the plans for building the towers.

Jack is spending much of his time working with Jim to plan, arrange and gain the security he believes will be necessary once the news conference hits the airwaves. He starts securing the land deals necessary at the proposed tower locations.

Savannah continues to hole up in her office during the day writing her newscast with consultation from Maggie and her team.

The rest of the team has been shopping as a group, sightseeing, and hanging at the hotel. The distractions outside the hotel don't deter from the anxiousness they all feel.

□□□

It is the day of taping the news conference. Maggie has arranged for the conduit team and the experts to meet at the studio for 9 am.

The conduits see the studio is abuzz as they enter. Technicians and camera personnel scurry around getting the set ready. Ang and Janet are in the room, and upon seeing the group enter, Janet motions them up to the anchor desk and welcomes them.

The desk is a large 'U' with the curved part at the rear and two ends pointing towards the gallery. There are name placards in front of the chairs aligned behind the desk, and Jack, Spencer, Alex, Jacob, Rosine and Sarah, take their seats to the right. Savannah sits in the middle anchor chair facing towards the camera.

Maggie seats three engineers, three astronomers and three astrophysicists at the anchor desk on the left side. Their name placards include their professional designation and place of work.

□□□

Janet hurries into the room. She instructs an attendant to place water glasses on the desk for the group, then says, "Ok folks, we're about to start. As we discussed, everyone looks at whoever is speaking, no one interrupts, and no exceptions, please. Savannah, are you ready?" Savannah nods affirmative. Janet continues, "Also, as I said earlier, please take your cues from Savannah. Even though this is a recorded session, we won't stop the recording at any point, whatever we say or do is what will get broadcast. We are not editing this broadcast; no one will accuse us of faking this story."

Janet looks over at her lead camera operator and says, "Karl, we good to go?" Karl does a thumbs up, which prompts Janet to say, "Lights down." The studio darkens. She then says, "On three, two, one, action."

The studio's branded news music plays, and the studio's lights brighten. There is a flood light highlighting Savannah. She lifts her head and looks into the camera. This is her moment; she is glowing.

Just as the music lowers, Savannah starts her story. "Hello, everyone, and thank you for tuning in to this special and important unscheduled news broadcast. My name is Savannah Davies and I'm a news correspondent here at London World News. This news story will rip your world apart, but I have to explain something first. I realize as you watch this broadcast it is later in the day on December 17th. For us here in this studio, it is 10 am on December 14th. Yes, you are watching a pre-recorded news broadcast we filmed three days ago. We needed to do this to prove we had advanced knowledge of certain events taking place in the future. So, I repeat, it is

December 14th here as we record this broadcast; what we tell you today hasn't happened, but we know it will. I would now like to introduce Jerry Stillman, an auditor and partner from the prestigious global accounting firm of Kendal McGrady."

A secondary camera goes green pointing at an opening side door. A well-groomed middle-aged man wearing an expensive suit and tie walks through the door towards the anchor desk. Savannah gets up from her chair and meets the man just as he reaches the desk's corner. The camera view switches to the two of them.

Savannah extends her hand and the two of them do a polite handshake.

"Thank you, Jerry, for coming here today." Pointing to a wall clock, Savannah asks, "Jerry, please look at our studio date and time as displayed on the wall behind the desk, state the date and time it displays, and confirm it is correct." The camera operator pans the clock on the wall.

Jerry looks at the clock which also displays a date, looks at his watch, then says, "Yes, Savannah. It is showing 9:22 am on December 14th, and it's the correct date and time."

"Thank you, Jerry." Savannah then looks into the main camera and says, "Jerry will remain with us in the studio here today so he can attest to the fact we will not stop the cameras from rolling and will not edit or alter the recording you are now watching. I realize this may all seem a little dramatic, but as you watch and listen to this story unfold, you will realize why this is necessary. When we finish here today, we will provide Jerry with a full copy of the recording for safe keeping so he can compare it to the original to ensure its authenticity as this is aired live on the 17th. Thank you again, Jerry. Please take a seat right over there." Savannah is pointing at a comfortable chair just out of camera view. She walks behind the desk and stops behind Alex and says, "Let's get this news story started."

She then says, "To repeat, I can't emphasize this enough, this news broadcast is being recorded here in our studio on December 14th, and we know you are watching this on December 17th. Before I introduce these guests I have up here with me today, I will preface this story by saying it is about three incredible ten-year-old children who have learned some amazing things and their story will shake the very foundation of your beliefs and how you feel about our very existence and the universe we live in. Yes, I know, ominous stuff. Stay tuned."

Savannah puts her hand on Alex's shoulder and says, "In no specific order, the first ten-year-old I will introduce is Alex here." Savannah's hand then moves from Alex to Spencer, and she continues, "Alex and his mother Spencer live in a small town in Ecuador."

Moving over and putting her hand on Jack, she continues, "This is Jack, Alex's father living in California."

Savannah then steps over and stands behind Jacob, putting her hand on his shoulder. "This is Jacob, he lives on a small island in Indonesia. Unfortunately, an event came up back home and Jacob's parents can't be with us, so Jacob is being a brave young man representing himself here on his own."

Sarah is next, and Savannah puts one hand on both Sarah and Rosine, saying, "Sarah here is from a city in the Democratic Republic of the Congo. Both her parents died from complications after exposure to the Ebola virus. Rosine here is Sarah's schoolteacher and confidant."

Savannah continues the story. "Now switching gears to what you may have just heard if you have been following today's news. When I say today, I mean December 17th, the day you are watching this recording. Two big scientific events just happened. Earth's astronomers and astrophysicists detected these events. The first was the detection of a massive gravity wave causing our planet to shudder for less than a second. It was a million times larger than any other gravity wave detected by, I hope I say this right, the Laser Interferometer Gravitational-Wave Observatory in the United States."

"The other huge and more noticeable event was the detection of a new large star in the center of our Milky Way Galaxy, which is the galaxy our solar system and our Earth reside in. The star is so big and bright, people will see it amongst all the other stars with the naked eye. Think about this, a new star, brighter than anything besides the sun and moon, became visible today."

"Now, if you have been paying attention, you will have noticed we are telling you this story on the day of this recording which is December 14th, three days prior to you hearing it now. Again, we haven't yet detected these events as we're sitting here telling you about them and making this recording. We know in advance! I'll say it again, as we sit here, we know this in advance. We have told the scientists these events will happen on December 17th and here today on the 14th, they doubt us. There is no known science for determining these events in space before we detect them, yet we know about it."

"Think about this everyone. These children here had knowledge of events in deep space before our scientists did. The fact you are watching this broadcast means the events happened, and the predictions were true. This is a startling revelation because it implies they knew about a future event. Stop and think about this for a moment; they knew of a future event! You may also wonder, what does this have to do with you and your daily life; why should you care? Keep watching, it will have a profound impact on everyone. Yes, I said *everyone*. Keep watching."

Savannah stops for a minute so the future audience can digest what they hear, and it provides her time for a quick sip of water.

She continues, describing in detail the story of the conduits, where they live, the surreal way they communicate and learn, and how over the past days they were brought together and arrived in London.

Subtly reading from her teleprompter, she continues, "So, you have been listening to this broadcast wondering, what is this really about? You don't need ten-year-old children calling themselves conduits to tell you about some space events having no apparent impact. Right? Hang in, there is more. So here we go; please listen carefully, your life won't be the same after this. What I'm about to say is a little technical, but it leads to an Earth-shattering climax."

"An event in space, not understood by our astrophysicists, created a supermassive star you can now see. The star's creation produced the gravity wave we felt today, and the conduits knew about it in advance. Again, I am telling you this message on December 14th, before anything has actually happened. Now listen to this; the conduits are telling us this new star was unstable. Please note, I'm using past tense here. The star *was* unstable. Our astronomers will confirm this. So, here is the big news; what they need to tell us, what this is really all about - take a deep breath as this is gut wrenching and profound. The new star was so unstable it exploded. Even though it looks like a brand-new star in the sky here on December 17th, it's already gone! It exploded over twenty-four thousand years ago, ten years after its creation. On Earth, we don't see or detect a star until the light from the star gets here. Space is a vast area, so even at the speed of light, it takes almost twenty-five thousand years for the light of this new star to reach us."

"Okay, so again, what is the big deal? Cutting to the chase, Earth won't feel the explosion until the energy from the blast reaches us. Travelling at the speed of light, it will take ten years. Now for the bad news, the gut-wrenching part. The explosion was so massive the energy it released when it exploded is destroying the entire galaxy and will destroy the Earth, too. I'll say this one more time - it will destroy the Earth too. In ten years, the explosion will reach us. One last time, our Earth will not exist in ten years. This is the apocalypse."

□□□

Around the world, hundreds of million people watching the newscast have gone silent. This is not something anyone expects to hear coming from a respected news source. There are no words to describe the gut wrench everyone feels as they hear this. Everyone is numb.

After a long ten second break, Savannah continues, "There is more. There is hope. There is still a chance for some of mankind. They - and we don't know who 'they' are yet - chose these children as conduits to pass this information on to us. The children proved their credibility by predicting the gravity event and the birth of a new star we detected today, something our scientists can't do."

Savannah stops and takes another drink. "I know I have just stunned all the viewers at this point. Folks, stay tuned, this story is not over. The purpose of the conduits is not to just scare everyone without offering some hope. They are here to help some of mankind escape the planet before the ten years is up. Yes, folks you heard me; the conduits are here to help mankind survive. I wouldn't be reporting this story, nor would this studio allow me to, if we didn't believe this information is credible, albeit almost impossible to believe. We are pre-recording to show the credibility of the conduits; it is paramount to the story."

Savannah changes her body posture, and her voice changes. "As I already mentioned, the conduits live on the equator in locations positioned around the planet. There is a reason for that. They are providing the instructions and the oversight for building towers at the locations where they live. They have already provided the engineers on this panel with much of the preliminary plans for the tower construction, no easy task given the towers need to be five miles high. We will discuss it in more detail in a few minutes and explain why the towers are important."

Savannah pauses and takes a deep breath. "Here is the information that for me was the most thought provoking while covering this story, and it comes from the mouths of ten-year-olds. They told me this entire operation of building three towers and conveying people off the planet is a test of mankind's fortitude. A test to see if mankind is capable of working together in total cooperation for self-preservation. A project needed for us to save ourselves. This is mankind's ultimate test."

She stops for a breath.

"And now I would like to hear from our panel of experts. I will start with Jerod McKennzie. Jerod is an astrophysics fellow at the University of Cambridge studying the makeup of our universe. Please introduce your associates and give us your team's opinion on what you have heard."

Jerod introduces his associates, one from the gravity monitoring experiment in the US called 'LIGO', and the other, another fellow from the local University of Cambridge. He says, "Thank you, Savannah, for inviting us to listen in and comment on the most tragic story ever told. As we are three days away from the actual events being forecast by these children here calling themselves conduits, we can only talk about things from the perspective of 'if' it happens. That said, based on your comments, if this conference is being aired on December 17th as planned, then the events did happen, so I will talk from that perspective. The three of us here interviewed the three conduits, each talking to a single child. We then met afterwards and compared notes. I want to make this very very clear." Jerod pauses for a second, and then continues. "These three children know more about quantum physics than we do, or any of our top scientists. From what we have just seen, they have verified many of the current scientific theories and have introduced new science. Traditional schooling could not teach what these children have learned. What is even more remarkable, they all understand this information equally well. We have no answer to how they could have this knowledge, especially at their age. As far as the gravity wave they have forecast to happen on December 17th, and the new star, we believe this could happen, based on what they told us. I'm assuming as you hear this, it's December 17th, and the events took place and you can all now see the star. As far as the ten-year warning, my colleagues and I concur on its composition and size. We have no idea how it could have been formed from a black hole, but we concur it will be volatile, no question. The star's mass will exceed that of our whole galaxy, so you can imagine the impact if it explodes. To summarize, we believe what these children have presented to us is credible."

Finishing his comments, Jerod sits back in his chair. Savannah takes this as her cue to continue. "Thank you, Jerod. I would now like to introduce Max Van Heusen. Max, along with his colleagues here, are astronomers and are part of the global team analyzing the data provided to the scientific community by NASA's Hubble telescope."

After introducing his colleagues, Max concurs with the astrophysicists that the conduits have more knowledge than his team could explain. He also concurs if a supermassive black hole becomes a star, it will be gigantic and unstable. They also agree the ten year prediction is credible if the December 17th events take place as forecast.

Savannah thanks Max and then looks towards James Houston, a principal in the local civil engineering firm of Houston Caldwell Engineering.

After the introductions, James says, "After spending about twelve hours total with each of these children, we have come away with the basic plans for building towers five miles high. The amazing thing about the plans are the detailed understanding of the foundations and the huge compression loads structures of this size will require. These structures also compensate for severe weather and have earthquake allowances. They even address security concerns. Just amazing. But the most astonishing thing I will show to you here today, is the construction material the conduits have specified and provided to us. Without this new construction material, it would be a herculean task to build towers that high, and the logistics to get materials to the tower locations would be monumental if not impossible within the timeframes."

James reaches beside his chair, grabs a small carry bag and pulls out a clear piece of plastic and a water pitcher. He says, "Please bear with me; what I have here is a long skinny bag called a poster sleeve, it's used for wrapping paper wall posters. Savannah, could you please have this pitcher filled with tap water and bring me an empty glass?" Savannah takes the pitcher from James and walks it over to an attendant who takes it away for filling. James reaches back into his bag and pulls out a small vial, and says, "Inside this vial is a catalyst provided to us by the conduits."

Spencer and Jack look at each other; they didn't know this.

James continues, "We haven't determined the composition of the catalyst, but we have measured its capability. Bear with me, what I'm about to show is unworldly."

The attendant brings the water pitcher back and hands it along with an empty glass to James. James pours a few ounces of water from the pitcher into the glass. He then says, "Savannah, please take a drink of this water to show everyone it is in fact just water."

Savannah drinks the water, setting the glass on the anchor desk. She says, "I'm pretty sure it's just water."

James then stands up holding the poster sleeve in front of him. He fills it with the remaining tap water from the pitcher. With humor in his voice, James then says, "I feel like I'm doing a magic act, but there is no magic here. Savannah please come around and confirm I have done no trickery, and this is still just a bag with water in it."

Savannah walks behind the desk and feels the plastic bag. She says, "It feels like a bag of water to me." She asks the auditor sitting next to the anchor desk, "Jerry, please come and see what James is doing." Jerry also feels the bag and confirms it feels like a bag of water.

James takes advantage of the auditor's presence, "Jerry, if you would be so kind as to hold the bag open from the top, so I can add some of this catalyst." Jerry holds the bag open. James unscrews the catalyst vial and pulls off the top. The lid has a small glass rod protruding downwards like a common vial of iodine. He pulls the glass rod from the vile, which is wet with catalyst, and swirls it within the bagged water. There is a slight crack-ling sound and the rod becomes stuck in what used to be water. Grabbing the bag in the middle, James takes it away from Jerry, and explains, "What has just happened here is literally out of this world. The catalyst has instantly changed this water's melting point from zero Celsius, which is thirty-two degrees Fahrenheit, to something much much higher. This water just froze at room temperature. Not only did it freeze, it has become as hard as any material we have ever tested. Let me demonstrate."

James pulls the frozen water out of the bag and places it on the floor in front of the anchor desk. In one quick movement, he lifts one leg and bangs his foot hard on the center of the frozen bar. The bar does not break. James says, "Why don't you try it, Jerry?" Jerry does the same thing with his foot. Again, the bar does not break.

James looks at the camera and says, "And there you have it. A construction material nothing but water, yet stronger than steel. It just takes a miniscule amount of catalyst, much less than a drop in this case, to turn water into a material stronger than anything we currently build with. Assuming the conduits here can provide adequate quantities of the catalyst, we have determined their plans to build five-mile-high towers with this material is workable. I just can't state strongly enough how astonishing this is. I've seen nothing like it. And yes, we tested it at our office with saltwater. It was just as effective. With adequate catalyst, our oceans will become the next building material. This is a game changer of colossal proportions."

Savannah takes over saying, "Wow! Thanks, James."

The catalyst demo caught Jack by surprise, and he leans over and whispers into Alex's ear, "I don't understand, where did the vial come from?"

"Dad, we can take things and bring stuff back with us each time we leave for our teachings."

"How large can these 'things' be?" Jack queries.

"Not sure Dad. So far, we've just brought back some of those vials."

Savannah walks back to her anchor chair while saying, "The story behind these vials will obviously be huge and we'll delve into them in subsequent newscasts. I now digress and discuss an event that happened almost a week back that many of you may have seen."

She pauses and gathers her thoughts. "Many of you know of the global news frenzy placing me on most everyone's television a few days back while I was in Indonesia. I was at a hospital in Sorong with Sarah and Rosine, who are with me today on my left. The reason we were at the hospital was because Sarah had suffered a brutal beating at the hands of some thugs and was near death with a severe brain hemorrhage. The hospital gave her an MRI to diagnose her injuries and gave her very little time to live without emergency surgery. While waiting for her surgery, it appeared Sarah had made a complete and miraculous recovery. She came out of her coma, and her bruising had gone away. She was lucid. For those of us on the conduit team, we knew what happened enabling Sarah to recover, but it wasn't at the time a story we could tell the world. As a result, the fire alarm was a spur-of-the-moment decision to create a diversion. We needed a distraction so we could get Sarah out of the hospital without her being turned into a lab rat."

"So, you ask, what happened to Sarah? Was it a miraculous recovery? I bring this up now, because as unbelievable as this will sound, it explains how these children are being taught, how they are learning their advanced knowledge, and where the information is coming from. I mentioned earlier they are conduits. They were chosen to channel and teach mankind information necessary to save itself. First, I will explain how they are learning it."

"Picture this - each day at the same time, the children freeze; they stop moving. While in this state, and we don't know why, their pupils fully dilate. Now here is where it gets surreal; during the few seconds the kids are in this state, they leave. They go to a different place, they actually call it a different dimension, a place we just don't understand. For these few seconds, their bodies do not appear to move. According to them, they are at this different place for weeks at a time learning what they learn. There is evidence they leave; we observe during the few seconds they freeze; their hair grows almost one third of an inch, and this is happening daily. They are growing hair at a rate greater than two inches per week. What does this mean? Well, for starters it means these children are aging many times faster than anyone else. They explain this is why they were chosen as ten-year-old children and not adults; they have more years ahead of them. When this story culminates in ten years, they will most likely appear to be in their fifties. Yes, I know this sounds like crazy talk, but the proof is in our observations and in speaking with the children; they know more than our scientists and they are unquestionably aging! This is not a time for denial, they have given us the opportunity to learn from them."

Savannah takes a breath and slows her delivery. "So how does this involve Sarah at the hospital in Indonesia? Well, while Sarah was lying on her gurney, close to death, waiting for her operation, she and the other two conduits went to their place of learning. According to them, on that specific episode, they left for over three weeks of 'Earth time'. While gone, Sarah was nursed back to health. So... although we didn't see her move, she left us for three weeks relative to her time. From our perspective it looked like a miraculous recovery, which I guess isn't too far from the truth. I hope you can appreciate what happened to Sarah would not have been explainable to the doctors at the hospital. We believed we had no choice but to create a distraction and get her out of there."

Savannah knows she might as well be talking about little green men from Mars. Her adrenaline is pumping, her heart is racing, and she attempts to minimize the effects of perspiration forming on her face, with napkins from the anchor desk. She looks into the camera and says, "I'm sorry, but as you might imagine, this is not easy, or for that matter, an enjoyable story to tell." Savannah pauses for a prolonged period, then looks up and says to the camera, "Enough of my talking, how about if I ask the conduits some questions?"

Savannah, moving towards the children, says, "Kids, tell us what it's like wherever it is you go. When did you first meet? When gone for extended periods, do you miss your family or surroundings here? Jacob, do you want to start?"

Jacob responds with, "Sure, Savannah. We don't know where we go and have no memory of being there. I know it sounds strange, they teach us, but control what we remember upon returning. The three of us are together, we remember that. Along with the learning, we share personal information we remember upon returning. We leave and meet every day. We're together for weeks while we're being taught and then when we return the time hasn't changed. I know it sounds strange, but we feel like we're always together. Space and time aren't understood by science. Where we go doesn't involve travel time. Hopefully we will learn more about it."

Savannah says, "This stuff is just so unreal it makes my head spin. Jacob, do you believe you are being taught by God?"

"Like I said, Savannah, we have no memory of who or where. We can't answer your question."

She asks Sarah, "Sarah, what do you believe the reason is you three are learning all this advanced information?"

"Sure, Ms. Davies. We have learned we are conduits, and our purpose is to explain to everyone the Earth will not last past the next ten years. Most important, we will show how select people get conveyed off Earth prior to its destruction."

Savannah says, "Wow, Sarah, that just doesn't seem possible. You have said not only will the explosion destroy the Earth but also the entire galaxy we live in. Where will people go when they leave?"

"We don't fully understand yet, Ms. Davies. We have learned there is an infinite number of universes, and they all overlap. Some theoretical astrophysicists have already been thinking about this; they are getting close to the correct understanding. Every universe is in its own dimension, but they all occupy the same space. I know it's not something humans can comprehend, but it appears possible to move between universes without actually going anywhere. I don't think mankind is ready to comprehend this yet, which is why we don't seem to learn these details."

"So, what I believe I hear you say, Sarah, is people will get saved by moving to a different universe. Correct?"

"Yes, Ms. Davies."

"People won't believe this. What is your plan for giving people the confidence they can actually do this?"

Sarah responds, "We go to a different universe every day for our training. We'll bring things back not of this world. We started today showing the catalyst turning water into a solid. When analyzed, the chemists will find the catalyst contains elements not from our planet. There is no one possessing the knowledge to bring unknown elements to our planet, yet we do it. It's a pretty strong statement for building confidence in what we're saying."

Savannah, keeping the momentum, looks at Alex next, "Alex, where will people actually go? What will it be like?"

Alex replies, "It will be a planet similar to Earth. Similar size and positioning within its own solar system, thus providing a similar climate. It's a stable planet, and like Earth, life has evolved. There is both vegetation and animal life although intelligent life capable of advanced reasoning has not yet evolved. There won't be territorial fights or anything like that."

"Alex, there are over seven billion people on Earth, and Sarah mentioned 'select' people will escape. Who gets to go?"

"Unfortunately, not everyone can go. It logically just isn't possible."

Savannah says, "Wow, Alex, NOT good news! How many will leave? Who chooses who can go?"

Alex continues, "Those are complex questions, Savannah, and will require committees to decide, with our guidance - we are being taught to lead the way. To be fair, the committee's decisions will need to transcend countries, borders, politics, race, language, creed and wealth. It will be complex and difficult. What we're just starting to understand is it will ultimately be skills based, and everyone leaving will have to contribute to the success of the exodus and have the necessary skills on the new planet. It's not just building the towers, but growing and providing food for the workers, learning pioneering skills necessary to function in the new world, etcetera. We will be figuring this all out while building the towers."

"You are being taught this?"

"Yes, Savannah. As conduits, we live equally dispersed around Earth. We will help coordinate creating the committees, followed by the selection processes. The amount we learn right now regarding this is amazing. We are learning weeks' worth of knowledge every day. And the way we're being taught, it doesn't appear we forget anything."

Spencer cries. Savannah looks over at her and then back towards the camera, "To all the parents out there, I think you can appreciate how devastating it would be to know your ten-year-old son or daughter is rapidly aging and will never be the same. With this, on top of all the other events happening, we can appreciate why Alex's mother is crying; it's obviously overwhelming. Spencer, we all understand how difficult this is, and I must commend you on your courage and strength thus far."

Spencer chokes out, "Thank you."

Savannah says, "Let's finish up with talking to Sarah. As we learned at the beginning, Sarah is from the Democratic Republic of the Congo. She is an orphan; her parents died from Ebola complications a few years back. Sarah, how are you feeling after the horrible beating you suffered that landed you in the hospital?"

Sarah responds, "When we leave here, we don't have a memory of actually being there, so I don't know what it was like while I was healing from my ordeal. I know Alex and Jacob were with me and I hear they helped a lot. I still feel pain here and there when I move, otherwise I am fine now."

Savannah, speaking with more emphasis, says, "It's just amazing, Sarah, you could leave and literally have your life saved, and then come back looking like nothing happened, all within just a few seconds. I know it happened because I was with you in the hospital and witnessed what looked like a miraculous recovery. Sarah, explain in your own words to the camera what happened and how you believe you got cured."

Sarah doesn't look at the camera; she continues to look at Savannah and starts in, "Well, Ms. Davies, I remember leaving my orphanage to find a phone as I believed Ms. Rosine here was at the airport and I needed to be there, too. From the other conduits I heard Alex had flown in, and he and his parents were there to find me. They had a plane at the airport. I was confident we would fly out to find Jacob, I just needed to get to the airport. So, soon after leaving the orphanage, I came across four boys who took me into their house. They said they had a phone inside I could use. When I got in, they grabbed me and tore my clothes off. They were all laughing. I told them to stop, but they didn't listen. They dragged me into a bedroom and tied me to the bed. They took turns climbing on me and doing things that made me really hurt. I remember bleeding a lot but couldn't tell how much because there was a rope around my throat, and I couldn't lift my head. I think I went unconscious after that because that's all I remember until I was sitting up in the hospital with you and Ms. Rosine here. I am sure whoever is teaching us, cured me. I'm happy about that." Sarah is smiling.

"Sarah, it doesn't appear like the attacks have affected you. Most young girls would be traumatized by what you endured, creating a permanent emotional wound. How are you dealing with it Sarah?" Savannah asks.

"Well Ms. Davies, I have very little memory of the incident or of healing. It just doesn't seem to have me upset. I think our teacher is making me feel this way so I'm not bothered by it. I don't feel any sadness."

"Thank you, Sarah. What a horrible situation and we're glad you survived ... you are a brave little girl. Now can you tell us about the plans you are learning for saving people. Where will they go? What will it be like? How long will travel time be?"

"Well, Ms. Davies, we know it will be a planet like Earth, but there won't be intelligent life already there. There will be plants and various animals. There is no travel time, we're just stepping into a different dimension."

Sarah digresses for a moment, "Our scientists believe there might be other universes, but have no direct evidence. The physical stuff we know of as matter, our bodies, the furniture, rocks, Earth, are all almost one hundred percent nothing; at the lowest levels it's just energy and infinite universes can coexist in the same space. Our scientists are getting closer to realizing this as they better understand quantum physics. Some call it the multiverse theory. At the quantum level, our physicists are missing a variable in their standard model equation factoring in dimensions. There are infinite dimensions and each dimension represents what we think of as universes. Our scientists will be closer to understanding this when they better understand dark matter, which has so far eluded them."

Sarah gets back to the question, "So the trip takes no time, we just step onto another planet with an equivalent climate. I know this seems pretty strange because it is. We need to build the towers because the new planet is slightly larger than the Earth, it has a larger radius, and when we step over to it, we need to land on the surface of the new planet at the correct location. The towers help compensate for the difference in size and spin rates between the planets. There is no other way to raise people en masse five miles up without towers."

"This is astounding stuff, Sarah. One last question; who is giving you this information?"

"We don't know, Ms. Davies. Whoever it is controls what we remember. We don't remember what it's like when we're there, or who they are."

Savannah turns back to the camera. "Thanks, Sarah. So there you have it folks. Let me recap. You are watching this pre-recorded news conference three days after we recorded it on December 14th. On December 17th, which is today for you the viewer, a massive gravity event has hit the earth and a new star has been born, visible in the middle of Earth's galaxy we call the Milky Way. These three children, calling themselves conduits, knew of these events weeks in advance. The children now know more about quantum physics than our scientists do and are being taught to help mankind deal with what lies ahead."

The camera pans across the three children.

"If you are wondering what quantum physics is, then join the club. We have three accomplished and published astrophysicists at the desk here today who all understand these sciences, and all three of them will tell you these three children have insights beyond any current human understanding. More amazing, the conduits learned it together while living eight thousand miles apart from each other. Think about it for a moment. All these events have led us to this news conference. We are recording it now on December 14th, three days before Earth's scientists had any idea the gravity and new star events would occur."

"Now, this story doesn't end here. The conduits are telling us the new star only lasted ten years before it exploded. They are telling us the new star you see in the sky is already gone; it literally doesn't exist anymore; you are seeing its light from when it did exist. The energy from the explosion is heading our way, destroying everything in its path. The conduits here are giving Earth a ten-year warning. They are also giving us plans to save some of us, but the vast majority of us will perish in ten years. So, what do we do? This story will receive disbelief, denial, fear and by some, outright anger. Even though we have in our possession, an out-of-this-world catalyst that turns water into warm ice, a forecast of future events in space that were accurate, and even with three children learning at an unprecedented rate, people will not believe this. I'm sure many of you will say we have somehow created what is called a deep fake. We didn't."

Savannah pauses and takes a big breath. She then lowers her pitch, saying, "Starting today, as a species, as mankind ... we are on notice to work together to save enough of ourselves to survive. You are in or you're out. It will be that simple."

Savannah looks at the individuals seated at the anchor desk and thanks them. She then talks back into the camera and explains the pre-recording session is now over, and the live broadcast will continue.

Maggie then says, "It's a wrap. Thanks, everyone. Ang, please make sure our auditor, Jerry Stillman here, gets a copy of the recording. Thanks! Oh, and give a copy to Jack here."

Savannah sees Maggie is sitting alone in the studio's gallery while everyone is scurrying around and preparing to leave the conference. She walks over and sits beside her. "What do you think, Maggie?"

"This makes me very sad," Maggie says in a subdued voice. "This message is horrible, and I don't want it to be true. It will change everyone's way of life. We might not have jobs after this story airs if everything falls apart. I don't want to think about death in ten years."

Savannah, trying to comfort Maggie, says, "I think things will become more difficult, but I don't think things will fall apart. People will need their income; they will continue to work. That alone will keep most things functioning. Ten years is a long time. After all, we all die eventually, it's the one certainty we all have."

"The problem will be the change in people's spending habits. If we are all going to disappear in ten years, everyone will cash in their long-term investments, and all unnecessary and strategic purchases will stop, replaced by toys and other short-term enjoyment items. This will cause a massive global adjustment. Business failures will force massive layoffs and unemployment. I hope these conduits here with their unworldly knowledge will have advice on solving these problems."

"Me too, Maggie, me too. I have to join the group now for the trip back to the hotel. Let's talk soon to discuss the airing on the 17th."

"Okay, thanks Savannah… and for what it's worth you did a good job today. I hope you realize your life will be very different in a few days. Lots of haters out there."

"I know, it scares the crap out of me. I'll call tomorrow." Savannah gets up and joins the conduit group who are chatting with the science experts milling around at the desk.

ꞏ∏∏∏ꞏ

There is no conversation as the team stares out the van windows on their way back to the hotel until Jack breaks the silence. "Hey everyone, I think as a team we did a great job today and you all should be proud. I have business to take care of tomorrow, but I think the rest of you should just stick around the hotel and relax for a few days. The engineers and scientists are most likely going to want to talk more to better understand your knowledge, but I'll hold them off until later. After this airs, we'll have no rest. Is everyone ok with this?"

Nobody speaks, their heads nod an affirmative.

∏∏∏

It is 7:45 am the following morning and Savannah is sitting up in bed with her laptop. She is reading news from various online feeds she follows, and then says, "Shit!"

Phoning Jack, she starts right in, "It's out, Jack. Maggie wasn't able to keep a lid on it; someone sold out. Multiple news outlets are saying the Earth will shake on the 17th, a new star is being born which explodes and it's the apocalypse in ten years, and three children talking with God will guide us through this and save mankind." She continues with a hint of cynicism, "That's pretty much it, Jack. Normal daily news stuff."

"Did it just hit the tabloids, or are the mainstream agencies covering the story?"

"I can't be sure yet, Jack, it's too early. I saw it on the tabloid site and I'm guessing the mainstream folks won't print something this sensational without bulletproof supporting facts."

Jack, thinking as fast as he can, “My concern now is the group’s safety. There will be reporters and crazies hunting us down in an attempt for details. I need to work faster than I had planned. I’m sure this goes without saying, Savannah, but let’s take a ‘no comment’ stance until after the 17th. Okay?”

“No worries there, Jack, Maggie will not stick her neck out any further than she already has.”

“Okay, good. I will get the group out of London today and focus on security. I’m now thinking for the live portion of the broadcast on the 17th, we will have the children speaking from a different and unknown location for their own safety. Can you and Maggie work with that? We all leave here ASAP this morning. The destination will be determined underway. No one returns to their homes until I have adequate security in place.”

“Wow, Jack, you don’t mess around. I will have to stay back and help Maggie coordinate this, and I’ll get back to you.”

Thinking things through, Jack asks, “Savannah, can you please phone Cahya and Bree and let them know the story is out. I know we didn’t mention specific details about where Jacob is from, but as you know, people weasel their way into getting the details. Give them a heads up, tell them not to mention anything. I’ll get security there as quick as possible. Also, tell them Jacob is fine and we’re moving the group to a different location. Will you do that for me?”

“Of course, Jack. I’ll see you when the group is loading into the van.”

“Okay, see ya.” Jack closes the call saying, “Damn it,” to himself.

It is early morning in Washington DC, and Jason Kravits receives an automated text message on his iPhone while vending his morning coffee. He routinely receives these messages from a computer application he helped conceive. The application scans the news feeds from across the globe and using available pattern recognition algorithms and artificial intelligence, it detects a myriad of trends. He trained it to watch for stories of importance to global populations and balance of power, especially when they show up from multiple news sources. On this day, he received his text message because his application flags the word 'apocalypse' and the fact eleven news feeds were reporting the same story. Jason's app maintains the links to the stories flagged in the notification he received, enabling him to review the stories from each of the various sources.

Jason steps over to his cubicle in the West Wing of the White House. He determines the main facts in the stories and sees it's a pre-recorded newscast to be aired on the 17th that was recorded at London World News. Savannah Davies is the anchor - someone reputable who Jason is familiar with. Given the world ending content and the fact it came from a reputable news reporter, it catches Jason's attention and he creates a reminder to himself on his iPhone to follow up on the 17th when the reported events are supposed to happen.

░░░

Jack has a busy morning working with Jim arranging for interim accommodation for the team. They decide on Halifax, an isolated yet modern city in the province of Nova Scotia in Canada. Jack also has Jim coordinating four security teams, one for each conduit, and a mobile team to follow himself and the team members while travelling. Jim will produce the mobile security team first and have them go straight to Halifax as soon as possible.

Jack calls the conduit team members to come over for a meeting in thirty minutes.

Half an hour later, the team congregates in Jack's room where he explains the story leaked and they have to leave for security reasons. He asks everyone to pack up and meet him in the lobby in thirty minutes. He explains the van will be ready, and the plane is waiting on the tarmac.

When asked by the team what their destination is, Jack says "I'll fill you in on the plane. It's best that way."

CHAPTER 7

HALIFAX

It has been a long and tiring trip travelling on Jack's jet to Canada. The team has checked into their prearranged rooms in the Prince George Hotel in downtown Halifax and have crashed in their beds. Jack asked the group to reconvene for an 8 am breakfast meeting in his room the following morning.

☐☐☐

It is four hours later in London. Jack is up at 5 am to check in with Maggie and Savannah before meeting with the group. He has lots of details to handle before the news conference scheduled for tomorrow, assuming the forecast events happen as planned. Jack wants to have a camera crew setup in Halifax who will live stream the conduits to the London World News studio. Maggie agrees to manage the logistics.

After completing discussions of the day's tasks, Jack asks if the leak of the news conference has created any negative effects.

Maggie responds with, "Oh Lord, Jack. I was just going to mention this. We have at least twenty people out front, but it's growing. The vast majority of them appear to be demonstrators and just crazies. I'm sure they really don't understand why they're here. The commotion is attracting lots of mobile news vehicles and reporters. My fear is the crowd will grow larger throughout the day. We have locked our front doors and taken our phones off the hook, as they won't stop ringing. We are receiving hundreds of emails per minute. If it's this bad now, Jack, I'm worried about what it will be like tomorrow after the event. We have no idea how to get to our cars, let alone get home. This will be rough Jack. I believe I'm speaking for everyone here when I say we're really scared. I'm calling the police; not sure how helpful they will be."

Jack has seen these gatherings in less stable countries and for different reasons. He thinks for a few moments and then responds, "Listen, Maggie, when you call the police you must insist on a senior police presence outside your building, literally at your doorstep. Insist on having a direct line of communication with whoever this officer is. Direct communication is essential so you can coordinate access to and from the building; it's a nightmare otherwise. Make sure they give you that. I will have a security team at your studio within hours. You will get a call with more information so you can have them let in. Jim will ensure the security guys bring overnight supplies. It may be better if you stay in the building for tonight until we can assess the situation and make plans."

"Jesus Jack, stay in the building? There are six of us here. There aren't enough couches. Really? Stay in the building?"

"I realize it won't be fun, but I can't protect you if you leave. I need you all in one place."

"Okay, okay, but this really sucks. I'm hoping nothing happens tomorrow. I would far sooner apologize to the world over a false newscast, then have to deal with what I'm pretty sure is coming."

Jack ends the call with, "I hear you." He then phones Jim to make the usual security magic happen. Jack requests a team large in physical stature who can handle themselves if the crowd breaches the studio's perimeter doors. Weapons are not an option in the UK, so nothing beats sheer size when trying to hold people back.

After the group enjoys their breakfast in Jack's room, Jack explains the aired news conference will broadcast out of London and Savannah will host it again. He describes how they will be live streamed from a banquet room within the hotel and finishes by saying he has arranged a guide to drive them around Halifax to enjoy the sights. He knows it's the final day before the world chaos begins and their last normal time together.

□□□

At just past 7 pm in London, a black Volvo XC60 screeches to a halt out front of the LWN studio. The driver uses his horn and almost has to bump the demonstrators to get the SUV to the front of the building. Three husky athletic looking men jump out. They have a central European look to them sporting groomed, near shoulder-length hair. Their attire is an all-black, casual look. They hustle to the back of the SUV and pull out three large size duffle bags and head for the studio's front door. The driver, still in the Volvo, drives off as abruptly as he had arrived.

The three-man security squad approaches the police officer standing guard at the door. Jack had called Maggie providing the information describing the team, and she had called the police officer as Jack had requested. The officer allows them access to the building without hesitation.

The duffle bags carried in contain overnight supplies as requested by Jack.

□□□

It is 7:10 am on December 17th in Livingston, Louisiana, when Maggie's correspondent on location at the Laser Interferometer Gravitational-wave Observatory picks up the phone to call her. It is after 1 pm local time in London and Maggie and Savannah can't sit and are pacing. When Maggie's phone rings, she grabs it, opens the call and blurts out, "Hello."

Her correspondent is almost yelling with excitement over the phone, "Holly shit, Maggie, this machine here just detected massive gravity waves ... they said it was off the chart. Hell, we didn't need the detector, Maggie, we just put our hands on the ground starting at five after seven. Right at 7:07 the whole fucking Earth shook. It wasn't even a whole second, but Maggie, the fucking Earth shook! The kids forecast a super massive gravity event and it happened within the minute they said it would. Jesus, Maggie, this is really spooky shit!"

Maggie ignores the correspondent's emotions and gets straight to business, reinforcing when they go live, she wants the scientists to clarify the conduits told them days in advance the exact time when the events would happen, and it happened within the forecast minute. She wants them to say to the camera they didn't know in advance, and don't understand how this could have been known.

Maggie places her phone in her hip pocket and looks at Savannah. "It's happening, Savannah. It's actually happening. Oh my God!"

Savannah immediately puts a call through to Jack. "It happened Jack, the kids were spot on. The scientists said the gravity waves were off the chart. We should hear from our guy at Hubble any moment. Since we got the gravity, I'm sure we'll get the new star. We'll be going live at 2 pm here. I'll ping you when we get the Hubble confirmation. Maggie has arranged for a crew to be at your hotel for 8:30 to cover the story at your end. They will call your room and you need to show them where to set up. I think she said they are from the CBC."

Jack asks, "How is it going with the security team and your demonstrators out front?"

"The mob didn't grow much larger and disbanded overnight. There was no trouble. We stayed here anyway as you suggested. The security team brought inflatable beds and blankets which was a nice touch. Thanks for making this happen. We even ordered food in, and the security guys were nice enough to make sure the delivery driver didn't get hassled. Thanks, Jack."

Jack ends his call with Savannah and then calls each of the hotel rooms and instructs everyone to eat and be in the banquet room he has set up for 8:30 am.

A few minutes later, he receives a text message from Maggie. The Hubble Telescope scientists confirmed the new star.

▯▯▯

"Three, two, one, action," Maggie says as she does with every newscast. The 2 pm news conference is now live.

Savannah lifts her head and looks into the camera. She is polished and professional and has a look of great concern, impersonating all newscasters when presenting a serious topic.

"Hello everyone, we are interrupting your regularly scheduled program to bring to you breaking news of global significance and importance that is literally out of this world. My name is Savannah Davies and I'm with London World News. I'm bringing you this story live from our studio here in London. This afternoon at seven minutes past one London local time, our scientists detected a gravity wave hitting the Earth. The wave was large enough to make the Earth shudder momentarily. Many of you may have felt it. At the same time a new star became visible in the center of our galaxy. This new star created the gravity wave we just mentioned, and it is now the brightest object in the night's sky except for the moon. Scientists at the Laser Interferometer Gravitational-Wave Observatory in the United States, called LIGO, confirmed the gravity wave just under an hour ago. The science community built LIGO as an experiment to measure gravity waves like the one just detected. NASA astronomers, using the Hubble space telescope, also just confirmed the new star's existence. London World News had correspondents at the scenes to capture these historic events, which we will show you momentarily."

Savannah pauses, takes a deep breath, and slowly says, "Now listen carefully. The real news in this story is NOT the actual events I just described; it is we knew these events would happen in advance. A select few knew of these events before they happened."

Savannah takes another pause, and then repeats, "Again, the *real news* is we knew these events would happen in advance."

"The beforehand knowledge of the star's birth is why we have news crews on the scenes. The scientists will tell you there is no known science or worldly way we could have known of these events in advance, especially when you consider they were predicted to the minute. Stay tuned, we will tell you how this came about and why it's of great global concern as part of this breaking news report. We will tell you a story unlike any story you have ever heard."

Savannah is functioning on pure adrenaline; her heart is pounding, and perspiration is forming on her body. This level of intensity is nothing she has felt during previous newscasts. She takes a deep breath, then sips from her water glass.

"We will now take you to Blake Johnson, our correspondent on location at the LIGO facility in the United States."

The live newscast switches to the LIGO facility and Blake introduces himself along with the two scientists responsible for monitoring and interpreting the results of gravitational waves. Taking turns talking into the microphone, the two scientists explain to the camera the gravity waves were millions of times stronger than anything previously detected and they don't have a good explanation for their source. They also explain they doubted the advance notice London World News provided them and they have no idea how predicting the event was possible. They explain gravity waves travel at the speed of light, and nothing observable travels faster than that, so no known science exists to have seen this event coming.

Blake thanks the scientists and takes back the microphone and finishes the LIGO newscast. "So there you have it. At seven minutes past seven this morning, which is seven minutes past one in London, the LIGO scientists here in Livingston, Louisiana detected by far, the largest gravity waves recorded since LIGO went operational. However, not to diminish this event, the outstanding news here is we knew of these gravity waves before they happened, a situation these scientists say is impossible, but yet we were here on the scene to witness it and record it happening. Back to you, Savannah."

Savannah then introduces the chief NASA astronomer who had received advance notice of the new star. Just as the LIGO scientists had done, the astronomer explains they couldn't have predicted this event; he also doubted the forecast. The astronomer concurs if Sagittarius-A is the basis for the star, its sheer size and young age, makes it unstable. He states he is not sure of its composition as he hasn't seen a star created this way. He explains what he observes has bewildered him.

The on-site correspondent thanks the astronomer and gives control back to Savannah.

"So you have just heard scientists state beyond a doubt a massive event has occurred in our galaxy. They also stated they received advance notice of the events. So how did we know in advance about the birth of a new star and resulting gravity waves? This is where the story becomes surreal. We here at London World News knew about this event more than a week ago. We couldn't report about it at the time because no one would have believed us, and frankly, we also questioned the prediction. What we did, however, was pre-record a news conference on December 14th. The pre-recorded news conference explains how we knew in advance this event today would happen. To appease the deep fake naysayers out there, we invited Jerry Stillman from the prestigious global accounting firm of Kendal McBride to sit in and observe the session. He is with us again today, and as a professional auditor, he and his firm will attest to the authenticity of our pre-recorded newscast. They have a copy of the original session as evidence, at their facility. Kendal McBride will play the December 14th copy alongside today's airing to assure its authenticity."

Savannah looks over at Maggie and says, "Are we ready to roll the December 14th recording?"

Maggie nods.

Savannah then looks at Janet, the studio director, and says, "Take it away."

The news story from December 14th plays.

After the recorded session ends, Savannah takes control as the anchor. "Hello, for those of you joining this newscast late, I'm Savannah Davies of London World News and we are now back to the live news program. As you have just witnessed, the story unfolding will have a profound impact on every living soul, and I mean everyone. To summarize, we have provided you information our planet Earth has only ten years of existence left. This information is coming to us via three children calling themselves conduits. Weeks prior they predicted, to the minute, the birth of a new star appearing today for the first time in our galaxy, the very star responsible for our upcoming demise. I am sure most of you watching this program are numb and in a state of disbelief or denial. I understand that, we understand that. People can't grasp this. We can't improve this story or its outcome. We will, however, provide additional information as it becomes available."

Savannah looks to her left to engage the same experts present at the desk during the pre-recorded session, "We introduced our experts here in the pre-recorded phase of this newscast. Are you ready to answer questions?"

They nod. Savannah then says, "The conduits are also available for questions. They have been watching this newscast from a separate location for their own personal protection and are available via live streaming. So, I'm opening this newscast up to the gallery. When asking a question, please stand and start by stating your name and affiliation. Also, please ask single answer questions. Who wants to go first?"

Two people in the gallery stand. Savannah sees a correspondent she doesn't recognize wearing a CNN badge. She says, "Let's start with CNN." The other correspondent yields and sits.

"My name is Melanie Franklin and I'm an affiliate with CNN. I'll direct my question at the experts here. How do you assure us the Earth has ten years left? We all understand the dire consequences of this happening, but it would horrify us to go through this and find out it's a false alarm."

Max Van Heusen, representing the astronomers, responds to the question. "There are many things to consider here. The first one is the new star's creation, and I use the term star loosely, which these children knew about in advance. We have no logical explanation for this. They say the star has already exploded; I believe them. Our initial observation, looking through the Hubble telescope, is it is large, larger than anything we have ever seen this close. It has many characteristics leading us to believe it is unstable. It's a billion times larger than our sun, so if it were to explode, there is no question the explosion would be enough to destroy us, and a ten-year time frame for how long the star existed, is feasible. Given what I've seen and heard, I believe this story."

Saying nothing, the other experts at the table are nodding their heads in support.

Melanie sits and Savannah points to the other correspondent, who stands again. "My name is Bandile Okafor and I represent ANA from South

Africa. I direct my question to the conduits. Where do you believe you are getting this information from?"

The children are visible to the studio's gallery via a projected image on a flat screen. Sarah, sitting in the middle, looks at each of the boys and whispers something. She then looks at the camera, saying, "I'll take this question, Ms. Davies. It's a simple answer; where or how we're learning what we learn, we don't remember. We remember only what helps us move this situation forward. The three of us have discussed this and believe people aren't ready to accept the answer, which is why we don't learn more regarding this. We as the people of Earth aren't ready to hear it. That's all we know."

Bandile says, "You are asking us to believe a story about our demise, and you don't even know where the story is coming from. Thank you," and sits while another correspondent stands.

"I am Albert Palmer and I represent the agency London Gossip. This question is for anyone with an opinion. Do you think it's possible the conduits are being manipulated, and this information is for nefarious intentions?"

Jack, at the table in Halifax with Alex and the rest of the team jumps on the question. "Look, Albert, with all due respect, Savannah, her colleagues, and all of us representing the conduits would not be putting our reputations at stake if we thought this was anything other than credible. Think about this for a second. How would people with nefarious intentions find three children born within the same minute, all living on the equator? Assuming they have some kind of mind-melding technology, how would they educate these children with knowledge exceeding that of our scientists? How did they freeze water at room temperature? The conduits have already said they don't know where their learning is coming from, so any suggestions are speculative. We won't accept any more questions asking about where this is coming from. We simply don't know, but it's undeniable it's happening."

Albert challenges, "With all due respect, sir, what if this isn't about saving the world, but rather destabilizing it? This information will create world chaos, which could provide the instigators with a means to change the global power landscape."

Jack, now upset, answers, "I wonder how they whipped up predicting a new star to help layout their sinister agenda. Think it through."

Savannah takes back control. "Thank you, gentlemen." She then looks into the gallery: "Any other questions?"

Another attendee stands. "I'm Sadia Anees from the CBC. I guess this question is for the conduits. What I have just witnessed is talking about mankind saving itself from an apocalypse. What are the plans for avoiding mass hysteria so people can work towards the tasks at hand? Isn't this going to be impossible to control?"

The team knew this question was coming. They had decided beforehand Spencer was the best person for the first response. She says, "Sadia, that is a good question and I'd like to respond on behalf of the conduits, and they can add to it. First, we emphasize there are many years ahead. We need to stay the course. For those of you out there who need your job to pay your bills, please don't change a thing. Again, stay the course and wait for the forthcoming guidance from the conduits. If we remain cool, we avoid anarchy and the need for governments to introduce martial law. The conduit team here is launching a website named conveyanceplan.com. It will contain all the information we have available and provide the guidance you will need as this situation plays out. This will test the will of mankind. Exercise patience and do nothing until guidance is available. It will be much worse if people panic. We need to focus on the things we can control."

Savannah says, "We have time for one more question."

An older man with bushy hair stands up. "I'm Hans Schmidt and I represent ABC. At my age, I thought I'd seen and heard it all. Now I learn you want the people of the world to believe they will be saved by transporting them to a different universe. A *different universe*! Come on! No one can tell you another universe even exists. How as a responsible news agency and professional journalists can you stand there reporting this story? I quite frankly find this shockingly irresponsible. It's deplorable, and I am disgusted. I hope your viewers see it for what it's worth. Flat out sensationalism. Unless you have factual evidence another universe exists that we can magically travel to, you should be arrested."

Jack doesn't give Savannah a chance to respond; he jumps right in. "Well Mr. Schmidt, you said Schmidt correct? I take pride operating with the highest ethical values and always act with integrity. Your comment angers me. My son is sitting here beside me and we have been living this. I see what they are going through; you don't. You calling this sensationalism is a flat-out insult to us; you are calling us liars. You say we're lying when we see it every day. These children leave for weeks at a time every single day. Their aging proves it. Do you understand that Mr. Schmidt ... proves it. Where do you think they are going, Mr. Schmidt, a magical trip to Disneyland? Frankly, I find your comments irresponsible because you say them with absolutely no understanding of this story's background. Please, sir, explain to the world, right here, right now, how these events are happening? How did we know in advance?" Jack doesn't wait for Mr. Schmidt to say anything and continues, "As parents and guardians, we watch these children go into a trance every day. During the seconds they are in that state they age weeks in front of our eyes. Lots of people have witnessed this. They return each time with more knowledge, highly advanced knowledge, and they actually communicate with each other while gone even though they live eight thousand miles apart. Mr. Schmidt, where do you think my child, and the others here, are going? It's not here on Earth, because they are learning things no one on this planet understands. There is no other place in our solar system, so given that you assume you are smarter and wiser than our panel here, please sir, give us your version, we're all ears."

Hans Schmidt knows he can't explain what is going on, but he is stubborn. Sitting, he concludes with, "This is all bogus."

Savannah ends the newscast and reinforces people stay calm and to check the 'conveyanceplan.com' website, available in a few days.

□□□

While walking towards his cubicle, Jason Kravitz's iPhone is buzzing. He sees it's the reminder notice he had set for himself to check out the strange story he had discovered on the 14th. Before he has time to reach his seat, Sowptik, Jason's co-worker yells out, "Holy shit," and then says, "Jason, you gotta see this!" Jason hurries over and sits in Sowptik's cubicle. The two of them watch the entire newscast on a computer screen.

Jason walks as fast as he can back to his cubicle and picks up his internal phone. He punches the button connecting him to Brian Donnelly, the Director of National Intelligence. Jason explains to Brian why the newscast is significant and suggests he should see it for himself. Brian turns on his large flat screen TV affixed to a wall in his office. It starts up already tuned to Fox News, and Brian sees Fox is in full coverage of the story. He changes channels to the other news networks; they are all covering it.

Brian watches a replay of the newscast and then picks up his phone. It's a direct line to the White House. As it is answered, he says, "Put me through to the President, this is urgent."

Michael Stanford is a tall imposing man, standing six foot four inches. He became a Democratic President in the 2020 Presidential election, defeating the Republican incumbent.

Just as his predecessor, and to the chagrin of his team, Michael seldom takes advice and makes the White House decisions himself. It concerns many cabinet members, especially the Democrats, his huge majority win and popularity is enabling him to rule as a dictator, using executive privilege to block everything he is in disagreement with.

He picks up his phone and says, "I'm busy, Brian, what is so urgent?"

"Mr. President, please turn on your television to any news channel. We need to pull the NSC together to discuss what is happening. This is a massive threat. I'm heading your way right now."

The National Security Council is an agency chaired by the President. It comprises all the top cabinet members and uses a staff of thousands to meet the tough demands of national security. It can create kill authorizations as happened when they targeted Osama bin Laden, the ISIS leader Abu Bakr al-Baghdadi, and more recently, the Iranian General, Qassem Soleimani.

The President responds, "Okay, I'll see you here."

□□□

It is 11 am and the NSC team has gathered in the West Wing operations room. President Stanford enters the room last. The team all rise and then sit again after he takes his seat at the head of the table.

Michael wastes no time. "I'm assuming you have all seen the newscast being covered on every flipping channel. Why the hell didn't we have any advance intel on this? Brian, has nothing come across your radar before today?"

Brian, not admitting he saw an early warning of this, sheepishly replies, "Absolutely nothing, Mr. President. I just heard today."

Michael, without discussion says, "Damn it, I don't know what we pay you people to do. I don't care what it takes, use every resource available, and I mean every resource. Find those kids for questioning. I want to know how and where they are getting their information and I want it on my desk tomorrow, so you better work fast. This shit doesn't happen on my watch. Put a stop to any further news coverage. I don't want this story to get bigger. Just shut it down. Do whatever it takes. Brian, take the reins and get results for a change. This is need-to-know for everyone. Interrogating those kids has to be top secret. This discussion doesn't leave this room; it never took place. Understood?"

The president stops his ranting, and everyone nods.

Michael gets up and walks towards the exit. He turns around and makes a final statement. "I want a social media campaign discrediting this bullshit. Hit everywhere and say anything. Make shit up. Like I already said, this isn't going down on my watch." He walks out of the room with no further discussion or conversation. The rest of the NSC team have blank looks on their faces. They hate working for Michael but have no choice but to do their job.

Brian is the first to break the silence, and blurts out, "Well, folks, I guess we have some work to do. We need to find where these kids are, so we work backwards from their last known location, which appears to be the pre-recorded newscast in London on the 14th. I'll have my team on it in ten minutes. As soon as I know what country they are in, assuming they left the UK, we will need to put an extraction team together. We are now in the business of kidnapping children. Let's move..."

▯▯▯

As the live newscast ends, Jack suggests to the team they go back and relax at the hotel and fly out the following morning. He knows the sensationalism around this story will create a crowd of people hunting for them for personalized interviews and inside stories, so he needs to keep them on the move and out of the limelight until things settle.

▯▯▯

It is 3 am in Washington, DC, and John McCallister, the White House Chief of Staff who has a seat at the NSC meetings, is sound asleep when his eyes open and his pupils dilate. Three seconds later, John's eyes are closed again. He didn't wake.

❑❑❑

Jack wakes Alex at 6 am to prepare for their next move. As Alex wakes, he looks up at his father and says, "Dad, I have some important information you need to hear right now."

"What's up, Alex. You haven't been updating me recently."

"I know, Dad, it's because we're learning really technical stuff now, and without learning the basics first, like we all have, it's almost impossible to explain. But I have something for you this time, Dad, and it's urgent. I have information from a man named John McCallister."

Little surprises have become the new normal for Jack, and he takes most of them in stride. Hearing his son mention the name of the US Chief of Staff, causes his adrenaline to spike.

Staying in control, Jack says, "Well, Alex, let's have it."

Alex starts. "The President convened the National Security Council in response to yesterday's newscast. He has ordered them to pick us conduits up for questioning. They want to know where and how we are learning. It is a covert operation, and he has literally ordered our kidnapping. He wants you to know the NSC has been on it since yesterday and have worked through the night, and they're pulling in every resource. They won't stop until they have us. He says we need to move fast and be smart because they will be close. It worries John what will happen to us if we're taken in. He suggests we run the second you get this message."

Without hesitation, Jack phones the rest of the team. He tells them to throw on clothes and meet in the lobby in three minutes, no later. He tells them to leave their bags; just get to the lobby fast.

In the minutes he has available, Jack orders two special Ubers on his iPhone that can accomodate the group, he then calls his pilot and instructs him to have the plane ready with clearance for takeoff.

The group assembles in the lobby looking disheveled; all were still in bed when Jack called. "Follow me," Jack says, leading them out the front door. A freezing drizzle permeates their light clothes as they cross Market Street and go into a small coffee shop in front of the hotel Jack had scoped out earlier. He knew it was open for business starting at 6 am.

The group orders biscuits, donuts and coffees for the adults. Jack has them sitting away from the windows and is keeping a sharp eye on the front of the hotel. Prior to finishing their makeshift breakfasts, two Uber vans pull up out front. Jack tells everyone to leave what they haven't finished and get in the vans. As he is closing the sliding side door behind Rosine, who is the last in, he notices two black SUV's pull up in front of the Prince George Hotel across the street. Stopping abruptly, two official-looking men emerge from each vehicle and run into the hotel.

Jack knows he just dodged a bullet. He instructs the driver to head for the Greenwood airport, an hour and a half drive. He calls Alma in the other van and requests they go to the same location. Greenwood is a Canadian Forces base also supporting general aviation. Jack had thought this through as Plan B, something he learned in the SEALS and still practices.

Once underway, Jack phones his pilot again, who has the Gulfstream ready to go at the Halifax Stanfield International Airport. He requests Andre get off the plane and then tells the pilot to take off immediately and set his flight plan for Iceland. He instructs the pilot to add everyone's name to the plane's disembarking manifest. If the US chases the team, Jack will not make it easy for them.

He's thinking and acting fast. He calls Jim to set up a charter flight originating out of the Greenwood airport with Sudbury in the province of Ontario as the destination. Jack chose Sudbury as it's an isolated Canadian city with adequate airport facilities within range from Greenwood for a smaller jet. From Sudbury, he reasons they can travel by vehicle. Jack cancels his request for a mobile security team and ends the call with Jim. Next call is Andre. Jack instructs Andre to Uber to Greenwood to meet them.

☐☐☐

It's 8 am and Brian sets his first report on the President's desk. Michael looks at the heading page and says, "What the fuck is this?"

Brian, confused, says, "It's an operational update on the status of bringing in the children, Mr. President."

"Jesus, Brian, I know that! I can read. What the fuck is it doing in writing? Erase it from whatever fucking computer it was written on, and shred whatever copies have been made. I thought I made it clear yesterday when I said the discussion never took place. Fuck! Now just tell me the update."

Brian despises the President but doesn't want to lose his position just yet. "We have tracked the last known position of the children to the pre-recorded news conference in London. Our analysts traced their arrival in London to a private jet owned by the billionaire Jack Campbell, who is part of the news story. His son is one of the kids you want brought in. After the newscast, the plane left for Halifax Canada. We have determined they're staying in the Prince George Hotel. They were there for the live newscast. They stayed at the hotel last night. We have a team arriving right about now. Our team will hold the children and their entourage inside the hotel until we assess the situation and have a means to extract them with stealth. We are running this out of the operations room and will advise you as each event unfolds."

Michael asks, "Where will they take the kids?"

"We are working on a location in Halifax. If this operation ever leaked, we're thinking we could better disavow our participation if the children never set foot on American soil."

The President thinks for a moment, and then says, "Are you planning to involve the Canadians?"

"No, sir."

"Check out this Jack Campbell, who are his accomplices? What is the motivation? Is he the ringleader or is there a foreign government involved? Need this info fast. As far as the kids go, send up a good interrogation team, and I want you there to oversee it. Find out everything. Make sure Jack Campbell is out of commission until this is stopped. If he needs to disappear, so be it. I don't want the Canadians knowing you were there. Given the coverage this story is getting, there will be an ongoing massive manhunt to find these kids. Christ, every network is talking about it non-stop. It's dominating the news; they are analyzing this thing to death. We need them first. What a fucking mess."

The President pauses for a moment, then says, "Every government will want these kids. Again, find them first. Don't fuck this up - I want this under our control."

Michael looks away thus signaling an end to the conversation. Brian takes this as a notice to leave and walks out of the oval office.

Just as he closes the door behind him, his cell phone buzzes. Brian takes the call and his assistant updates him on the miss in Halifax. He is told they appear to have left in a hurry without their luggage, and Jack's plane flew out early this morning for Iceland with a manifest containing the children and their entourage. Brian tells the assistant to have people on the ground in Iceland on standby, and to have a plane ready in thirty minutes large enough for himself, his assistants and an interrogation team. He also explains the flight has to be unofficial under the guise of a government sanctioned business trip. No one is to know US intelligence is on the flight. Handling covert flights to foreign countries is standard procedure for the NSC.

The children and their entourage leaving their luggage behind has Brian concerned. The only reason for leaving quickly would be knowledge of the impending US abduction plans, or maybe one or more other foreign powers are also searching for them and it was their intelligence who leaked. Either way, someone warned them. Brian is getting the feeling this covert operation won't go as easy as he thought. He is not looking forward to walking back into the oval office and explaining the latest news. He knows he's in for a tongue lashing; the President has no patience or finesse.

☐☐☐

The scene in front of London World News is out of hand. Hundreds of demonstrators are out front, holding signs declaring the work of the devil, the return of Jesus, blasphemy and every other crazy thought conjured up in the minds of the excitable. Not only are they yelling LWN, they are fighting amongst themselves, when their messages don't align.

The police have positioned twenty officers in riot gear around the building, but it didn't stop a demonstrator from throwing a Molotov cocktail through a front window. With effort, just using janitor supply hoses and fire extinguishers, the security team Jack provided gets the resultant fire under control, but now a broken window has become a bullseye for anything throwable a demonstrator can find. Debris is flying through the window non-stop. The riot is making world news, captured both by LWN's own cameras and by the assemblage of mobile news trucks arriving to capture the commotion.

Maggie is meeting with her colleagues and the security team in the boardroom, discussing plans to abandon the studio. They know if the crowd grows, there will be an assault on the building; the situation will become untenable. They are discussing the logistics for getting to one or more of the studio's four mobile news trucks; where they can continue their coverage.

Although never used, the LWN building was designed with a heliport on the roof. They decide if they can round up a charter helicopter, it will be their best evacuation method. The logistics challenge is the lack of helicopter landing areas anywhere near where they have parked their mobile news trucks.

□□□

Cardinal Lorenzo is sitting at his magnificently sculptured desk reviewing the Book of Revelation while watching CNN on his TV, a dichotomy of these times. He has been receiving communications from many of the church's top clergy, concerned by the recent events dominating the news. They haven't experienced an event of this magnitude polarizing the established faith over the advent of an extraterrestrial message. They are fearful.

Lorenzo will distribute an encrypted message to the church's ultra-secret '*Group of Nine*'. It outlines the steps the church will take in preparation for Satan and the Antichrist, whom Lorenzo now believes the conduits to be. The letter states the church will refrain from action until the outcome of the United States NSC involvement is concluded.

CHAPTER 8

ESCAPE

While in flight to Sudbury on the chartered Learjet, Jack is thinking through plans for getting the conduits returned to their homes. He knows the NSC will leave no stone unturned until they have custody of the children and will watch both chartered and commercial flights; the border will be impossible

Jack phones Jim and instructs him to buy two high-end ocean crossing sailboats in the sixty-foot range. He explains one boat will need both a qualified ocean crossing captain and first mate and the passengers will include Spencer, Alex and Andre. He explains he will skipper the second boat himself, but he'll need a first mate to help with standing watch, and the passengers will be Sarah, Jacob, Rosine and Alma. Jack asks Jim to provision each boat for five weeks at sea and be ready to go with food provisions, water makers, safety gear, storm gear, satellite communications and electronics. Jim will purchase the boats through Jack's various shell companies.

Jim says, "And I suppose you want this all in two days."

"Yup, you're the man, Jim."

"Jesus, Jack."

"Oh, and one more thing. I also want a large crewed decoy charter yacht sailing out of Vancouver. It will go up the inner passage to Kodiak, Alaska. Make it more real by calling a talent agency and populate the boat with extras all appearing like members of the Conduit team. We'll slip a little nugget to the news agencies after it leaves port saying the conduits are onboard. Should create a distraction. Gotta love decoys!"

"Three boats is a tall fucking order, Jack."

"You can handle it, Jim. The group will arrive in the Vancouver area in two days. We will jump on the boats and head out fast because the NSC is hot on our tails."

"What the fuck, Jack! You didn't tell me the NSC was involved! Those spooky people can kill you. They better not find out this involves me! The fucking NSC? Jesus! When they torture you, Jack, make sure you don't fucking mention me. Jesus!"

"Just have the boats ready. Call me with locations. These folks need to get on boats, and I need to know locations."

"You know the sad part about all this, Jack, is I will only have ten years to spend all the money you will pay me."

"Call me soon, Jim. I gotta go." Jack closes his call and opens his news feeds. He reads there has been a massive stock selloff and the markets have dropped thirty percent, the largest one-day sell off since the great depression. He is pensive, knowing the market fall was his doing. He reads it started with a few large significant sells, making the smaller traders skittish. The recent doomsday news hasn't helped. The markets have always been a follow-the-leader practice; the reason leaders do well. The bottom dwellers of the markets do well during good times; a time they will never see again.

000

The Learjet arrives in Sudbury without incident, and Jack puts the team up in a local hotel. He explains they will drive out the following evening, heading for Winnipeg, a large city in the Canadian province of Manitoba. Jack explains the trip is eighteen hours and they will drive it non-stop, mostly under the cover of darkness. He requests Andre and Alma to help with the driving.

Jack uses a regular taxi to travel to a local car dealership in Sudbury. Cash taxi rides are more difficult to trace than an Uber having credit card fingerprints all over the transactions, something the prying eyes of the NSC can find. Jack knows he has to work under the radar from this point forward.

At the Ford dealership, Jack wires money from a shell company to purchase a large ten passenger van. He can keep a vehicle purchase much less visible than if he rents. Jack knows the NSC will track the purchase, but it won't be easy, and it will buy him time. It takes Jack into the early evening to complete the purchase.

He drives his purchased van to the nearest Hertz rent-a-car location and rents another large passenger van as a decoy. He asks if the attendants know anyone willing to do a round-trip drive in the rented van to Toronto and back to pick up and return passengers. He explains the fee is $1500, paid in cash. Good money for an eight-hour round trip. As Jack expected, one attendant offers to make the trip after his work shift ends. He provides the attendant a Toronto address and then heads back in his purchased van to pick up the conduit team. Jack smiles to himself as he muses over the new decoy he has just established.

While driving, Jack calls Jim to have waiting another chartered jet, obtained from Private Jet Air Charter Ltd., a company based out of Winnipeg's James Armstrong Richardson International Airport. Jack instructs Jim to lie about the jet's destination. The eventual destination will be Boundary Bay Airport near Vancouver, British Columbia.

Jack instructs Jim to provide a phone call tip to the NSC saying the conduit team is heading for the US in a white passenger van.

▢▢▢

Within three hours of Jack's Gulfstream leaving for Iceland, the NSC had their own plane in the air. They determined via Jack's flight plan that Reykjavík Airport was the destination. Four hours into the flight, Brian Donnelly receives a call from Jason in the Operations Room. Jason informs Brian their operatives working through the American Embassy in Iceland have determined the flight manifest was incorrect and there were no passengers onboard Jack's plane when it landed. Brian curses. He is now wondering how Jack is getting his inside information. Jason explains they have received more credible intelligence the children are taking a land route to the United States via the Niagara Falls border crossing. Jason is instructed to put the border on high-alert and detain anyone matching the pictures or description of the team members. Jason also explains the operatives in Iceland interrogated Jack's two pilots and determined they didn't possess information about Jack's plans or whereabouts.

Brian tells Jason he wants concrete evidence of the children's travel, including vehicle information; no more false trails. He is now concerned; his conversation with the President over the Halifax fiasco was difficult. Brian now has to call and tell the President of another operational screw up, explaining the flight to Iceland was a decoy and they have lost time and have temporarily lost the trail. He knows Stanford will lose it over this information.

Brian procrastinates on phoning the President by first instructing his plane's pilots to return. The pilots inform him they don't have the fuel range necessary for a simple turnaround and must first touchdown in Greenland for refueling. Brian realizes he won't make it back to Washington for hours.

He knows he is being played; Jack and the children are one step ahead of him.

His call to the President is as expected ... not good. The President can't fathom a group of civilians including three children can outfox the NSC. He makes this very clear to Brian and tells him his job is on the line if he can't deliver on this operation soon. Stanford ends his conversation with Brian by asking what is happening with the shutdown of any further news stories from being broadcast. Brian explains he has placed a covert team at the LWN studios but hasn't instructed them to intervene yet. He tells the President a plan to stop the studio is underway. He also expresses his concern that closing one studio may not slow the story, and very well could fuel it. Michael tells Brian to just handle it.

As Brian ends his call with the President, he receives another call from Jason in the Operations Room. The operatives outside of the LWN studio have informed Brian they have intercepted cell phone communications showing the news crew is planning to vacate the studio via a rooftop helicopter due to the protesting commotion on the street.

Brian feels a knot in the pit of his stomach. If the news crew leaves the studio and continues to broadcast from an alternative location, the President will remove him from command.

Brian tells Jason to draft documentation declaring the children, their entourage and any groups promoting the conduit story or sensationalizing it as a terrorist threat to the domestic interests of the United States. Brian knows with this declaration in place, signed by the President, the NSC can legally use lethal force to stop it. He also asks to use normal diplomatic channels with the UK's National Security Council and Canada's Department of National Defense to inform them of the US position.

Brian tells his assistant to make sure under no circumstances does the news crew at LWN make any more broadcasts, either from their studio or from any other location. He reiterates to his assistant, who will communicate it to the rest of the team, that the NSC's authority can stomp out this story using whatever means deemed necessary.

□□□

Maggie can only get a Bell 206L helicopter with seating for seven people, including the pilot, so they have to split the evacuation into two trips. She also found a heliport on a rooftop within a few miles of where LWN keeps its mobile news trucks. The team decides once the helicopters leave the studio, the demonstrators will have no means to follow them and ground transportation via Uber shouldn't be a problem once at the destination. They decide Maggie, Janet, Ang and two security personnel and a staffer will leave first. Savannah, the third security person and the remaining staff will leave on the second trip.

Maggie tells the group the helicopter will arrive within the hour.

The group moves to the roof to prepare for the helicopter's arrival. Jack's security team has placed themselves at the only rooftop entrance to prevent intruders.

While the news team waits for their helicopter ride, the NSC has been busy getting a team in place to prevent their departure. The NSC communication team is already out front of the studio and intercepting the cell phone calls is providing intelligence back to the Operations Room in the US, who are using the information to coordinate the covert team interception.

Forty minutes after gathering on the rooftop, Maggie can hear the undeniable thump, thump, thump sound of an approaching helicopter. Minutes later the requested Bell 206L settles on the center of the 'H' painted on the rooftop. Maggie and the others designated for the first trip duck their heads and run to the waiting chopper. Once aboard, the helicopter lifts off and disappears into the distance.

After forty minutes, an eternity to Savannah, the helicopter returns and lands. She and the others also duck their heads as they run to the aircraft. As the chopper lifts off, moving forward to clear the edge of the rooftop, a large explosion numbs the occupant's senses and the big bird shakes violently. The explosion has taken out the tail section and multiple cockpit alarms are wailing. Without a functioning tail rotor, the helicopter starts spinning from the torque of the large spinning propeller; the pilot has no control and yells, "Brace yourselves, we're going down."

It falls and hits the street hard outback of the LWN building. Fortunately, the building wasn't tall. Savannah, sitting in the front seat, is the first one out, just as a fire starts at the rear. Blaine, the one security operative on board, is sitting in the 2nd row and opens his door. Just as it opens, the chopper explodes. The shock wave from the blast launches Blaine out onto the street. No one else makes it out. The blast knocks Savannah to her knees and stuns her. When she regains consciousness, she sees Blaine not moving face down on the pavement. He is perilously close to the burning helicopter, so Savannah runs over, turns him onto his back, throws off her heeled shoes, and struggles to pull him away. She can't hear a thing; her ears are ringing from the loud explosion and heat from the burning helicopter is almost overwhelming her; she doesn't quit and pulls Blaine clear.

Moments later, a dark van pulls up beside Savannah. Three men jump out and force her into the vehicle while the other two pick up Blaine, throwing him through the opened rear door. The three men jump back in the van and it speeds off before the crowds can engulf it.

Above, the crowd sees another black unmarked helicopter hovering while it watches the event unfold. After it sees the crash and the abduction of Savannah, it disappears into the night's sky.

〇〇〇

The on-site news crews capture the downing of the Bell helicopter above the LWN studio and the subsequent crash. They broadcast the action live to the worldwide audience glued to the story. The conduit entourage have been watching the non-stop news coverage from their provided iPhones while they sit enduring their long road trip to Winnipeg.

The angle of the helicopter crash prevented the news crews from viewing the exit of Savannah and Blaine and their subsequent abduction. From the news viewer's perspective, there appeared to be no survivors. Jack and the group weren't aware there were two rooftop pickups made by the helicopter; from their perspective, all LWN personnel have perished.

Jack compartmentalizes the event as his focus and concern needs to stay tactical. It concerns him there was an additional helicopter hovering above the crash scene and then flew away before the event had ended. Had it been a police or news helicopter, it would have stayed hovering to capture the entire news story, or if police, to monitor the situation. He determines the hovering helicopter must have caused the crash, and therefore the culprits aboard would have used a handheld air-to-air missile. Jack knows it takes a government backed operation to pull this off so quickly; a government willing to use lethal force. He's worried but says nothing to the group. He knows nothing is gained by telling them how precarious their situation is. Jack is hoping Jim comes through with the boats and he can stay ahead of their pursuers for a few more days.

He didn't foresee being chased by the NSC and hadn't planned for it.

❚❚❚

The team spends their time watching the endless unfolding news dissecting every word of their message and the events at LWN. They are restless as they drive to Winnipeg along the remote Northern shores of Lake Superior.

Alex is sleeping sitting upright in the uncomfortable van seats. Just after 4 am he wakes and sees his father driving; he doesn't remember seeing the driver switch from Andre to Jack. He immediately says, "Dad, we got more information from John McCallister."

"Let's have it."

"They must have exited LWN with two helicopters because there were only four people in the helicopter crash. Two unidentified men died - Savannah and one male survived. There is no accounting for the rest of the team."

"Maggie must have made it?" Jack asks.

"Don't know Dad, but Savannah is in trouble. She was taken by the group who shot down the helicopter. It was a covert operation ordered by the NSC. It is really frustrating the US President the NSC's can't bring us in so he has signed an executive order declaring us a terrorist threat to the interests of the US. The NSC has authorized lethal force to stop us."

Jack says, "shit," under his breath, and then focuses, "Alex, do you know where they have taken Savannah?"

"Yes. It's a small office building in London. John says they will most likely move her soon. He also said security will be light as they won't be expecting anyone to come after them. They also took the other survivor; his name is Blaine."

"Alex do you have the actual address of the office building?"

"Yes, it's …"

"Tell me in a minute," Jack interrupts. "I won't remember it." He then slows the van down and stops on the shoulder. They are in a desolate region of Western Ontario and only one vehicle whisks by this late in the night. Jack gets out and opens the door where Alma is sleeping. The opening door wakes her, and Jack apologizes explaining she needs to drive for a few minutes, as he has important business to handle. They switch places, and Alma floors the accelerator getting the van back to cruising speed.

Jack places a call to Jim, who as always, immediately answers. Jim knows it is Jack, and starts right in, "Do you have any idea what kind of mess you and your band of misfits are causing?"

Jack doesn't acknowledge the comment. "Jim, you obviously have been watching the news, and therefore know they shot down a helicopter in London. Did you see it?"

"Fuck, pretty hard to miss Jack. Every news channel is covering it non-stop, and most regular stations are giving it time, too. Biggest news story I've ever seen. Only you could cause this one, Jack. You said 'they'. Who is it?"

"The NSC, they're going crazy over us. Now listen up. Savannah survived the crash and Maggie wasn't in the helicopter that crashed, so she should be okay too. The NSC has captured Savannah and one of your security team, his name is Blaine. They are being held in an office building in London. We need them out before they're moved. It should be easy; they won't be expecting anyone. They will torture Savannah to find us, which won't work because she doesn't know where we are. After they're done with her, they'll make her disappear. You gotta get a team in their fast, Jim."

"Well, Jack, you're lucky they're in London and not France. I'm a little low on French operatives." Jim pauses and then says, "Give me the address, should be able to get boots over there within two hours. Simple extraction, correct? How many bad guys?"

"Our intelligence believes there are three, and you will extract Savannah and Blaine. If you have the element of surprise, it should be simple."

"Sure, Jack. Your operations are always simple, yet my teams seem to disappear. Where do you want Savannah to be taken to?"

"Get her to a local airport where we can fly her out. Arrange an international charter and get her a fake passport. If you can round up a wig for her to wear, that would be helpful. Her face is on every TV as we speak."

"Your shit is just never easy, Jack. Christ. Okay, I'll call you after we get them out."

Jack gets the office address from Alex and gives it to Jim. They close the call.

▯▯▯

It is 8 am as Brian Donnelly walks into the Oval Office to update the President on the 'situation'. He tells Michael they haven't located the team, and there has been no sign of them anywhere near the Niagara Falls border. Stanford yells and swears at Brian. Brian sucks it up, as he always has. The President simmers down when Brian explains they have in custody the primary reporter who broke the story and has been working with the children from the beginning. Through interrogation, they will know everything she knows within the next few hours. In addition, Brian explains they have thousands of aides working non-stop scrutinizing, with the help of computers, all available transportation transactions to find where and how the team left Halifax, and how they're getting to Niagara Falls, assuming the tip is legitimate. He assures the President they are leaving no stone unturned.

▯▯▯

At the same time Brian is talking to the President, Jim's extraction team arrives at the office in London where Savannah and Blaine are being held by the NSC covert operatives. One of the team members is wearing a courier driver's uniform. He walks through the front door and sees the building is an office co-op, where individual businesses rent single spaces. The supplied office number shows a main floor office. The fake courier approaches and turns the handle; it's locked as expected. He knocks on the door.

During this time, the extraction team has been communicating with each other via earpieces and stealth microphones. Once the fake courier determines and communicates there are no office windows with visibility in the hallway, the three other team members run up and stand to each side of the doorway.

They hear the door's lock bolt slide from inside. The anticipation creates racing hearts and pumping adrenaline within the team; they know what is about to transpire. As the door opens, the fake courier throws a small concussion bomb into the office room followed by a tear gas canister. The bomb temporarily stuns the occupants from the loud explosion; it harms no one. The occupants become incapacitated from extreme eye pain from the tear gas.

After the bomb explodes, the fake courier steps aside and the extraction team leaps into the room wearing gas masks. The blast temporarily stuns the NSC operatives in the room they don't have their guns at the ready. Jim's team gains control of the room and handcuffs the operatives to the desk and puts tape over their mouths. The overtaken operatives are reeling with eye pain from the gas. Jim's team takes their guns and phones.

Savannah and Blaine are sitting in chairs with their hands tied by plastic straps and gag balls stuffed in their mouths. The fake courier leads them from the room, removes their gags and provides eye drops to ease the severe burning they are experiencing. After cutting the wrist straps, the extraction team whisks them down the hall and out to the awaiting vehicle.

ꖛꖛꖛ

It took the NSC operatives just over thirty minutes for the fire department to find them and for them to gain access to phones needed to notify the Operations Room back in the States. As the news from London arrives, Brian is at the table with the NSC leadership. Brian tells the group no way this could have happened without a mole or leak originating from within the NSC team. He says someone, either in the room, or a senior assistant, is providing intelligence to the 'Conduit Team'.

Brian directs the NSC leadership to communicate need-to-know until they find the leak. Leaks in the NSC are just not supposed to happen.

The NSC computers are grinding through millions of bits of electronic information looking for trends to help identify where and how the conduits are travelling. Brian's senior assistant walks into the Operations Room and whispers into his ear. Brian responds, "Go ahead Jason, tell them."

Jason addresses the group, "We have been through every transaction available to us showing transportation the Conduit Team could be using. We have determined someone got off Jack Campbell's jet prior to its flight to Iceland, and we believe that same person used an Uber ride to travel to Greenwood Airport, which is about eighty miles West of Halifax. We then focused on Greenwood and found a large capacity Uber van also left from Halifax to Greenwood. In about the time it would take to drive to Greenwood, a charter Learjet flew into Greenwood, picked up a party of ten people and flew them to Sudbury, Ontario. Sudbury is a small isolated city North West of Toronto, above Lake Huron. The plane touched down there late yesterday, and we have found one transaction for a large passenger rental van leaving Sudbury and travelling Southeast to Toronto. It aligns with the tip we received regarding crossing the US border at Niagara Falls. The rental agents said they needed the van for transporting some people back from Toronto, but we believe it was a ruse. There are only two main highways going East and West through the city, so we're analyzing all satellite video taken from yesterday until now looking for vans, focusing on ones heading to Toronto. Our video analysis should be completed in a few more hours."

Brian responds with, "Thank you. Please light a fire under your team."

"Yes sir," Jason replies, while leaving the room.

Brian then addresses the leaders again. "I'm not liking this. Jack Campbell is a highly decorated ex-SEAL, and he knows someone is after him. He is using decoys; our little joy ride to Iceland is a case in point, so I'm not confident with any of the intelligence we have coming in. Consider nothing without definitive evidence. We can't afford to go down rabbit holes while they continue to leave us in the dust. I want a media campaign setup targeting the Canadian news outlets. Word the message saying we want the conduit team brought in for questioning. Show all their pictures and provide a 1-800 number for people to call. They are a big group; someone has to have seen them. We need results, folks, and we need it fast."

Within an hour the NSC establishes the messaging and contacts the Canadian news outlets.

000

As the conduit team closes in on the Winnipeg airport, Spencer pipes up for the first time. She is looking down at her iPhone as she follows the news event engulfing them. Using a voice loud enough to overcome the van's significant road noise, Spencer says, "What else could happen! We're now considered fugitives and wanted for questioning by the police! There is a 1-800 number for anyone to call who recognizes us. It's all over the news! I thought we were the good guys!"

Jack is back behind the wheel and hears Spencer. He responds, "That is actually good news, Spencer. It means the NSC doesn't have smart people calling the shots, and they haven't narrowed down where we are."

Jack's comment leaves Spencer and the rest of the group confused; how could any of that be good news?

He has seen this desperate knee jerk reaction before, and it makes him smile. Jack then reaches down and picks up his iPhone and asks Siri, his automated phone assistant, to phone Jim. After Jim answers, Jack explains to him about the 1-800 number and requests Jim to have his team make anonymous calls. He tells Jim he wants it to appear at least twenty different people make calls in and spoof the call-in area codes to align with those near Parry Sound, a city on the highway between Sudbury and Toronto. Using the same technology as phone spammers, Jim will setup calls appearing to originate from the local area code and will show fake callback numbers.

Jack tells Jim that as a decoy he wants a coordinated sighting of the whole team at a McDonald's restaurant and a service station. He wants the callers to have information about the white van, the number of occupants and other tidbits to make the visual accounts appear consistent and real. Jack describes the decoy van he had rented in Sudbury to Jim so Jim can pass on the message. As the call to Jim finishes, he smiles again.

Jack knows the team is far from safe; the 1-800 distraction only works if others don't see them in their current location. Jack's plan is to drive straight to the next plane at the airport. He is hoping the NSC won't get a satellite position of them before flying out from Winnipeg.

ㅁㅁㅁ

Jack gets a phone call from Savannah as she and Blaine get transported to the airport. She describes the harrowing studio incident and thanks Jack for coordinating their escape. She also informs Jack that Blaine will stick by her until he deems her situation safe wherever that leads them. Jack asks Savannah where she wants to go. After thinking for a moment, she concludes she needs to leave the UK; she knows the pressure on her in London will be unbearable. Savannah knows her days of reporting in the Congo are over, so she asks Jack what Spencer's plans are because they haven't touched base in a day. He explains he's trying to get Spencer and Alex back to Ecuador. Savannah asks if she can be flown there to join them. Jack observed Savannah and Spencer have become close. He immediately agrees.

☐☐☐

Jack gets a call from Jim, informing him he had the money Jacob's mother stole returned to Cahya, and Indah was removed from the bank account. He thanks Jim and then makes a call to Cahya to inform him of the good news. Jack learns from Cahya that even though Jacob has not yet returned, a large security contingent of twelve men have set-up camp out back of the house. Cahya is comforted hearing every effort is being taken to get Jacob home. He asks Cahya if he's heard from his wife, Indah. Cahya says, "no."

"If you ever hear from her again it will be now you have your money back. My bet is she will call, apologize and ask for forgiveness and want to return. Don't engage her Cahya, she played her cards and showed her hand. She was not only willing to abandon your children; she was also willing to leave you all destitute. Please don't engage her. I understand how loneliness and emotions can play into this. Don't be sucked in."

"I won't, Jack."

☐☐☐

The NSC receives a significant number of phone calls based on the 1-800 number they put out to the media. Most of the calls are being received from areas near the #400 highway between Sudbury and Toronto, provided by Jim, just as Jack had planned. They treat most of the calls as credible because of the consistency of the sightings. A significant effort targets finding the van en route. Satellite imagery is being used to find Jack's rental van, not knowing it is another decoy. Based on the exceptional volume of intelligence being gathered and corroborated, Brian is confident they are getting close; they have limited their search to three vans that could be potentials. Brian instructs his resources to coordinate with the local Canadian Mounted Police to intercept them before they reach Toronto. He updates the President with this information.

000

Now in Winnipeg, the transfer from the van to the Learjet taking the team to British Columbia goes without incident; no one pays enough attention to recognize the entourage as the conduit team; they are not expected to be in the Winnipeg area.

Jack knows the NSC will relentlessly try to locate the decoy van on its way to Toronto and designs a plan to stretch out the ruse. Jack calls Jim after studying Google Maps for a few minutes. As soon as Jim picks up, he says his usual "Speak to me."

Jack jumps right in. "Your phone calls worked like a charm. I've been watching the news and they are reporting your sightings near Parry Sound. They will assume we're heading to Toronto, en route to the Niagara Falls border. Before they find the van, I want you to do another round of sightings near a small village named Baysville, it will get them refocused and its remote enough to make it challenging for them to do an interception. I'm guessing they are trying to bring in the Canadian authorities to assist."

Jack continues, "How are my boats progressing?"

"I have yacht brokers in Vancouver checking available inventory. We have one good candidate so far. There aren't a ton of qualified boats out there, you know that, right? My team is trying to find you some crew, and I have some locals purchasing your provisions. I had to find a fucking refrigerated truck, Jack; this is a logistics nightmare. With this short notice, don't come whining if some of your crew end up being axe murderers."

"Sure, Jim."

Jack hangs up. He doesn't tell Jim they are now flying en route to British Columbia. Not that Jack doesn't trust Jim; he doesn't need to know it ... yet.

000

Brian Donnelly gets a good news bad news update from his assistant Jason who tells him the van hasn't shown up at the traffic stop they coordinated with the Canadian police. The good news Brian hears is they are receiving a new round of credible sightings near a tiny town called Baysville where the conduits appear to have stopped for fuel and a restroom break.

The new sightings has Brian smelling a rat. Why have they turned away from Niagara Falls? He asks his assistant to have all the sighting phone calls traced. He wants to know where they are originating. If this new twist is real, Brian is wondering where they plan to drive - maybe to a remote airfield? If it's another rabbit hole, someone is doing a hell of a good job of playing him.

Before Jason leaves, he says, "Oh, and one more thing, Brian. We found a large passenger van purchased in Sudbury yesterday. It was a white 2019 Ford Transit. It was purchased cash via a wire transfer. We're chasing down the source of the funds."

"Jesus, Jason. Are you looking for it?"

"Yes, we're scouring our available satellite coverage and not finding anything yet. I'll let you know if we spot anything."

Brian just got another pain in the pit of his stomach. He knows he is continually being played.

"Jason, calculate how far the van could have travelled since yesterday's purchase. Work with the Canadians and establish spot checks on every single road thirty minutes beyond where they could have reached by now. Do this fast. Also start with the primary roads leading out of Sudbury and look at the satellite imagery starting from first light this morning. I'm guessing they drove in the dark to avoid satellite detection. Damn it! Find that van. I can't believe they have this kind of jump on us."

☐☐☐

At the same time the NSC is establishing spot checks on the Canadian highways and scouring through endless hours of satellite video, the Learjet accommodating the conduit team is on final approach into Boundary Bay Airport near Vancouver in British Columbia.

Jack, now aware of the dangers of being identified, explains to the group the need to split up four ways, each staying at a different motel within the area. Before the plane stops on the tarmac, Jack is again on the phone renting a small van. He uses a new credit card from his arsenal. He knows the NSC is tracking his previous cards. As is normal operating procedure with private jets, the rental agency delivers the van to the jet where they handle the rental transaction. Jack has also done research looking for a rental car agency residing in a retail mall with covered garage parking. In addition to the van, he also rents a car, this time a small economy car, and again with a different credit card.

Andre and Alma have received no news exposure as-of-yet, so Andre is the designated driver, the most noticeable position in a vehicle. Andre's first commuter trip is to take everyone from the jet to the mall where the rental car is waiting under cover. They all wait in the van while Andre and Alma drive team members, two at a time, to their prospective motels using the smaller car. If the NSC is close, they will lose hours first identifying the car, and then tracking its movements. Jack knows he's just buying time, because the NSC will figure it out.

Prior to the team disbanding to their motels, Jack explains all food is to be ordered in; no one is to be out and about except for Andre and Alma. To facilitate this, Jack withdraws Canadian money from an ATM at the mall, again using a clean card, and distributes ample cash to the group.

Everyone settles into their motel rooms for the night, still wearing the same crusty clothes they had on when they scurried out of the hotel almost two days earlier in Halifax.

Andre returns the rental car and takes a taxicab back to his motel.

ᗑᗑᗑ

"We found the van Brian!" Jason says after Brian picks up his phone. "We spotted it via satellite just outside Winnipeg this morning. It drove to the private aircraft terminal at the Winnipeg airport and it appears the occupants climbed onto a Learjet. The registered flight plan for the Learjet is Kelowna, in the interior of British Columbia, Canada. We're arranging an interception team there as we speak. The images we received are clear, Brian, it's them; this is the best intelligence we have received yet."

"Good work, Jason. What about the other van? Have you found it yet?"

"Yes, it was a decoy as suspected, and it wasn't spotted because it only had a single occupant. They instructed the driver to pick up passengers in Toronto and return them, but when the driver arrived at the pickup address, he realized it was bogus, and then returned to Sudbury. When shown a picture, the driver identified Jack Campbell as the person who hired him."

Brian asks, "What about all the 1-800 phone-in sightings?"

"We're still working on tracking down the calls. We believe they spoofed the caller IDs with legitimate local numbers. It is almost impossible for us to find the spoofing culprits. It's a flaw in the system. The phone spammers love it."

Brian thinks for a moment and says, "We need to find out who is facilitating Jack Campbell. He is not doing this alone while on the run. A phone spoofing campaign is no small feat. Put some people on that. Have you received any word yet on Jack's financial sources? It would be helpful to shut him down financially."

Jason pauses before responding, and then says, "I haven't heard yet about Jack's finances. I will check." Brian knows Jason dropped the ball.

"Please stay on top of it all, Jason. This is the President's number one priority, and you know what will happen if this operation doesn't go well." Brian is referring to the President's tendency to make reckless staff replacements when he loses confidence in someone's ability to deliver.

ⵔⵔⵔ

Just as Jack had predicted, Indah makes a call to her husband. When Cahya picks up the phone, she meekly says, "Hi, Cahya."

Hearing her voice, Cahya feels his heart hurting, and he gets tears in his eyes. "You left us, Indah. You left your children. Where do I put that?"

"I have no answers, Cahya. I do know I still love you. It took what I've done for me to really understand my feelings."

It doesn't go unnoticed by Cahya she didn't mention the children.

She continues, "I have grown depressed over the years with my lot in life; I thought I deserved more, and I felt the world was passing me by. It wasn't your fault Cahya. You did what you could, and you always provided. I saw the money in the bank, and I saw the caretaker watching over the kids and I just didn't think. I turned into a robot. I am so sorry, I know it was horribly wrong. I don't understand my feelings at the time and I don't know why I did it."

"Why did you wait until you lost the money to call me?"

"It's because I needed a wake-up call. It was when I saw my bank account empty that I actually woke up and realized what I've done. It hit me like a rock. I've been crying ever since. It's not because I lost the money, it's because of what I've done. I've lost you; I've lost my children. I'm so sorry. I'm now sick over it and want to fix it, but I don't know how. Help me fix it, Cahya."

The conversation is killing Cahya, his heartache is nothing he has ever experienced, but he doesn't cave. "Indah, maybe over time we can fix this, but right now I'm not ready to see you. I'm not prepared to make it that easy for you after what you did."

"I'm broke, Cahya, I don't know what to do."

Cahya is thinking to himself, 'Ahha, and there you have it, the real reason for the call.'

He says, "Call your family, they will take you in until you can figure things out."

Indah takes a different tactic, as she is not making any headway. "How are the kids doing? Are they eating well and doing their homework?"

"Yes, Indah, they are doing fine. As expected, they miss their mother and ask about you every day. I tell them mommy went away for a while."

Cahya can hear through the phone she is crying. "How about Jacob? I can't believe he's mixed up in this crazy doomsday stuff. The news is going crazy over it. How is he handling it? Will he be home soon?"

Without thinking, Cahya says, "Jacob is about to have a little adventure. He is heading out on a small boat from Canada, an adventure of a lifetime. Should take about a month. I'll be so happy to see him again."

"Why can't he just fly home, like the way he left?"

Cahya goes into a nervous sweat; he realizes what he has just done. He knows the answer for not flying home is because the authorities are after the children. When he and Jacob last talked, which they do daily, Jacob had confided in his father about the sailboat trip, but he had been adamant with his father not to tell anyone.

Cahya tries to retract, "Well, it's not for sure yet. I think they were trying to figure out a way of giving the kids a little adventure before things get crazier. I doubt they will actually do it."

Indah can sense Cahya's retraction in the tone of his voice. She knows he just said something he is now regretting.

Flustered, Cahya ends the call, "Listen, Indah, phone your family and ask for help and you take care of yourself."

Indah doesn't say goodbye as the call didn't go her way and she doesn't know how to end it. She hangs up on Cahya.

▯▯▯

Jack phones Jim from his motel room, and says, "Jim, I need some good news. I've got lots of folks here needing to sail out ASAP. Tell me something."

Jim responds, "Jack, Jack, Jack, you know I'm the miracle worker. Have some faith."

"I need more than faith right now, I need results. What do you have?"

Jim responds in a lighthearted almost excited voice; he is proud of his accomplishment. "Jack, I have a Hallberg-Rassy 64 for you and your group needing to head to Indonesia, and I have a brand-new Oyster 565, hull #2, for Spencer and Alex to get back to Ecuador. It's a super sexy model new to the market. It's the second one they built. Both are outfit for serious offshore passage making."

"Good job, Jim. How soon until we can push off?"

"Day after tomorrow, Jack. I still have to complete the purchases, you know, like getting the money to them. I mean we're only moving a little over six million dollars, a piece of cake. I'm pretty sure I can get the provisioning completed by end-of-day tomorrow. Damn, you owe me."

Jack continues, "Jim, it will only be a day or two before the NSC tracks us to Vancouver. They will watch all outbound air flights and will have increased security at the border. It won't be too long before they figure out we could leave by boat. I want the decoy charter yacht I requested to head out one day after we leave. You can call the NSC's convenient 1-800 number a day after it leaves with a sighting."

"It's already penned it into my schedule, Jack. You just worry about your tribe; I've got the rest."

"You're a good man, Jim."

"No, Jack, I'm an expensive man."

"Yeah, yeah. Send me the boat addresses so I can plan logistics."

"Okay," and the call ends.

□□□

Indah knows her family won't help her, and she is now desperate. She looks up the phone number for the Jakarta Post. After placing the call, she asks for the lead editor of the news desk, stating she has valuable information about the 'Conduit Team'. The editor perks up upon hearing this because it is currently the number one world news story. In no uncertain terms, she tells the editor she will sell her story. He agrees to an interview.

□□□

Andre and Alma get up early, they need to purchase a new wardrobe for everyone. Jack has instructed them to buy warm clothes and foul weather gear suitable for a sailboat voyage leaving from the damp cold of the Pacific Northwest, and also suitable for a return to the hot equator climate. Jack asks Alma to purchase both male and female wigs, hair scissors, makeup, hair color, fake moustaches and duffle bags to hold everything for getting it to the boats. They travel by untraceable taxicab to make their purchases and decide the best choice for a store is West Marine; their clothing section will have everything they need and good quality.

When Alex wakes up, he sees his father sitting at the motel room table drinking a cup of coffee. "I have more information from John McCallister, Dad."

"Does John McCallister know he is helping us?"

"I don't think so, Dad. He tells us stuff during our episodes, but I don't think he remembers. I believe this because when we see him during the episodes, previous info isn't discussed. It's like we're seeing him for the first time, each time."

Jack, as always, is dumbfounded with the whole situation. "Wow, so John McCallister doesn't know he is helping us. That is just wild. So what's happening, Alex?"

"Well, the NSC knows we went to Winnipeg, where we got on a jet for Kelowna. John says if that wasn't our actual destination, by the time I tell you this, they will have figured out where the plane actually went. So, they will know we're in Vancouver, Dad. We need to be careful and hope they take a while to catch up. The scary thing, Dad, is John says the President is so upset by this whole thing, which he doesn't believe, he just wants it gone. John says if the NSC captures us, we should fear for our lives, because after we're interrogated, they will just make us disappear. The President is positive we're working for a foreign government wanting to weaken the US by creating anarchy. He believes this because democracies will have the hardest time maintaining civilian control if this whole thing spins out of control … autocratic countries will just clamp down. If democratic societies become weak, it will be much easier for the autocrats to step in. This is so big, the President thinks whoever we're working for is after world domination. Oh, and Dad, they want to shut down your finances, and they're looking for whoever is assisting you, because they know you can't be doing this alone."

"Wow, Alex, I can't believe you can explain this stuff the way you do. It just blows me away every time you talk these days."

He pauses, then says, "Are you scared, Alex?"

"Yeah."

"Don't worry. We'll keep ahead of them and sort this all out. Your teachers will have seen this coming and have a plan." Jack wants to stay strong in front of his son, but he knows the noose is tightening around the team; the dash to the boats will be tight; Jack feels it. He knows it is near impossible to stay invisible to the NSC for more than a short time. He just needs to get everyone three hundred miles offshore - soon.

Jack makes phone calls to move his money around and to warn Jim to operate with extreme stealth.

▯▯▯

"They are in Vancouver, Brian, they changed their flight plan and didn't land in Kelowna, just as we expected. Intelligence just came in." Jason is explaining this to Brian over the phone. "It appears they are getting sloppy. We have satellite images of them getting into a van from their jet, but we lost them because of darkness once they left the airport. We have every resource available looking through satellite images wherever there is enough light. Based on pattern recognition, our computers can reduce the number of target vehicles in the whole of Vancouver to around forty. We'll get them, Brian. Maybe we'll get lucky with an actual sighting or a slip up with a credit card; we can't count that out."

"Thanks, Jason." Although Jason sounded positive, Brian isn't. He knows they just lost the trail again in a city of over two and a half million people in a foreign country. Brian knows they are chasing an elusive group understanding how not to get caught, and he is worried. He is wondering if he will have a job tomorrow after the next status report with the President.

▯▯▯

Alma and Andre use multiple taxi rides to get the clothes and supplies they purchased, and deliver them, motel by motel, to the team.

Everyone hunkers down watching the never-ending news of their plight while they wait out the rest of the day and evening. Short of facts, the team gets enjoyment watching all the theories the news anchors and their expert panels, come up with.

Via phone calls, Jack tells everyone to be ready in the morning with altered looks using the provided wigs and makeup. He also tells the group to be careful and on high alert with everything and anything they do. He tells them if anyone gets caught, they should fear for their lives, and to do anything to avoid capture.

❚❚❚

Jack's iPhone rings before Alex wakes up. It relieves him when he sees the call is from Jim. "Are we good?"

"Got a pen and paper?" Jim says.

Jack puts his iPhone on speaker, and then opens the 'notes' app and says, "Go."

"I've got two addresses for you, they are a fair way apart, but it should be helpful; if I were you, I would not want the boats leaving together."

Jim gives Jack the addresses, which he records in his phone.

Jim then says, "The boats are fully provisioned, and hopefully it's mostly edible stuff. Water and fuel tanks are full. The crews should be onboard. We told them they are assisting owners to deliver their new boat purchases home. They have no idea who you guys actually are, and I have no idea how they will react to it, if, or when they find out."

Jack says, "What are the crew names? It will be kinda nice to know we're getting on the correct boat when we arrive at the docks."

"Just details, Jack, but if you insist. The Oyster has Bradley Cox as the captain and his wife, Shirley. They are seasoned ocean passage makers, and Shirley is handy both in the galley and about the boat. Your first mate is Ben Foster, he's been on two previous long crossings, that's all I know about him."

Jack enters the names in his phone and says, "I'll call you from the dock as we head out," and then closes the call.

He walks over and gives Alex a nudge. As Alex wakes, Jack says, "You got anything more for me this morning, pal?"

Alex was in a deep sleep and dreaming when his father woke him, so he sits up and looks around disoriented before he can respond to his father. He snaps to life and looks at Jack. "Mornin, Dad."

Jack repeats his question to Alex.

"Good news, Dad. The NSC lost track of the van we used after we left the jet. They didn't see us go into the mall parking lot with it. They are going through all their imagery and expect to have some leads soon."

"Thanks, Alex. It means they have no idea about the motel rooms. Get dressed and put your wig on. We're leaving for the boat right away." Alma had purchased Alex a wig with shoulder length hair, totally altering the boy's look.

Jack then calls the other groups and asks them to get ready. He wants everyone to use taxi cabs and to leave within two hours. He gives them the address of the boat locations and also says he believes the NSC may have lost their trail.

⧄⧄⧄

Jack was wrong. During the night, and after John McCallister's session, the NSC narrowed the search for the van. Working with local law enforcement in Vancouver, they tracked as many vans as they could using satellite images and pictures from intersection and infrastructure cameras. Of the dozens of vans the NSC were following, they saw one enter a parking garage at a mall. When it came out, it was traced back to a car rental agency. It raised a flag, and the NSC focused energy in that direction.

Over a few hours, the NSC noticed the same small car came and went from the parking garage four times. That raised another flag. They focused on the specific car and lost track of it three of its four trips. On the trip they could follow, they saw it go to a Motel where two adult women got out and went into the motel office. Because of the motel's overhanging eaves, the NSC surveillance lost visibility.

Not wanting to complicate things with the local authorities, the NSC scrambled their own local operatives. The operatives are en route to the motel as Spencer and Alma are getting ready to leave.

□□□

Alma, not needing as much alteration to her appearance, is ready and waiting while Spencer is finishing with her makeup in the washroom.

Sitting in a chair near the door, Alma hears its knob turn. She hears it click twice as the handle hits its detent on both a left and right turn. The locked door doesn't open. Alma's hair on the back of her neck stands and her adrenaline runs.

A voice outside says, "Room service."

Alma gets up silently and tells Spencer to go to close and lock the washroom door. She looks out the entrance door peephole and sees a single male who is clearly not room service. Alma knows not opening the door will only make the situation worse, as reinforcements are likely on their way. Not knowing how many she may have to handle; she goes for it.

Alma unlatches the door and stands behind it as it's opened. The man she saw through the peephole forcefully enters with his arm outstretched holding a gun. Alma needed only to see the gun. Her elite military training taught her to react instinctively, and she immediately kicks the gun out of his hand as she simultaneously swings the butt of her gun and hits him hard in the center of his forehead; she hears his skull bone crack. The man falls. He hadn't even seen her.

A second man, both stupid and bold, charges the room. Alma chooses not to fight and says, "Hey!" He turns to face the voice and Alma shoots him in the chest before he has a chance. He also falls. She looks out the door; there doesn't appear to be others.

Alma yells for Spencer. As Spencer comes running out of the wash-room, Alma picks up her duffle bag and says, "Grab your bag and follow me."

Spencer steps over the dead bodies and doesn't say a word.

They both run to a Chevy Impala, the car driven by the two men. They throw their bags into the backseat. Alma yells at Spencer, "Get in," as she jumps into the driver's seat.

The Impala is a late model version and doesn't have an ignition key. Alma pushes on the brake pedal while simultaneously pressing the start button. Nothing happens.

"Fuck, they took the key fob with them. Let's go get it."

As they run from the car, Alma says, "You check the guy at the door, I'll check the one I shot."

Their hearts are pounding as they sprint back into the motel room and check for the key fob in the pockets of the two dead men.

Within seconds, Spencer yells, "I got it." They sprint back to the car.

Alma starts the car and spins the tires as she squeals away from the scene. She looks at Spencer and tells her to phone Jack.

Jack answers right away, and Spencer, almost yelling, explains what has happened.

Jack says, "Shit, Spencer, the NSC is probably watching this go down from their satellites. You need to ditch the car. Leave your bags in it and get away on foot. I'll have Andre pick you up. When you run, try to pick a place where you're not visible from the sky, like under trees, and make it look like you're out for a morning run; no one notices joggers. I know this will be hard but figure it out. You can't let the NSC see you being picked up or they will follow you to the boat. Go fast, they have probably called in the local police. They will brand you both as cop killers; you gotta stay ahead of them."

Spencer has never been so scared.

Alma drives the car for a couple of miles and pulls into the first parking garage she sees. They both get out, leaving behind their bags.

Jack assumes the NSC has identified the other motel rooms. He calls the others and tells everyone to get out. He tells them to be quick and walk around the back or just go anywhere where they can hide from sight.

Everyone scrambles to get out of their rooms.

One reason Jack had provided the team with iPhones back in London was to provide GPS tracking and location capability between the team members if they got separated. They now need it. Jack phones Andre and tells him to commandeer a car and drive to Alma and Spencer's location and pick them up. He asks Andre to phone the women once his iPhone shows he is close to them as they will be on foot running.

Jack ends the call with, "Go now, grab Jacob and get the hell away from the motel - fast. Get the women. Go. Do this fast!"

Andre looks at Jacob and tells him to grab both bags and be waiting out front. He then runs out the door. Andre has to think and act fast. Commandeering a car without a plan can end badly. Andre runs into the motel office where the day clerk has just started his shift. He does a quick scan and sees nobody other than the clerk.

Andre says to the clerk, "There is a little problem in the lot. What car is yours?"

"It's the Nissan Altima," the clerk says with a quizzical look. "Why?"

Andre responds, "I thought so. Quick, grab your keys, there is smoke coming from it. Could be electrical."

They run from the office towards the car.

The clerk gets halfway to the car and stops running, and with an annoyed look, says, "What the fuck, man, it's not smoking!"

Andre has already pulled out his gun and shoves it hard into the clerk's side ribs and says, "Look, dude, I hate to do this but listen carefully. I'm an assassin and I'm in a pinch. You're not my target but I will kill you if

I have to. Yelling out would be a reason. Now give me your keys and walk towards your car without making a scene. Do nothing stupid; I can kill you without using the gun. Be smart and live. I need to borrow your car."

The clerk, now trembling, says, "It's yours, man. Just take it and leave me the fuck alone."

"Sorry, not that easy," Andre says as he takes the clerk's keys and leads him to the back of the car where he asks him for his phone. The Clerk says he left it inside, and Andre believes him.

Andre opens the trunk and tells the Clerk to get in. "Look, dude, I don't want to do this and I won't kill you unless you make me. I'll let you out when we're away from the motel. So please, don't make me kill you, which I will if you don't cooperate. Now hurry!"

Andre is bluffing, but the clerk believes him and climbs into the small trunk. The only thing the clerk says is, "Please don't leave me here."

"I won't." Andre feels bad because the trunk is small, and the clerk is all scrunched up to fit. The clerk is too scared to realize a real assassin doesn't reveal his trade, nor do they leave anyone behind alive to identify them. Andre took him to ensure his silence for the next few minutes.

Andre jumps in the driver's seat, starts the Altima and drives back to their room where Jacob is waiting with the bags.

He jumps out and yells at Jacob to get in the front seat while he throws the bags in the back seat. Andre races off looking for a spot to stop. Within a few blocks he sees a parking garage without a gate next to an apartment complex. He pulls in and screeches to a stop.

Andre pulls out his iPhone and goes to the messenger app and searches for Alma. He then goes to her information which shows her location on a Google map; she is about three miles away. Andre jumps out, goes to the trunk and tells the clerk to get out. Andre then says, "Look, kid, like I said, I'm a professional. I could have killed you at the motel, I could kill you right here, right now, but I don't need to, so I won't. But listen and listen very very carefully."

Andre's performance has the young clerk trembling.

"Wait one hour before you call the police. Tell them your car was stolen. The police and your insurance will ask how the thief got your keys. Make up a story someone stole your keys from behind your desk when you stepped away. Do not mention me. Understand? Do not mention me! If you do, and I learn the police hear about me through you, and trust me, I will know, I will hunt you down, whether or not you stay working at the motel, I will find you and I will kill you, and I will kill everyone associated to you. Do not test me on this. Do you understand?"

The clerk, shaking, nods his head.

"Now get lost and wait one hour. One hour - got it?"

Again, the clerk nods.

"Okay, go." The clerk runs off.

Andre closes the trunk, jumps back in the car and drives towards Alma based on her iPhone's location.

"You're probably wondering what that was all about," he says to Jacob.

"I'm assuming you needed a car, and you got one."

Andre smiles.

▯▯▯

As a distraction and to make it harder for the NSC to see them, Spencer and Alma set off the fire alarm at the apartment building where they pulled in. They wait for a significant number of people to exit the building, then walk casually away. With a block behind them, they jog. They are attempting to stay under coverage from above wherever possible, using trees, parking garages when they see them and overhanging building eaves. Direction changes are made when not visible from above, at which time they stop and catch their breath; the delay and direction changes make it more difficult for the hawks above to follow them. They are anxious, not knowing how much time they have.

Within five minutes of dumping the motel clerk, Andre phones Alma; he knows he's within a city block from their location. Andre asks if a parking garage is available to use as a pickup point. Andre explains the car can't be seen from above as they enter it.

Alma says she doesn't immediately see anything providing good protection such as a garage. Andre then explains he will drive past them as they are jogging. He says he will keep driving until he finds a good stopping location and asks Alma to stay on the call.

He keeps driving and sees the two ladies jogging; Alma is holding her phone to her ear. Andre tells her he's driving past them now. Alma takes notice of the car going by while barely moving her head as she looks.

Two blocks ahead, Andre sees another parking garage. He pulls in and parks explaining to Alma where he is. They close the call and Andre jumps out and throws the bags from the back seat into the trunk.

Jacob, being polite, jumps in the backseat without being asked.

While they wait for the ladies to jog in, Andre brings up Google Maps on his iPhone and enters the Oyster sailboat's location taking him, Spencer and Alex to Ecuador. The map app estimates the trip to the Vancouver Marina, near the international airport, at thirty-five minutes.

As the two ladies approach the car, Andre asks Alma to go into the adjoining apartment building and set off the fire alarm.

"Sure Andre, we're getting pretty good with fire alarms."

Alma sets off the alarm and strides back to the car. Andre waits for the first two vehicles to leave the parking garage before heading out.

☐☐☐

As soon as Jack closes the call with Alma, he and Alex grab their bags and head outside where they cross the street from the motel and walk a block away. While walking, Jack calls for a taxicab and provides a street corner as the pickup address. He then calls Rosine, telling her to be on a street corner one block North of her motel address. He will swing by and pick her and Sarah up with his taxicab.

Jack, not knowing if all the motel locations were compromised, worries about the prying NSC eyes from above. If they see him and Alex get into the cab and travel to the boat, the boat location will also be compromised; the escape would then be impossible. As Jack is thinking this through, he receives a call from Andre who explains he has Spencer, Alma and Jacob and are heading for the Oyster's location in the Vancouver Marina. He tells Jack he doesn't know if the NSC identified his commandeered car and whether it's being tracked, but he has no choice but to just go for it.

Jack doesn't like it. He tells Andre to have Spencer find the closest shopping mall on his route to the marina with covered parking, and pull in. He requests a callback once they know which shopping center it is.

Two minutes later Jack gets the return call. Spencer tells Jack they are going to Oakridge Centre and provides the address. Jack calls Avis and rents a Chrysler minivan to be dropped off at the mall; a service Avis provides. The drop off location instruction is the mall's front entrance.

☐☐☐

Andre pulls his stolen Altima into the parking garage at the Oakridge Centre. He calls Jack back and provides the parking location where they are. Jack tells Andre to get everyone out of the car and wait in a non-conspicuous and sheltered location at the pedestrian entrance where the mall and the garage join. He then asks Andre to keep his eye on the car, but to stay out of sight.

Jack explains he's still forty-five minutes away and his cab hasn't arrived yet. He then has to swing by and pick up Rosine and Sarah. Jack has learned to hate cabs, preferring the prompt pickups offered by Uber and Lyft.

☐☐☐

The entire NSC leadership team is in the Operations Room, including President Stanford. When they received the update that two conduit team members were located at a motel, everyone came together to watch the operation unfold. The entire Counsel's eyes are on the large 200-inch screen streaming a live feed from a US spy satellite focused on the front of the motel where Spencer and Alma have spent the night. Watching events this way by the NSC and the president has become a regular procedure with Bin Laden and Abu Bakr al-Baghdadi being two recent examples.

The image is clear as they all see a dark vehicle pull up to the motel. Two operatives get out of the car. They walk to a motel door where one tries the door and then knocks. They see him enter the room followed immediately by the other. The NSC team watches, waiting with bated breath for the outcome. The next thing they see is Spencer and Alma run out from the motel with their duffle bags to the car. They watch the whole thing - the loading of the duffle bags, the run back into the motel, followed by the run back out and driving off.

Everyone in the room is dumbfounded.

The first person to speak is President Standford, "What the fuck! Who the hell were those two dumb fucks? Jesus fucking Christ! This is fucking amateur hour. Make sure you track that car. Fuck! Call me when you have them."

The President stomps out of the room.

Brian, trying to stay calm says, "Follow the car," and also gets up and walks out of the room. He has had better moments.

The NSC follows the car until it enters a parking garage. Jason establishes communication with the Canadian police to get them to the area and broadcast an all-points bulletin. In the interim, the NSC team sees people by the dozens streaming out of the building next to the parking garage. Jason knows they pulled a fire alarm and now realizes it will take time to identify the two ladies from the car in the crowd forming. He's thinking these people know how to avoid being caught.

After twenty minutes of replaying the images, the NSC analysts spot two women leaving the scene of the gathering outside of the building. They are on foot. Jason has to hustle as the women now have a significant lead.

Twenty minutes after it happened, the NSC sees Spencer and Alma get into the stolen Altima Andre was driving. They track it to the parking garage at the shopping mall.

□□□

Jack's taxicab finally arrives, and he and Alex have the cab swing by the location where Rosine and Sarah are waiting. After a twenty-five-minute uneventful drive, they get dropped off at the shopping mall. Jack sees the Avis van he ordered waiting out front.

Jack has waited until he's at the mall and out of the cab to call Andre as he didn't want to say anything within earshot of the cab driver. Andre picks up his buzzing phone just as he sees a police car pull up and stop behind the abandoned stolen Nissan Altima.

Andre answers the call without a hello, "Jack, you were right. The police just pulled in and stopped behind the car I was driving. That was way too fucking close!"

Jack says, "Okay, listen, they will probably put the mall into a lockdown here real soon and this place will crawl with cops looking for us. Walk in pairs to the front of the mall. Don't draw attention to yourselves and spread out. I saw the van, it's at the front entrance waiting. I'll see you there."

He closes the call and immediately speed dials Jim. As Jim picks up, Jack is looking for a random vehicle leaving the mall. He spots a Lexus and tells Jim to call the NSC's 1-800 number and tell them he spotted the team jumping into a blue Lexus SUV now just leaving the mall heading West.

Following the others, Andre walks through the mall entrance and glances over his shoulder. He sees the police car race off.

◻◻◻

The team walks through the mall and into the van without incident. After Jack completes the rental agreement with the van delivery driver, Andre drives the van to the Vancouver Marina where he, Spencer and Alex get out. They rush their sad goodbyes, and Alma gets behind the wheel to drive to the awaiting Hallberg-Rassy at the Maritime Market & Marina, a 30-minute drive North. This drive also goes without incident. Jack is hoping they finally catch a break and have another jump on the NSC.

After dropping off everyone near the boat, Jack takes the van and drives a mile inland. He locks the doors and places the keys inside a fender. He runs back to the boat, a distance he covers in nine minutes. While running, Jack calls Avis and arranges for them to pick up the van; he doesn't need a missing van report to speed up the NSC's hunt.

◻◻◻

After introductions, Spencer explains to her captain it's important to untie and get going immediately because she is already a week behind schedule and is in a huge rush to get the boat home. Captain Cox agrees and within the hour they untie and leave the dock.

Spencer is hoping Andre is into sharing because she had to leave her duffle bag behind and isn't looking forward to not having adequate clothing or any of her personal items.

They motor West down the freshwater of the Fraser River which spills into the Strait of Georgia. From there they will set sail to the Strait of Juan de Fuca which empties into the Pacific Ocean where they travel nonstop South to Ecuador.

▢▢▢

Jack's new crew member Ben Foster is waiting for the team as they walk up to the Hallberg-Rassy. They do their introductions as they shake hands. Jack takes thirty minutes checking out Jim's provisioning, and without further adieu, they untie and go. They will sail out through Burrard Inlet and then follow Spencer's tracks. Once on the Pacific Ocean, they head West nonstop to Indonesia. Jack has checked the marine weather and its looking favorable for the next few days with a south wind at 12 knots which is excellent for sailing, although for the first twenty-four hours the boat's engine will also run to increase speed and put as many miles behind them as possible.

As Jack steers his new boat through the Burrard Inlet, he is hoping they've made a clean escape. He's also hoping the conduits will come up with a plan to get the NSC off their backs because Jack knows the sailing adventure ahead is only an interim measure and he has run out of ideas.

▢▢▢

Indah is waiting in the front lobby for her appointment with the editor-in-chief of the Jakarta Post office in Sorong. After a few minutes, the editor's assistant asks Indah to follow him. Indah is led into an office which overlooks the Sorong commercial shipping docks and is introduced to the editor. She tells him she is the mother of one conduit. She also tells the editor she can help the United States in locating the children as she has seen the news reports and knows they are requesting information as to their whereabouts. The editor agrees to a twenty-thousand-dollar payment, paid half up front and half if the story pans out. Indah tells the editor her son is leaving Vancouver Canada by small boat.

CHAPTER 9

THE NSC

Ben has the helm of the large Hallberg-Rassy sailing yacht as it makes its way through the San Juan Islands bordering the coast of Washington, en route to the Pacific Ocean. He is accompanied by Rosine, Sarah and Jacob in the boat's center cockpit where they consume the majestic scenery passing by. The endless lush cedar covered islands against a mountainous backdrop, framed by clear blue skies, has them spellbound; it's a brush-stroke of nature they have never seen. The oddity of a sun-filled day graces them as the Pacific Northwest is usually heavy overcast and drizzling rain this time of year.

Alma is asleep in her cabin resting before her first night shift stand-ing watch at the helm. Jack is down below at the boat's large navigation desk plotting the team's sailing route to Indonesia. A cell phone call from Maggie interrupts his concentration.

"Hello, Maggie, are you staying safe?"

"Jesus, Jack, this fiasco you're running almost got my entire team killed. I just heard from Savannah; thank God she escaped the crash, but I lost two of my crew. Someone killed two of my crew, Jack! They were family men. I had to talk with their wives, and I had no answers for them. Who the fuck is trying to kill us? We are scared to death!"

"Slow down, Maggie. For starters I'm sorry for your crew but I'm not running the fiasco, it's running us. None of us asked for this. As for who's trying to kill us, it's the NSC, I'm sure they're responsible for the helicopter attack. I hear idiot President Stanford has his knickers in a knot over us and believes we're involved in a plot to destabilize the United States. That's his argument to stop us. Anyone associated is in danger, and I'm guessing he's attempting to remove the sources of the story, explaining the helicopter attack."

"So, he's solving it by killing off civilians?" Maggie asks.

"It's becoming apparently clear, Maggie, mental stability or working within the system isn't a qualification for Presidents' these days. I'm guessing Stanford sidelined Congress and has the NSC running this operation covertly. He chased our asses clear across Canada. Not sure if we got away cleanly, only time will tell. After what we've been through, I totally understand your team being scared; stay under the radar for a while. What are your plans?"

"My crew got to the mobile news trucks and we're monitoring the story. We haven't chimed in again yet; still a little gun shy. How certain are you the NSC shot down our helicopter? Can you prove it? It's huge news if true. Because of the NSC's request for help in bringing in the Conduits for questioning, CNN asked the White House if they were involved here in London; of course, they denied it."

"We need to figure out a way to implicate them, Maggie. It's the only way we will get them off our backs. I'm afraid if we're captured in the meantime, we won't see the light of day again. I am intimately knowledgeable on how the NSC runs covert operations, and we don't want to be on the receiving end - people mysteriously disappear, and it's never sanctioned or acknowledged."

"You're *NOT* very reassuring, Jack. Jesus! Have you been watching what is happening? As the news agencies feed on the frenzy we've churned up, the world financial markets are tanking. There have been multiple reports of stockbrokers committing suicides. The CDC and Britain's National Health Service have gotten their hands on the water catalyst from the engineers who presented our story and are freaking out over the possibility of interplanetary contamination. The world's scientists are freaking because they don't understand what just happened, they've never seen a black hole change state, and they've never seen a star like the one now occupying the center of our galaxy, not to mention where did the advance warning coming from. On top of everything, Jack, there is a social media storm out there saying our pre-taping of space events was a deep fake, even though the scientists know otherwise, and we provided the evidence it wasn't. The churches are all screaming foul and everyone else believes God is talking to us through kids. It's a mess."

"Yeah, we know, Maggie. We've been following it on TV, too. Not sure what it will take to swing this around. At the very least, the governments need to acknowledge what we're saying. This is a tough nut to crack, and honestly, Maggie, I can't worry about it right now; I need to stay focused on keeping this group together and away from the NSC. It's almost impossible these days to stay hidden if they really want to find us, so I'm just buying time."

"I hear you, Jack. Have you heard from Savannah since heading out?"

"No, I will call her a little later today."

Maggie finishes with, "Okay. I'll ping you if something comes up. If you can figure out how to pin the helicopter attack on the NSC, let me know."

"Will do. Bye for now."

As Jack sets his cell phone down, Sarah appears coming down the companionway stairs. "Mr. Campbell, Ben says his shift is over and is asking if you can relieve him. The rest of us are thinking of coming down as we're all starting to get chilled. Will it be okay if we turn on the TV and catch up on our news?"

"Tell Ben I'll be right up, I just need five minutes to finish up my route planning, and yes, by all means, you guys can come down and catch some TV. You don't need to ask, we're on this boat together."

Sarah disappears back up the steep companionway steps.

Jack finishes his planning and joins the crew in the cockpit. After getting his 'change-of-post' update from Ben, he takes the helm as the group heads down to the warmth offered within the lavishly appointed main salon. Ben clicks on a remote control and raises the large satellite enabled flat-screen television hidden within the teak cabinetry. A minute later, they are glued to the non-stop CNN news coverage their exploits have created. Their timing couldn't have been better; CNN anchor Robert Malone is announcing they are switching over to a live broadcast coming from one of their affiliate stations in Sorong Indonesia. Standing in front of a large plate-glass window overlooking the Sorong harbor, the news scene shows two people. The CNN anchor says, "Hello, Farrell, what do you have for us today?"

"Thank you, Robert, and hello everyone," Farrell says in accented English. "I'm Farrell Karokaro, a correspondent for the Jakarta Post here in Sorong Indonesia. I'm accompanied today by Indah Mendoza, the mother of the Conduit named Jacob."

Jacob jumps from the salon's settee, "That's my mom! Look everyone, that's my mom on TV! I can't believe she's on TV! Look! That's her!"

Farrell continues, "We have all been following the story of the three Conduits who claim to have knowledge for saving mankind prior to the alleged apocalypse. We are bringing you an exclusive first, talking here with Indah, a Conduit parent."

Jacob can't hold his excitement back. "I can't believe my mom in on TV. This is just crazy. Wait until my friends see this; they won't believe it!"

Rosine interjects, "Jacob, let's give the team a chance to hear what your mom has to say."

"I'm sorry, Ms. Rosine, this is just so exciting!" Jacob regains his composure and settles back down.

Farrell turns from the camera and faces Indah, "Indah, tell us about yourself and explain what is happening."

"As you said Farrell, I'm Indah Mendoza and I live with my husband Cahya and my five children in a small village on the northern shores of the island of Waigeo. My son Jacob is the oldest of the five. He confided in me some weeks back he is mysteriously learning about things, things of great magnitude he can't possibly be making up."

Jacob's look of excitement has vanished. He doesn't understand why his mother is saying things he knows are not true.

Indah continues, "About a week back, two Americans, whom we've all learned are Jack Campbell and Spencer Graham, the parents of the Conduit named Alex, came looking for Jacob. After explaining to my husband Cahya and me the need to take Jacob away for a news conference, Cahya and Jacob, left the same day with the Americans and flew to London."

Farrell jumps in, "What were your thoughts knowing something astronomically big was happening, involving your son, and your husband takes him and flies off?"

"It was difficult, Farrell. I was trying to come to terms with what Jacob was telling me, and then to find myself alone to deal with my bewilderment while managing the children without their father has been difficult. I felt alone and isolated. It has been troubling for me."

Jacob, upset, can't hold back, "That's not true! Why is my mom saying that? I didn't tell her what I was learning, and Mr. Campbell provided an assistant to help her. I don't understand; Dad went right back to help her. He's there now."

Rosine, not understanding the recent events involving Indah, attempts to console Jacob, "It's okay, Jacob. Your mom will have good reasons for saying these things. You can ask her yourself, soon."

Jacob isn't convinced.

Farrell keeps the interview going, "Indah, what are your thoughts regarding your son, the other conduits, and their message? This has to be overwhelming for a parent."

"I don't know what to think. I know something is happening to my son I can't explain, and the story has people either bewildered or exceptionally upset. I can't believe they actually have the United States government looking for them. I think the US is scared of this story and wants to know where it's coming from."

"Why don't the Conduits just reach out to the US government and talk to them about it?" Farrell asks.

"I don't know the answer, Farrell. The US seems to have them spooked and they don't want to cooperate right now, and I don't understand why. It obviously concerns them for some reason."

Farrell has pre-interviewed Indah prior to the live broadcast and isn't asking questions he doesn't already have the answer to. "If the Conduit team is on the run, what do you think their plan is?"

"Well, I know they found their way to Vancouver, Canada, and from there they have headed out on a private ocean-going boat. I'm guessing they are trying to find their way back here to Indonesia."

"Wow, Indah, they really are trying hard not to be found … not the easiest way to get home."

"I just hope Jacob stays safe."

Farrell asks one last question, "Indah, do you think God is talking to your son and the other Conduits?"

"I know this sounds outrageous, but if these kids are learning things that can't be learned here on Earth, who else could it be?"

Farrell finishes up the interview, "Thank you, Indah, for speaking with us today." He faces the camera and says, "Well there you have it. Indah here, the mother of Jacob, a Conduit, has told us her son, along with the rest of the Conduit team, is running from the United States government, and she believes they communicate directly with God. And with that, I will end this broadcast by saying, may God help us. Back to you Robert."

The scene switches back to Robert in the CNN newsroom who says, "Wow! I'm literally speechless."

As they always do, the news anchor introduces other speaking guests sitting at the desk, jumping in to dissect the story they just heard from Indonesia.

Jacob is upset, gets up and walks to his cabin.

Rosine climbs the companionway to the cockpit where Jack is manning the helm. "How's it going Jack?" It's more a salutation than a question, and she doesn't wait for Jack's response. "We just watched Jacob's mother Indah being interviewed on CNN. She said we're being chased by the United States government and we've escaped Canada heading out-to-sea in a private ocean-going boat."

"Jesus Christ." Jack snipes. "That stupid bitch. Did she give any specific details? How in hell did she find out about us boarding a boat?"

"She didn't say what kind of boat we're on other than a private ocean-going one and she didn't say how she got her information. It upset Jacob because she's saying things on TV that are not true, and he doesn't understand why."

"Okay, thanks, Rosine. I have to make a phone call. Please continue to keep an eye on the news."

"Sure, Jack." Rosine drops back into the boat's salon.

Just as Jack attempts to call Jim, his phone starts ringing. He sees its Cahya. "Hello, Cahya, I'm assuming you're calling regarding the little news interview your wife just gave."

"I'm so sorry, Jack. Indah called me when she lost the money, just like you said she would. I didn't placate her, but when she asked about Jacob, I slipped and said he was on an adventure of a lifetime heading out on a small boat from Vancouver. I'm sorry. I knew I slipped the second I said it. I realize the danger I've put the group in."

"We have to be careful, Cahya. These are difficult times. But listen, I can't talk now; I have to make a call. I'm sure you'll be hearing from Jacob, and I'll touch base with you soon."

"Okay, Jack, and again I'm really sorry about this." The call ends.

Jack calls Jim who answers without an acknowledgement, "Just saw the news, Jack, and because I'm clairvoyant, I believe you're calling to get a status on the third boat you requested, right?"

"Listen Jim, I need the charter boat heading out ASAP because we need another two days to get further out to sea making it harder for the NSC to find us. Push to get the decoy folks from a talent agency onto the boat. Make sure there are three kids; two boys, one girl. One boy and the girl being of color. You get the idea. In the meantime, call the NSC's 1-800 number and tell them you've caught wind the group is about to head North by yacht. Let them think we actually haven't left yet and provide a little tease to the media. Do this quickly, Jim; we're in a pickle here."

"Jack, I wonder if there will be time before we all fry to make a movie of your exploits. It has all the ingredients of a box office hit."

"Just make it happen, Jim." ending the call without a goodbye.

In the salon, Ben has remained quiet as he watches the news with the group. As the CNN anchor moves away from the immediate topic, he says to the group, "You didn't tell me you were the Conduits. Are you actually being chased by the US government?"

Rosine answers, "We couldn't tell you Ben, or anyone for that matter, because of the precariousness of our situation. To understand what is happening, please talk to Jack first before discussing this with Sarah and Jacob. Would you do that?"

"Sure Rosine. Holy crap! I can't believe I'm here with you people. You are world news right now and I'm in the thick of it. I can't believe this is happening to me. Your story is the only thing being talked about. I have to admit I didn't think it was real, and then here you are. This is just wild! I'll be famous over this; I think I'll go talk to Jack right now. Holy shit!" Ben gets up and heads for the cockpit.

Sitting in the cockpit with Ben, Jack has no choice but to fill him in on the details of their plight. While telling the story, Jack doesn't get a good feeling for how Ben is accepting the story. Ben doesn't ask questions and just sits listening. When the story is complete, and without commenting on the enormousness of the Conduit's mission, Ben finishes with, "You know, Jack, you put me in harm's way without my knowledge. I'm not sure how I feel about that."

"Sorry, Ben," is all Jack says as Ben gets up and returns to the salon.

Once Ben's returns, Rosine heads out to speak alone with Jack. She sits as close to him as possible to keep her voice low. "So, I guess Ben now knows all about us."

"It was bound to happen at some point," Jack responds, "But I was hoping it would take a few more days. I'd feel much more comfortable if we were further out to sea."

"Did you notice anything odd about Ben?" Rosine asks.

"Only he didn't ask many questions, or to care about the magnitude of what is actually happening; not a response I would expect when hearing this story for the first time. He seemed more concerned about his own notoriety and personal safety, and he let me know."

"That's my point, Jack. In my opinion, when we were down below and he saw the newscast and realized who we were, his behavior was strange.

It was all about him, and what was happening to him. It was just a small thing, but like you're saying, it wasn't behavior I would have expected."

"If he does anything, and I mean anything, you don't believe is normal, or you don't like, you tell me right away - okay Rosine?"

"Absolutely, Jack."

▯▯▯

Brian, feeling an instant increase in anxiety, walks into the president's office to provide a Conduit update. Before Brian can get a word out, President Stanford says, "So what have you and your group of misfits screwed up this time, Brian?"

If it wasn't for Brian's own craving for power and recognition, he would have walked from this administration long ago. He knows he can outlast the President, so he sucks it up and plays the yes-man.

"Well sir, it appears the leak we have is coming from the top. We have tightened the information to be need-to-know, yet some armed group rescued the reporter we had in custody in London. They knew exactly where to find her."

"What the fuck, Brian! What are you doing about it? How in Christ's name can we run anything if someone is broadcasting our every move? This is like watching a fucking episode for Laurel and Hardy."

Brian doesn't know who the president is referring to, and is about to speak, but the president cuts him off and continues, "Here is what I want you to do Brian, and this stays between you and me. Please don't fuck it up again. I want every ranking member of the NSC bugged and tailed. I want every word they say or text, recorded. I want to know everyone they talk to. Whoever this snitch is, they're communicating with someone and I want the bastard found. In no uncertain terms, you tell your people doing the spying if they speak about this, I will charge them with treason, and they will spend the rest of their miserable lives in jail. Got that Brian? I don't want this coming back to haunt me."

Stanford continues, "Whoever this snitch is, they are most likely informing their source on a near daily basis. If the premise is true, I expect results on this little witch hunt in two days. Brian, you're letting this whole thing slide out from under us; find the snitch and get those kids. I need to understand who is behind this mess before we lose control. Christ, have you seen what is going on out there? The masses are looking for leadership. I need answers. If you can't come back with results, come back with your resignation notice. Now go."

▯▯▯

Jim had to scramble to up the schedule for the chartered decoy yacht to depart Vancouver. The charter company worked through the night to clean and provision the yacht to earn an additional handsome fee. Jim went through the same hassle from the talent agencies attempting to recruit guests resembling the Conduit team. Extra cash on the table provided the motivation to make it happen fast. On the morning of the second day, the decoy yacht with its disparate tribe of Conduit lookalikes departs Coal Harbor Marina in downtown Vancouver.

Six hours after departure, Jim's team calls the NSC 1-800 number three times from spoofed phone numbers, saying they saw a group of people resembling the Conduits, board a large luxury yacht. Jim further promotes the decoy by making an anonymous call to CTV News, Vancouver, to offer his eyewitness account. Jim even offers up the yacht's name, 'Blue Moon'.

▯▯▯

"Brian, I think we've found them again. This makes sense and explains why they went to Vancouver. They have chartered a large yacht and have headed North. It also corroborates the story out of Sorong by a mother of a conduit who described their departure by boat."

The excitement in Jason's voice doesn't go unnoticed by Brian. He cautions Jason, reminding him on how skilled the Conduit Team has been on deploying decoys and false leads.

"Jason, find out who has marine jurisdiction up there and coordinate a boarding of the boat. Have plans in place to extract them."

"Yes, Brian, I'm on it."

ꟷꟷꟷ

Jack, Rosine, Sarah and Jacob have gone to their sleeping cabins for the night. Alma has taken over the watch in the cockpit, and Ben is still watching the news, dreaming of his new found fame sitting at a news anchor desk while interviewed and seen by the world.

The CNN anchor announces a breaking story. The coverage switches to a CTV News broadcast out of Vancouver, Canada, where a correspondent is standing on a marina dock surrounded by large yachts.

"Hello, I'm George Caldwell of CTV News, and I'm here on the docks of the Coal Harbor Marina here in Vancouver. According to an eyewitness accounting, a large yacht left this very spot earlier today with guests matching the descriptions of the Conduit Team. According to the witness, there were three children appearing to be about ten years old, and two of them were children of color. There were five adults, also matching team descriptions. This information comes on the heels of Indah Mendoza, the mother of Jacob, a Conduit Team member, telling us her son is departing Vancouver via boat. The yacht's name they departed on is 'Blue Moon.'"

George ends his newscast displaying the 1-800 hotline phone number on the screen with a reminder to call it with any information useful for locating the Conduits.

Ben jumps off the settee and leaps to the navigation station to get a pen and paper. He writes down the 1-800 number. After calling the number and providing his name, Ben tells the phone agent he saw the CTV newscast and explained it's not correct. He says 'Blue Moon' is just a coincidence and explains he's on a sailboat heading out to sea with two of the real conduits and three adults. Ben tells the agent he'll provide an exact GPS location comprising a latitude and longitude if the United States agrees to pay him one-hundred-thousand dollars. He also explains he can't deal with phone calls, and from this point forward all correspondence must be text messages. The agent dismisses Ben as another call-in crazy person and quickly ends the call.

ooo

"We have them Brian! The Canadian RCMP has redirected the boat into Deep Bay on Vancouver Island. They have confined the guests and crew to the boat, awaiting guidance from us. It's definitely the boat that left Coal Harbor Marina and it's named 'Blue Moon' as described by an eyewitness. We have confirmed three ten-year-old's are aboard. How do you want to proceed? I have already done some legwork, and the closest airport where you can land your jet is Nanaimo, about forty miles south. Do you want your plane ready, Brian?"

"You bet, and good work, Jason. Let's go, you're joining me. Grab four operatives. Call the pilot and get the Canadian clearances. Let's get this ordeal over with."

"What about packing, Brian?"

"There is toothpaste and brushes on the plane. Let's go."

"I do have a wife, you know. Jesus, Brian, how long will we be gone?

"As long as it takes, Jason." Brian says without empathy.

🯄🯄🯄

Jack wakes from his restless sleep, picks up his cell and calls Spencer.

The ringing of Spencer's cell wakes her; she answers in a groggy state. "Hi, Jack, you guys okay? Alex and I are really enjoying our trip, it's beautiful out here, and what a relief to be away from the stress of running, we were exhausted."

"I don't want to add stress back, Spencer, but in all likelihood the NSC knows we left Vancouver by boat. Cahya's wife Indah found out Jacob was heading home this way and spilled the beans to a news outlet in Sorong, she most likely sold her story."

"What a witch. I'm sorry for Jacob, his mom is so callous. What does that mean for us, Jack?"

"Don't know yet. Jim has sent out a decoy boat loaded with passengers resembling us. The idea is to get them looking in the wrong place so we can get some sea-room. Once out far enough, we're a needle in a haystack. Let Andre know, and you may also want to come clean with your captain. I'm telling you all this in case we have to do something quick; I don't want to explain things in a hurry."

"I understand, Jack. So I think what I'm hearing is stay the course, tell my crewmates, and cross my fingers."

"Exactly." Jack says. "I'll keep you informed as this unfolds so you're never caught off guard. Now get back to sleep. I'm sorry I woke you."

"It's okay, Jack. How is your crew making out?"

"Everything is fine so far, but we had to come clean with Ben, and I'm not getting a warm and fuzzy feeling with him. Something isn't right. I'll be watching."

"Okay, good night, Jack. Talk soon."

000

Ben's alarm notifies him of his next watch at the helm. He saunters up to the cockpit to relieve Alma who provides him a quick watch update.

"Pretty crazy being with Conduits, hey?" Ben says.

"So I guess you know all about it now?"

"Yeah, I'm a little put out I was misled, given how dangerous running from the NSC must be."

"Jack has had to make a lot of tough calls, Ben, to keep us all safe. I can understand your concern, but I'm confident he can handle it and he says and does everything for a reason."

"I guess I just don't understand why the team doesn't let the NSC talk with them and get it over with. Why run?"

"You need to ask Jack, Ben. I know he has his reasons, and trust me when I say, they will be good ones."

"Well, I'm sure they will catch us, so I hope he's made plans."

"What makes you so sure they will catch us, Ben? Jack has done a pretty good job of outmaneuvering them so far."

"It's just a feeling I have. I've heard the NSC is a pretty tough group to stay hidden from. They found Bin Laden in the middle of Pakistan, and al-Qaeda knew how to hide people."

"Well, Ben, I don't know anything about that, but like I said, Jack knows what he is doing." For Alma, the conversation is over, and she gets up and goes below. Ben unnerves her. She didn't like his confidence that they will be found. He has a creepy way about him, she senses it, but can't put words together describing it.

The salon is empty as Alma descends the companionway stairs. She fixes herself a hot chocolate which she heats in the microwave. After completing her drink, she walks to the owner's stateroom at the aft end of the boat where she knows Jack is lying down. Without knocking, she gently turns the latch of his cabin door, opening it as she steps in, and closing it behind her. Jack is sound asleep on his berth as she silently slips her clothes to the floor and climbs up onto the berth. She straddles Jack moving forward on her hands and knees. As she gets positioned over Jack's chest, her movements wake him. Just as Jack is about to yell, Alma gently puts her hand over his mouth and says, "Shhh."

Jack quickly sees what is happening and succumbs to the advance.

ꊢꊢꊢ

Brian and Jason accompanied by four NSC operatives pull up to the docks in Deep Bay on Vancouver Island. They see the huge luxury yacht at the end of the large pier with two uniformed RCMP officers standing watch. At the entrance to the pier, a small group of news reporters and camera men have gathered. As Brian's team approaches, the NSC operatives flank them, protecting Jason and Brian from the reporters who shout out questions about the Conduits being aboard. The questions go unanswered as the team makes it way forward. Brian shows an officer his NSC credentials who then explains the circumstances and events leading up to the impounding of the boat. They are intercepted by the yacht captain as Brian leads the way up the gangplank. Obviously annoyed by the impounding of his boat, the captain asks what is happening. Without providing an explanation, Brian tells him he is the Director of the US National Security Council and wants all the crew and guests brought together. The captain makes a radio call to the boat's bridge which is immediately followed by an announcement over the yacht's intercom system for all personnel to gather in the main salon. "Follow me," the captain says, as he leads them into the spacious and luxurious socializing lounge. Crew and guests meander in and congregate. The proxy Conduit Team hired from the talent agency don't know each other, and no one is talking. They look bewildered and concerned.

Brian introduces himself and his team, and then says to Jason, "Please ask the adults here for their names and request photo ID, then wait for me to return. You three children, follow me." Brian walks to the doors at the rear end of the salon leading to the yacht's aft cockpit. The children look at their parents who came as chaperones, for approval, which they get in the form of nods. Displaying reluctance, the children follow Brian out to the cockpit where he says, "Your name must be Sarah?" looking straight at the young girl.

She responds with no noticeable accent, "No sir, my name is Janet Hopewell."

"Nice to meet you, Janet, can you tell me where you live?"

"I live in North Vancouver."

"How long have you lived there?

"All my life."

"Do you know what your parents do for a living?"

"My father is an accountant and my mom is a nurse."

Brian can feel sweat forming under his clothes. He is frustrated as yet again he's being played. Not establishing the guest identities in advance was foolish, and he knows it.

"Janet, do you know why you are on this yacht?"

"My parents have me registered with a talent agency, and they told us there was an opportunity to be extras on a film scene being shot on this boat."

Brian looks at the other two children, "Is it the same story for you two?"

They both respond together saying, "Yes."

"Did you kids know each other prior to this boat trip?"

The children look at each other shaking their heads indicating, 'No'.

Brian asks one last question, "Have any of you ever lived in Africa or Indonesia?"

Again, 'No.'

"Thanks kids, you can return to the others."

As the kids walk back into the salon, Brain calls for Jason to join him in the cockpit. Jason, who has been getting the adult's information, walks back sheepishly.

"Jason, when we get back to Washington, go straight home, don't go back to the office. I will ensure we deliver your desk belongings. You're done. I don't want to see you again. This has been a colossal screw up."

Jason is about to speak to defend himself, but Brian cuts him off while backing him as he walks into the salon, "We're done here Jason."

Brian says to his operatives, "Let's go. We're out'a here," and walks out and down the gangplank.

Upon seeing Brian, the reporters shout out questions. Through the ruckus, Brian clearly hears two repeated statements, "Are you the NSC? Are the Conduits on board?" Again, Brian ignores the reporters and walks straight to his rental vehicle. He is now wondering if he will out-survive the president in Washington.

⧄⧄⧄

After his helm watch, Ben retires to his sleeping cabin. The small cabin comprises an over and under bunk arrangement, a small hanging locker and a vanity with a set of drawers built into it. Ben has the upper bunk and shares the cabin with Alma, although they never occupy the cabin at the same time because of their overlapping shift schedules, setup by Jack.

Ben is sitting up and unwinding on his bunk prior to sleep while checking the conduit news from his iPad tablet computer. As usual, all the news agencies are mercilessly covering the story, and the latest development being televised is from Deep Bay where the NSC agents are leaving the scene empty handed. The CTV news correspondent makes an assumption, suggesting the Conduit Team were not present on the yacht and 'Blue Moon' was a false lead.

Ben climbs off his bunk and pulls the paper out of his pants pocket containing the NSC 1-800 number. He calls the number and again an agent answers right away. Ben explains he had called yesterday, and had they listened to him, the NSC wouldn't have wasted their time with the yacht named 'Blue Moon'. The new agent Ben is speaking with is more interested in his story and wants details. Ben requests to continue the conversation with text messaging; the same unheeded request he made the previous day. The agent agrees and verifies with Ben the caller id is the correct number to text back on. Ben confirms and ends the call. Within seconds a text arrives, "is this ben?"

"yes"

"u said u with conduits, correct?"

"yes"

"what is your location?"

"as said, put $100k in bank account first"

"can't make that happen"

"If u want location, make happen. i have location and sure thing. i am cheaper then screw ups."

000

Ben is sound asleep when he's awoken by the vibrating of his phone. He looks and sees it's a return response from the NSC. His adrenaline spikes. His phone shows it's been two hours since his last correspondence.

The message is terse, "enter routing number and account number for wire."

Ben's heart is racing. The thought he's helping the NSC and receiving a hundred grand for his efforts is overwhelming. He takes a deep breath and jumps off his bunk to find his wallet. He texts the account information from a blank check into his phone.

The response comes immediately, "midnight est funds clear. provide location now."

Like most people who are untrustworthy, Ben doesn't trust. He responds with, "will give location after funds clear."

The NSC sends one final message, "okay do not mess up"

Ben's heart is pounding.

□□□

Brian has just ended his call authorizing one-hundred-thousand dollars to a person calling himself Ben Foster. He has a better feeling about this information because it came from a satellite uplink in the US Pacific Northwest, a location that could coincide with a boat location. In addition, a background check on Foster shows he's clean and contracts as a small boat crewmember. Brian is not happy he has to wait for the funds to clear before he gets the location. If this doesn't pan out, Brian knows he's done.

□□□

Sowptik, Jason's co-worker picks up his ringing phone and hears, "Hello Sowptik." He recognizes Brian's voice.

"Hi, Brian, I hear your recent trip to Canada didn't go well."

"Nope, it sure didn't. Listen, Sowptik, I had to let Jason go. The trip was grossly mishandled, but in the meantime, we have new intelligence the Conduits are on a sailboat that embarked Vancouver. We're guessing they are a few hundred miles into the Pacific by now via the Strait of Juan de Fuca, heading West. Sometime after midnight Eastern Time, we should receive the exact latitude and longitude of the boat's position. I need you to pick this operation up and find the closest navy asset we have that can intercept them. Once we have definitive knowledge, they've found the team, I need you to arrange logistics to get us, including my interrogator, onto the navy boat. We'll need something like a destroyer. Is this something you can handle?"

"Not a problem, Brian. I will call you when the arrangements are in place.

ⵔⵔⵔ

Rosine is the first morning riser, the rest of the crew is sleeping except for Alma who is standing watch in the cockpit. A refreshing shower has helped reduce Rosine's anxiety that's been festering within her. She proceeds to the galley for morning meal preparations, a crewing responsibility assigned to her by Jack.

Sarah is the next to wake to the unmistakable pungent aroma of the scrambled eggs and bacon. She leaves her cabin walking through the main salon to the galley where Rosine is hard at work.

"Hi, Ms. Rosine. Did you sleep as well as I did?"

"Well, Sarah, I have to admit being chased by the United States, seeing you learn unworldly things, and knowing the Earth is ending in ten years, hasn't made for great sleeps lately."

Sarah, displaying her natural empathy says, "I understand, Ms. Rosine. This whole thing has uprooted your life and changed everything. I feel so bad you got dragged into this. I'm sure this has you quite scared."

"Oh Sarah, you are growing up so fast. Please don't feel bad for me, I wouldn't have it any other way. I love we're here for each other, and yes, I'm a little scared."

"We'll get through this, Ms. Rosine. Oh, and one more thing, we have learned a bit more about who is teaching us, and we have a message for Mr Campbell.

"I think Jack is still sleeping, I'm dying to hear more about your teacher!"

"Well, we learned our teacher refers to itself as the 'Spirit-of-Life'. We were told it can be shortened to 'SOL', pronounced the same as the word 'soul', as in the human soul. The thing about SOL, Ms. Rosine, is he sees everything, regardless of how far away it is, that's how we know about the black hole explosion in the Milky Way."

Sarah continues, "SOL impregnated single cell life forms on the Earth billions of years ago, just as our planet's oceans were forming. SOL has been doing this on endless planets in all the universes, providing life the opportunity to evolve. SOL sits back and watches life evolve and intervenes occasionally to assist and provide opportunities for survival when environments collapse due to natural catastrophes like what is happening to our Milky Way."

Rosine turns off her stove, walks to the salon and sits down. Although it's always been assumed the Conduits are communicating with something, it overwhelms Rosine to hear it so succinctly.

Sarah sees she has disturbed Rosine and asks, "Are you okay, Ms. Rosine? Did I upset you? I didn't mean to."

"Oh, Sarah, this isn't your fault. I'm not upset by what you say, I'm just overwhelmed by the gravity of the whole situation. Your definition of SOL is like you're describing God, and you and the others are directly talking with him. Do you understand that? Is this not affecting you kids knowing you are the chosen ones?"

"We haven't talked about it that way, Ms. Rosine. We are learning what needs doing and will try to accomplish it. It's the only way we're thinking about it. We realize we know things others don't, but we don't consider ourselves special, or to use your term, 'chosen.'"

"Aren't you at least scared by what is happening? This whole burden is on you three kids, and there are lots of angry people out there."

"I think SOL is purposely training us not to think of it that way. None of us are scared, and we think this adventure is kinda cool. We're all having fun doing it. We know Mr. Campbell is worried the NSC might catch us, but for some reason we're confident things will work out. It's the only way I can explain it."

"Oh, Sarah, you're talking like an adult. It's so easy to see why you three are the ones. SOL obviously knew what he was doing."

Rosine allows herself a small smile, then finishes with, "I better park these emotions and get you people fed." She heads back to the galley.

▯▯▯

Brian picks up his ringing phone, and without a salutation, Sowptik starts speaking, "Brian, we have the destroyer USS Kidd departing its base at Everett Washington tomorrow on a regularly scheduled deployment with its strike group. Navy operations says we can borrow it for a few days to accomplish your mission as long as the intercept point isn't too far off course for them."

"That's great, Sowptik. Have you planned for helicopter transportation? Not only do I have to get to the destroyer, but we will have to extract the Conduit team. From reports, there could be up to ten of them."

"I thought this through, Brian, and have arranged for our largest helicopter the navy has; the size of the team we extract won't be a problem. Because of range limitations, I've arranged for it to be secured to the deck of the USS Kidd on the way out; it therefore only needs to do a one-way return trip with the Conduit team and a security detail. Your chopper will rendezvous with the Kidd, refuel, and return with you and your team."

"Excellent, Sowptik. When is the Kidd departing?"

"O eight hundred tomorrow. Assuming we have the interception coordinates from your source, it should reach the Conduits by fourteen hundred hours, give or take. We can have you standing by at the base in Everett, and when a boarding team from the Kidd establishes the Conduit's identities, you can be on the destroyer within ninety minutes."

"God, I hope this finally goes as planned."

"I'm sure it will, Brian."

"Please make arrangements for us to fly to Everett tonight."

"You want me to join you?" Sowptik queries.

"Yes."

□□□

Ben sitting on his bunk, waiting for his next helm shift, looks at his watch; it is 7:59. He has anxiously been waiting for 8 pm, which is midnight in the Eastern Standard time zone; the time banks transact their money transfers. Ben runs his Wells Fargo banking app on his iPad and goes to his checking account. He gasps when he sees a six-figure balance. The burden of responsibility placed on him hasn't sunk in until this moment, his next breath is difficult. Ben is sweating. He is now in a high-stakes game.

Ben switches over to his Navionics iPad app. As a seaman, he routinely runs Navionics which provides him a GPS map view of where he is on the ocean. It's used by small boat captains to assist with navigation or to provide a backup to the larger more expensive systems. Most importantly, it provides his current latitude and longitude. Ben copies the two location numbers and then creates a new text message, "47-21.967n/129-23.679w,64' hallberg-rassy sailboat,heading 248,11kts,adults:Jack,rosine,alma-children:sarah,jacob-crew:me-don't divulge it was me."

Ben gets an immediate response simply stating "send latitude and longitude screenshot from app." The NSC wants to see visual evidence of the location.

Ben goes back to his navigation app and does as requested.

▯▯▯

Brian is sitting beside Sowptik on their government jet en route to Everett Washington. It's just past 8:15 pm when Brian's phone rings. After speaking with the caller, Brian says thank you and hangs up. "Sowptik, we got the location. They're about two hundred and thirty miles West of the Strait of Juan de Fuca heading West on a sailboat, just as we suspected. The downside is it's not the whole team. It appears Alex and his mother Spencer are not onboard; we still need to find them. Maybe we'll know more after the initial interrogation." Accompanying Brian and Sowptik on the plane is Brian's lead interrogator. Although deemed illegal in the United States, the NSC uses truth serums they forcibly inject into their subjects to assist with secret interrogation results. Brian knows this, but never witnesses it. Deniability of illegal acts is an art form thoroughly practiced by the senior bureaucrats.

▯▯▯

Jacob, smelling the bacon originating from the boat's galley, jumps from his berth and joins Sarah and Rosine in the galley. He asks Sarah, "Did you tell Ms. Rosine about SOL?"

"Yeah, she now knows all about it. I haven't talked with Mr. Campbell yet though."

Jacob, almost cutting her off says, "I think we need to tell him right now, it's urgent. Ms. Rosine, do you think it will be ok if we knock on Mr. Campbell's door?"

"If it's important, I'm pretty sure Jack won't mind."

Jack's cabin door is on the other end of the narrow galley, and Sarah and Jacob squeeze past Rosine to get to it. Sarah knocks."

Without hesitation, Jack responds with, "Come in."

As the Conduits enter his cabin, they see Jack sitting up with his computer on his lap. "What's up kids?"

Jacob says to Sarah, "Should I tell him?"

"Sure."

"Well, Mr. Campbell, we've heard from John McCallister again, and he says we will need to act quickly on this information. He told us the NSC knows our exact location and they have dispatched a destroyer to intercept us. It will catch up with us about 2 pm today. They know Alex and Spencer are not onboard."

"Did John tell you how he knows this? Did he provide a source of information?"

"No, Mr. Campbell. We only know what we just told you."

This information has put Jack in a funk; he knows his options are limited. "Thanks kids, give me a minute to think about this and then we'll hold a team meeting."

Jack is processing this latest turn of events, "How did they get a location? How do they know who's aboard?" He knows if the NSC has a position fix of the boat, it either came from a source on board or from a satellite, but he's concerned about the passenger knowledge, a satellite couldn't provide that. Jack can't come up with any other solution other than Ben selling them out, he knows it wouldn't have been Alma or Rosine.

Jack phones Jim and gets the normal, "Talk to me," response.

"Got another problem, Jim."

"Of course, you do, Jack."

"The NSC is sending a destroyer to intercept us. I need the kids off the boat. We don't have time for you to send a fast boat to us. Do you know what a 'Spot' is Jim?"

"If you're talking about the spots on the front of my pants, Jack, I get them all the time."

"Be serious, Jim, we have little time."

"Are you talking about the satellite uplink device used for tracking people, that I was clever enough to have put on your boat?"

"That was a good call, Jim. I'm putting everyone in the boat's tender, and we'll steer a South East course back towards land. We won't have enough fuel to make it, and we won't last long in this cold weather, so I need you to send a go-fast boat and pick us up at our 'Spot' location. Your pickup boat can take us to rendezvous with Spencer and Alex which will still be in range. I'm turning on the Spot right now and I need you to verify you're seeing it on the Spot web portal. Once I hear from you it's working, we're out'a here. We will also have the portable VHF radio and will answer to the call-sign of 'ReelFun' on channel sixteen. I hope you're taking notes Jim; I also need you to call Spencer and Andre and tell them they will have company for the rest of their trip to Ecuador. In addition, you need to send out a second go-fast boat to Spencer with additional food and clothing provisions for us."

"Holy Christ, Jack! Does this shit just never end with you?"

"Hurry, Jim, I'm waiting for your callback."

Within minutes Jim calls Jack back and says he sees their 'Spot' track on the website. It shows as little breadcrumb dots on a Google Earth display.

Jack quickly dresses and joins the others in the salon. He mentions to Rosine how great her eggs and bacon smell. He then excuses himself and goes to Ben's cabin. Jack has to be sure it was Ben who turned them in. He knocks on the door. The knock wakes Ben from his sleep but Jack doesn't wait for a response as he walks in and stands beside Ben laying on his bunk.

"What the fuck, Jack, you always just bust into people's cabin?"

Jack knows how to handle these situations and goes for the immediate bluff. He knows it's much better to appear to know the answer rather than ask a question. "Why did you sell us out, Ben?"

"What are you talking about?"

"Look, Ben, I have my sources and I know what is going down, so we do this the easy way or the hard way, it's up to you, and you don't want to know how the hard way works, trust me. So, tell me, why did you sell us out?"

Ben, now scared and feeling cornered, goes straight to the truth, "Because they gave me one-hundred-thousand dollars, Jack, that's why. Anyone would do it for that, and besides, you shouldn't be running anyway. If they want to talk to you, you should let them. You brought this on yourself."

"You sold out two young children, and the rest of us for money? Do you have any understanding at all what you're dealing with here? These kids will never see the light of day after they're taken. You sicken me. Get off the bunk."

Just as Ben's feet touch the cabin floor, Jack grabs him around the neck giving it a twist, killing him instantly. As Ben's body goes limp, Jack drops him onto Alma's lower bunk and covers him with a blanket. Jack had quickly thought this scenario through and couldn't come up with any other option to pull off their next move; Jack needs Ben out of the equation. He can't take him, and he can't leave him behind to talk. This isn't the first time Jack has killed, and he sweeps it into the back of his mind where his other skeletons are stored.

Jack returns to the salon, "Man, breakfast smells good. I'm famished! Is it ready, Rosine?"

Rosine answers by way of an instruction, "Sit down everyone, I will bring it to the table, and you can serve yourselves. Jacob, can you take a plate up for Alma?"

"Sure, Ms. Rosine."

Jack eats quickly so he can address the group. "Keep eating everyone but listen to what I have to say. We're about to embark on another adventure."

This captures everyone's attention.

"Unfortunately, Ben told the NSC our location, and they have dispatched a Naval Destroyer to intercept us. It will reach here by 2pm today. There is no way to avoid them if we stay on this boat."

Everyone stops eating to take in Jack's words.

"Please finish eating, it may be the last good warm meal we get for some time."

Jack waits a moment, then continues, "We will launch the boat's tender. It's a small inflatable boat stored in a compartment at the back. It's our new home as we head back towards shore. My facilitator Jim is sending out a go-fast boat to pick us up. The destroyer heading for us hopefully won't see us making our way East in such a small boat, and they won't find this boat because I'm sinking it."

Everyone's eyes widen. The thought of being hundreds of miles offshore and having their home scuttled creates instant anxiety.

Rosine says, "What about our stuff, Jack? Are we leaving everything behind?"

"Yes, Rosine, we take water and a few snacks. I'm sorry. I can't think of any other way to save us. After everything that has transpired, if the NSC captures us, they won't let us go; we have to do this."

Jacob asks, "When do we leave?"

"Right now, Jacob. The quicker we get going, the more miles we can put between us and the NSC. You all finish up; I'm going to brief Alma and get the tender ready. When you're done eating, layer on as many clothes as you can; it's going to be wet and bone chilling cold. Grab six gallons of water and any small packaged food items you can find and bring it all to the back of the boat. I want everyone on deck waiting. No personal stuff except your ID, your phones and their chargers."

Jack gets up, climbs the companionway and informs Alma on the change of plans. She immediately starts pulling the sails in while Jack opens the tender garage. Within five minutes Jack has the tender floating, tethered to a cleat with its outboard engine purring at idle speed. Jack calculates they have enough gasoline in the outboard engine tank and one auxiliary tank to go about sixty miles - not near far enough to reach shore.

After removing the primary electrical cable from the boat's battery bank to disable the boat's sump pumps, Jack goes from locker to locker throughout the boat closing each thru-hull tap called a seacock, followed by cutting through the rubber connecting hose with a hacksaw, and then reopening the seacock. Seawater pours in. It will take the boat over twenty minutes to sink, so Jack performs his scuttling task methodically.

With water pouring into the boat, Jack collects the Spot, his phone, the portable VHF radio and a pair of binoculars and heads for the back. Rosine is helped onto the tender first, followed by Sarah, Jacob and then Alma; it's a snug tight fit. Jack unties the painter and climbs in last. He steers South East towards shore trying to put distance between them and where the NSC expects the yacht to be.

"Jack, What about Ben?" Rosine queries.

"Ben won't be joining us," Jack responds without further explanation.

The team has learned to respect Jack's judgement and actions; Ben's fate is not mentioned again.

Twenty minutes later, they no longer see the sailboat in the distance behind them.

□□□

"What do you mean they can't find the fucking sailboat? It's 64 feet long! Tell them to keep looking. This cannot be happening; boats don't just disappear. Fuck! The boat is there so call me when you find it." Brian can't get his head wrapped around this. He ends the call with the Navy tactician by throwing his cell phone on the cushioned chair beside him. He gets up and paces.

000

Jack has been running the tender at two thirds throttle towards the coast. He uses the sun as his bearing and occasionally does a sanity check using his iPhone's compass app.

The outside temperature is just a handful of degrees above freezing and occasional water spray has rendered the team wet and miserable; they are chilled to the bone and shivering. Looking around, they see nothing but horizon and this scares them, they know they can't last more than a few days; Jack's resource needs to come through. The group remains silent.

Three hours into the trip, Jack fills the motor's fuel tank from the auxiliary supply. Three hours later, just as Jack tops a wave crest, the engine sputters and seconds later stops. Jack simply says, "And now we wait." He reassures by saying, "Jim's people know our exact location and are most likely already on their way."

They all hear Jack, but their discomfort and early onset hypothermia is keeping them quiet; no one responds.

000

"I just heard from the Navy, we found them via satellite, Brian! They are floating about 120 miles offshore in their boat's tender. They are 80 miles East of the fix we were provided. Our guess is they scuttled their boat to avoid detection. They are not making additional headway so they either broke down or ran out of fuel."

"Thanks, Sowptik. They had to know we were coming. Where are they getting their intel from?" Sowptik has no answers and doesn't respond.

"Jack Campbell must have arranged for them to be picked up. He's too smart to go sixty miles from his mother ship, run out of gas and just float around with no plan. Send out two fast boats, one to pick up the Conduit Team, and the other to find and grab whoever is picking them up; this could be our best chance yet to find who is supporting Jack."

Brian processes for a second and then makes another request, "Put a chopper in the air and have them watch this whole thing go down. We're not going to fuck this up again."

"Sure, Brian, I'll ensure a bird is scrambled ASAP."

"Have them initially do a flyby and hang out beyond eye site, I don't want whoever is picking them up to get spooked and take off when they see a helicopter hovering"

"Sure, Brian."

ᏆᏆᏆ

Within three hours of the Conduit Team abandoning their boat, Jim's crew is underway.

It's only been twenty minutes since their engine quit and Jack can see the rendezvous boat near the horizon speeding towards them. Jack manages a smile as he thinks of how Jim always comes through. The team is hailed on their VHF with the prearranged call-sign; the two boats verify themselves.

Fifteen minutes later, and to the relief of everyone, they have abandoned the tender and are speeding towards the shores of Washington at over 50mph.

252 DAVID W. DRAPER

⬜⬜⬜

"Brian, we didn't get to them soon enough. Satellite is showing they rendezvoused with another boat about 20 minutes back. At the speed they are traveling, they will be on shore in an hour."

"Where is the fucking helicopter?" Brian asks with exasperation.

"It's headed out from Everett and should be close." Sowptik says.

"Ok, have the coordinates obtained from the satellite sent to the helicopter and our chase boat. Don't let the damn satellite lose them; we need these people to stop waiving their damned magic wand. When the helicopter gets to them, force the Conduits to stop until the chase boat arrives. Tell the chopper to shoot at them if they have to; I want them stopped."

⬜⬜⬜

Jack is the first one to see the low altitude helicopter flying straight towards them. He sighs knowing what is coming down. As expected, the helicopter confronts them flying barely twenty feet off the water behind their rescue boat still maintaining 50 mph.

Everyone on the boat hears the helicopters loud hailer as they are instructed to stop. Jack motions to the boat captain recruited by Jim to throttle back. He knows if they don't, the helicopter will shoot at them aiming to disable the engines, but he also knows about the high probability of someone accidentally getting shot with that low precision maneuver.

The helicopter follows the Conduit Team as they idle along. Jack knows the NSC will have sent an intercept boat and the helicopter is just biding its time until it arrives. He can't notify Jim of the situation because they are beyond cell phone reception range and he no longer has the benefit of his sailboat's satellite communications capability.

Pulling the group into a huddle, Jack explains the NSC will be taking them in for questioning. He simply requests everyone tells the truth as that's all there is. He also describes a complex plan to Sarah and Jacob they will tell Alex during their next 'episode'. Alex can then tell Spencer, who will carry it out.

▯▯▯

The next morning, Alex walks out of his stateroom and sees his Mom in the galley, "Mom the rest of the team is in trouble, I also have a bunch of instructions from Jack through Sarah and Jacob. I got it last night during our episode."

"What kind of trouble?" Spencer asks.

"The NSC captured them, Mom. They have been taken to the United States Navy station in Everett Washington. They need your help."

"Oh my God. What will happen to them? What can I possibly do? I can't get them out." Spencer is rambling.

"Well, Mom, you have to phone Jim and have him bring me two small wireless video cameras. I know the model numbers. It has to happen today, so you need to get Captain Cox to start steering towards shore to meet Jim's boat. You will have to coordinate the position of our boat for a rendezvous with the boat Jim is sending. Jacob and Sarah will get the cameras from me tonight during our next 'episode' and they will use them to live stream their NSC interrogation tomorrow. In addition, you need to tell Jim to have a vehicle parked outside the Everett base to pick up and transmit the video streaming from our cameras over the Internet to Maggie. And speaking of Maggie, you have to call her and have her capture our recording from the Internet and broadcast it live to the world; Jim and Maggie will need to talk directly to get this all coordinated. Do you need me to write all this stuff down, Mom?"

"Geez Alex, I'm sure if we work together on it, writing it down won't be necessary. How did you come up with all that?"

"This was all Dad's idea Mom; he told Jacob and Sarah on their boat before they were taken captive."

"Well Alex, for starters I don't know how to call Jim. Your Dad never gave me his number. I have no idea how to handle any of this."

"Oh, I forgot to tell you mom. Dad had an app installed on all our phones called 'Beetle Bash'. If you run it, there is a small ten-digit number called 'serial number' on the app's 'About' page. It's Jim's phone number."

"Of course, it is."

"Dad's pretty clever, hey, Mom?"

"You could call it that. I have different words for it," Spencer says, talking above Alex's understanding.

"Alex, you said we're telling Jim to bring two small video cameras to the boat today. I didn't understand what you said they are for."

"I will give Sarah and Jacob the cameras in our next episode, and they will secretly use the cameras to video their interrogation with the NSC. Maggie will then broadcast it to the news networks for everyone to watch. Dad is hoping to expose what the NSC is doing because he thinks their actions are illegal, and the video will expose them ending their harassment of us."

"Wow." Spencer says.

❑❑❑

The Conduit Team transfers to a Homeland Security boat that has rendezvoused with them. Once ashore, they are driven to Everett, where the adults are separated from Sarah and Jacob. Jim's operatives and their boat are taken to Homeland Security's Washington base, where the boat is impounded, and the crew held for questioning.

□□□

Brian, walking to the interrogation room where the Conduits are seated is feeling euphoric; he knows he is finally getting his chance. He shows the guard at the door his credentials and tells him no-one enters the room while the door is closed.

As Brian walks in, he says, "Hi kids, you must be Sarah and Jacob, correct?" Brian doesn't wait for an answer and continues, "My name is Brian Donnelly, and I must say it's a pleasure to meet two of the three most famous people on the planet right now."

Sarah and Jacob look at Brian with deadpan expressions, saying nothing nor providing physical acknowledgement to his statement.

"I would like to spend some time talking with you two about a few things, is that okay?" Brian is showing no finesse for dealing with ten-year-old's.

"Mr. Donnelly, we will talk with you and tell you anything you want to know, but first we need to rest. We have been through a lot over the past few weeks and it would be respectful of you to allow us this request before we proceed." Jack had coached the kids on what to say in order to buy time, and Jacob is pulling it off perfectly. Brian is surprised by the maturity Jacob exhibits in his phrasing of the request.

Not wanting to alienate the kids before getting started, Brian responds, "I'm sorry, kids, that wasn't nice of me. Can we maybe do this in a couple of hours?"

Sarah responds, "With all due respect, Mr. Donnelly, we were think-ing of tomorrow morning. We could both use a night's sleep, a shower, and we will be much clearer and more focused in the morning after a good rest."

This disappoints Brian, but he wants to show the kids he's compas-sionate and not a threat, hoping it helps the interrogation to go smoothly. Knowing they're finally contained, he controls his impatience, "Sure, kids, I totally understand. You two get your rest, and I'll make sure there is a nice warm breakfast waiting for you in the morning. How does that sound?"

Again, the kids show no response.

As Brian is about to leave the room, Jacob asks, "Can we see Jack and Rosine please? Being here alone and separated has us pretty scared."

Brian needs to deflect, "Absolutely, but let's do that tomorrow after you two kids are rested up. I'm sure the adults will appreciate the chance to rest as well. No need to be scared, everyone is being taken care of."

Sarah and Jacob know Brian is lying.

▯▯▯

Spencer comes clean with her captain and first mate, explaining the events leading up to their current circumstance taking them home to Ecuador. She also explains the need for a course change to rendezvous with Jim's boat from shore. After the initial introduction to the Conduit's story, Alex explains to Bradley and Shirley, at a high level, all the things they have learned. After getting to know Spencer and Alex, and then hearing the details, the crew believes the story and are enthusiastic to help. Spencer spends her time coordinating with Jim.

Captain Cox is the first to observe Jim's rendezvous boat approaching, appearing as a dot on his radar screen. Within thirty minutes, the boats are close enough to pass over the little cargo package containing the video cameras. The entire operation takes less than a minute and goes without a hitch. As quickly as it approached, the delivery boat is racing towards the horizon.

▯▯▯

Alex, earlier than normal, jumps from his sleeping berth and enters his Mom's stateroom. "Get up, Mom! The live broadcast will be starting soon, and you need to call Maggie. I have important information from John McCallister."

Spencer sits up looking disoriented, "What time is it, Alex?"

"It's 6:30, Mom. You need to call Maggie right now."

"All right, all right! What am I talking to her about?"

"I gave a video camera to both Sarah and Jacob last night and they will be ready to start broadcasting soon. John McCallister says Maggie can't pre-announce the NSC's interrogation - it's important the NSC doesn't know in advance or they will stop it before it happens. Also, tell her not to start live streaming until Brian Donnelly enters the room and closes the door."

"Is that it?"

"Yeah, Mom, but you have to do it right now in case Maggie starts broadcasting early."

"Okay, okay... geez." Spencer immediately places a call to Maggie and conveys Alex's request from John McCallister.

▯▯▯

Sarah and Alex are taken from their cell, disguised as a sleeping dorm, and led to the same meeting room as the previous day. Shortly after entering the room, a uniformed private brings in two dishes containing grits, a piece of toast and scrambled eggs. After the plates are set down, Sarah looks at the private and asks if they can get orange juice.

"Yes." is all the private says as he leaves the room.

The stress of the situation has wiped out Sarah's appetite. She pokes at the eggs and takes a small bite. The eggs are bland and cold, and she thinks to herself, "So much for a warm breakfast." Neither of them eats the food.

Precisely at 7 am, Brian arrives. As he said the previous day, he instructs the guard for no interruptions. He enters the room followed by the same private who had brought in the food. The private sets down two orange juice glasses, removes the breakfast plates and immediately leaves. Brian closes and clicks the lock from the inside.

"Well hello again. I hope you two got the rest you needed. Were the beds comfortable?"

"Not really," Jacob says.

"I'll have to have that looked in to," Brian says, trying to be funny. "Are you ready to talk with me? We here in the United States are looking forward to getting to know the famous Conduits and learn of your message. All we know at this point is what we hear and see on TV. Do you think we can do that?"

▯▯▯

President Stanford, while drinking his second cup of coffee, is sitting in his Oval Office enjoying his executive time watching the day's news unfold on Fox News, his network of choice. The program is interrupted by a "Breaking News" alert displaying across the TV. The scene quickly switches to a news anchor, saying, "We interrupt your scheduled program to bring you this special live news report involving the Conduit Team. The report comes from the US Naval Base in Everett Washington where it appears the Conduits are broadcasting an interview they are having with Brian Donnelly, the director of the United States National Security Council."

Michael Stanford, alone in the room, reacts so suddenly he spits coffee over his pants, followed by yelling, "What the fuck!"

▯▯▯

Sarah and Jacob have to be careful and play Brian. Jack coached them and explained they need Brian Donnelly to confess information incriminating himself and the President. Brian doesn't know his subjects are wearing small video microphones transmitting a live streaming of his interrogation to the world.

Maggie has called all the major news networks in advance and prompted them to be ready to receive the video feed. As Brian closes the door to the room, a large number of the major television networks are receiving and forwarding the broadcast. Brian Donnelly is front and center as the world watches.

Sarah starts, "We will answer your questions, Mr. Donnelly, but it has to be done in a spirit of cooperation. If we believe you are not being transparent with us, we won't cooperate."

Brian is immediately taken aback. He didn't expect ten-year-old children to act anything other than a little scared and willing to spill the beans to get back with their parents. Brian has no idea what he is dealing with.

"Of course, Sarah, we are here to help you. If we don't fully understand your story, we can't help you achieve your goals. It's that simple."

"Good Mr. Donnelly, we were hoping that would be the case. So before we start, and as mentioned yesterday, can we first get together with Jack and Rosine? They will be able to help answer some of your questions."

"Not quite yet, Sarah. Jack and Rosine are talking with one of my associates, and when they're done, we'll get you all together. In the meantime, can we talk alone?"

"Sure, Mr. Donnelly, but you need to be transparent as promised, so can I ask you a question first?"

Brian sees no harm in this and says, "Sure."

"Why did you and the NSC chase us and arrest us using guns rather than just ask us to meet and discuss our story?"

Brian cannot believe the level of comprehension coming from Sarah. He answers directly as she won't be repeating this publicly any time soon. "Well Sarah, your story has the potential for disrupting the entire world, we needed to bring you in for questioning to ensure the authenticity of your story before things get out of hand."

"Couldn't you have done that in cooperation with other governments and without resorting to force? Innocent people have died as a result of your actions."

Brian is wondering where this is coming from, "What do you mean people have died, Sarah?"

"Well, Mr. Donnelly, in your attempt to stop the story, people died in the helicopter the NSC shot down in London. You killed innocent people because they were helping us."

"What makes you think it was the NSC, Sarah? Anyone could have done that."

"It would take a large organization to have arranged shooting down the helicopter in such a short time frame, right? And besides, our informant told us it was you."

Not caring what he says, he slips. "Well Sarah, bringing you and your team in for questioning was only half of the problem we were faced with. The other half is squashing the spreading of your story from those who intimately know the details. Unfortunately, London World News needed to be stopped. And who is this informant you mention?"

'Gotcha,' Sarah is thinking.

▯▯▯

President Stanford watches Brian Donnelly admit the NSC's involvement in the London helicopter shooting. He again screams, "What the fuck!"

He collects his thoughts and requests his assistant to call his Naval Operations Chief. When he hears the Chief say, "Hello, Mr. President," Michael becomes unglued. He yells into the phone, "Stop the fucking broadcast from Everett. Right fucking now!"

"I'm not sure what you are referring to, Mr. President." The naval chief isn't currently watching the news.

"There is an unauthorized signal coming out of the Everett Naval Base being broadcast to the world. Make it stop. Now! Right fucking now!" Michael slams his phone down.

▯▯▯

Taking over from Sarah, Jacob says, "So, Mr. Donnelly, you are actually admitting the NSC shot down a helicopter in London and you had us kidnapped?"

"Well, Jacob, I wouldn't exactly call it kidnapping. You have been brought in for questioning."

Before Brian can say another word, Jacob takes advantage of the timing, "What would happen if President Stanford knew what you were doing?" Jacob is hoping to trap Brain.

Brian, falls for it, "Jacob, do you think I'm doing this on my own? It's President Stanford who is most concerned about you kids. He sees you as a threat."

Jacob keeps pushing, "So you're saying President Stanford ordered the shooting in London and our kidnapping because we're a threat? Did the whole National Security Council stand behind this?"

"Wow, Jacob, you're a pretty bright and knowledgeable boy for only ten years old." Brian is enjoying the authority he believes he has over the children. "Sometimes operations need to be done quickly. Involving the full council would quite frankly be too slow; the council is not capable of quick decisions, or in some cases, the correct decisions. In situations like this, we need to take things into our own hands and give directives without the team's involvement; it's for the greater good."

"Isn't that illegal Mr. Donnelly? Doesn't the NSC have rules you have to follow?"

"Like I said Jacob, we had to act fast."

"So, this isn't really an NSC operation, it's a clandestine operation mandated by you and President Stanford. Correct?" Jacob continues knowing he can fluster Brian. "Mr. Donnelly, you asked about our informant a minute ago, do any of your NSC members know you and President Stanford are secretly eavesdropping on them, while you try to find our informant?"

"You can't possibly know we're eavesdropping to find the informant? How the hell do you know about that?" Brian is frustrated, because the mole seems to know everything, and is somehow passing it to the children.

"Well, Mr. Donnelly, we do know, and you're not understanding. In dealing with us, you are dealing with powers beyond anyone's level of understanding. We speak directly with the 'Spirit-of-Life' daily, we actually call him 'SOL', and SOL tells us what is going on. You're not fighting a mole, Mr. Donnelly, you're fighting a higher power."

"That's your interpretation. I will find out how much you know about our mole, and we will catch the traitor. In any event, you kids are upsetting some powerful people."

Jacob, continually pressing to have Brian incriminate himself, continues, "So, Mr. Donnelly, to be clear, it was you and the President who sanctioned this, not the NSC. Correct?"

"We do unauthorized operations all the time without involving the full NSC. This is how we get things done quickly."

Sarah, putting nails in the coffin, says, "Mr. Donnelly, if this is an unauthorized operation, that means it's secret ... nobody knows about it, correct?"

"You two have completely surprised me. I thought I'd be talking with two children crying to see their parents again. Yes, nobody knows about this right now."

"Then you can't let us go, right? You can't risk this illegal operation becoming public ... you need it to stay secret. You just told us stuff that can't be repeated. Are you going to hide us in some cell somewhere, or just kill us, Mr. Donnelly?" Sarah asks.

"Wow! You're being a little over dramatic, Sarah. I'm sure once we figure this all out, and put a stop to it, we can get your lives back to normal."

"Mr. Donnelly, the part you're not understanding, or just not seeing, is there is no putting a stop to this. It's happening and there is nothing the United States or any other government is going to be able to do about it. We either work with SOL to save some people or we don't. Either way, in ten years it's all over. We have provided ample evidence to support this."

"Well Sarah, we're not ready to believe your story and go down that path."

"So, your answer is to abduct the whole team and hope it goes away?"

"You have me feeling like I'm the one under interrogation. This has been fun kids, but now I ask the questions."

They don't give Brian control, "Mr. Donnelly, given you have admitted to an illegal covert operation killing innocent people, and then forcefully abducting us, I don't think Sarah and I are willing to cooperate." Jacob can hardly wait to see how Brian handles this one.

"Jacob, you're being a little melodramatic and I don't want this interview to be like that. If you cooperate with me, I'll make sure this goes as well as possible for you two. It's your choice because I have the means to make you talk. I don't think either of you would want to see harm come to Jack or Rosine, right?"

"Harm Jack or Rosine? What are you talking about? You would actually hurt them in order to make us talk? Are you serious? You mean like torture them so we will talk? People in the United States actually do that?"

Brian is now frustrated. "Come on kids, nothing has to happen to anyone if we just talk in the spirit of cooperation, is that too much to ask?"

Brian has no idea how to lead an interrogation with children, especially Sarah and Jacob who surpass his intellect.

"But you would torture them to make us talk if you had to. Right, Mr. Donnelly? That's the point we're trying to make."

"Okay, look kids, I don't care what you think of me, I'm the person that gets results. We do what it takes. You're now going to answer my questions fully and to my satisfaction. Please understand this because it's your only option. It either goes smooth, or it gets ugly, and none of us want ugly. It's your choice."

Not relenting, and believing Brian has incriminated himself enough, Sarah says, "Mr. Donnelly, I don't think the United States Government, nor the rest of the world for that matter, is going to like what you're doing here. You are breaking laws at every move, and I believe they will be stopping you shortly."

"No one will be stopping me Sarah. We are alone here."

"Well, actually, Mr. Donnelly, we're not. You are on a global stage. Jacob and I are wearing video cameras, and this meeting has been live streamed to the world, for all to see. I'm sure President Stanford is watching right now. Why don't you give him a little wave. We're not alone at all."

Sarah toys with Brian by taking off her video camera, letting Brian see it for the first time, and holds it in front of her in a 'selfie' position. "Hello, President Stanford," Sarah says defiantly. "Do you want to come and join in on the torture?"

Brian's face contorts as he says. "You little brat, do you think this is a game here?"

Jacob says, "Mr. Donnelly, please go to any news station on your phone and see. Don't make it any worse for yourself; I'm sure most of the world is tuned in. Go ahead, Mr. Donnelly, take a look."

Brian is sweating and has a sinking feeling. He pulls out his phone and navigates to his CNN app. He immediately sees himself from the point of view of the children's cameras. From his view, he sees the room's door behind him come flying off its hinges.

□□□

President Stanford is sitting at his oval office desk, frantically making damage control phone calls. Without a knock, Vice President Harrison enters the room along with the Chief of Staff, John McCallister. They are accompanied by two secret service agents.

President Stanford looks up knowing what is happening.

Vice President Harrison starts talking before the President can get a word in. "Mr. President, under Section 4 of the 25th Amendment, it has been determined you are unfit to discharge the powers and duties of this office. I have a letter here stating this, signed by a majority of the Cabinet Secretaries. Effective right now, I am assuming the Office of the President." Looking behind him, the new President Harrison speaks to the secret service agents, "Gentlemen, please walk Mr. Stanford here to the Lindsay Room for debriefing."

Michael is defiant. "I am the president. I run things, and I do what's needed. Please do not refer to me as 'mister.'"

"Yes sir, please go with them."

□□□

After the military police remove Brian from the room, Rosine, Alma, and Jack walk through the broken interrogation room's door. Sarah runs to Rosine and gives her a lasting heartfelt hug. Rosine is crying with happiness that she's able to embrace Sarah again. Jack puts his arm around Jacob who says, "You don't look very good Mr. Campbell. Are you going to be ok?"

"I'll be fine Jacob; it takes more than a few NSC thugs to get the better of me. It looks like you and Sarah got things straightened out."

"Yeah, I guess we did pretty good, hey, Mr. Campbell. Do you think we can get back to being normal again?"

Jack has a smile on his bruised and bloodied face as he looks down at Jacob, "Yes, Jacob, it appears you and Sarah were amazing. I'm pretty sure the chase is over, but I doubt things will ever be normal again, but at least we should now be able to get you home."

The Conduit's cameras keep transmitting.

A uniformed statuesque man walks into the room, "Hello everyone, I'm Base Commander Phillips, and before I say anything, I want to apologize for the treatment you folks have been receiving lately. We had no idea there were no legitimate authorizations in place regarding how we have handled your situation. My job is to get you home as quickly and comfortably as possible. Again, on behalf of my entire staff, and the United States Government, I hope you accept our apology."

Commander Phillips shakes everyone's hands. He saves a handshake with Jack until last. "Well, I finally get to meet the infamous Jack Campbell. I wish it could have been under better circumstances. Looks like you received quite a beating, Jack. We'll make sure your interrogation friends won't be practicing their trade anytime soon. That just isn't supposed to happen."

"It's okay, Commander, I've had it worse."

"You're a tough one, Jack. Hell, there is barely a single serviceman out there that hasn't heard of you and your exploits."

"Not sure if that is a good thing or not, Commander," Jack says with a smile."

"You set a good example Jack, and again, please accept our apology."

"Apology accepted. We know this had nothing to do with you, or any of our great service men for that matter; we take orders, it's the only way the system can work. Now if you can just get us all home, we'll be eternally grateful."

After a long hand shaking embrace, Commander Phillips tells the group he'll send in his administrator to handle the logistics for everyone to get home. He salutes Jack and exits the room.

"Let's get home and build some towers," Jack says just before he asks for the video cameras to be turned off.

CHAPTER 10

THE ANTICHRIST

Cardinal Luca Lorenzo, the Pope's personal assistant, is enjoying his morning tea in the private Vatican courtyard as Cardinal Matteo Rossi enters
and approaches. Matteo leans over and discreetly speaks into Luca's ear.

Upon hearing Matteo's message, Luca has a grave look and quietly
says, "It is happening Matteo. Satan has awoken and placed the Antichrist
amongst us. He is moving fast; you say he used trickery and deceit to take
down the United States Presidency? Satan is strong. We must mobilize
quickly and move carefully; we are fighting for the very existence of the
Holy Spirit and we cannot lose. It's been a long time Matteo, but we now
convene the 'Group of Nine'. Only the group has the strength to match what
appears to be Satan's final onslaught. Let us hope we are not too late. Now,
Matteo, we pray."

Luca extends his hand to Matteo as he kneels beside him. From
memory, he recites the famous 'Prayer to Defeat the Work of Satan'.

"O Divine Eternal Father, in union with your Divine Son and the
Holy Spirit, and through the Immaculate Heart of Mary, I beg You to
destroy the Power of your greatest enemy - the evil spirits. Cast them into

the deepest recesses of hell and chain them there forever! Take possession of your Kingdom which You have created, and which is rightfully yours. In the name of the Father, and of the Son, and of the Holy Spirit. Amen."

"Matteo, I fear the prophecies were correct, this could be the final war. We are entering a dark time. Pull the group together, right away."

THE END